T0376128

ZONE ROUGE

A NOVEL

MICHAEL JEROME PLUNKETT

THE UNNAMED PRESS
LOS ANGELES, CA

AN UNNAMED PRESS BOOK

Published in North America by the Unnamed Press.

www.unnamedpress.com

Unnamed Press, and the colophon, are registered trademarks of Unnamed Media LLC.

Hardcover ISBN: 978-1-961884-55-7
EBook ISBN: 978-1-961884-56-4
LCCN: 2025940188

Cover design and typeset by Jaya Nicely

Manufactured in the United States of America by Sheridan

Distributed by Publishers Group West
First Edition

For Margaret Plunkett
who gave me stories.

"The struggle itself toward the heights is enough to fill a man's heart. One must imagine Sisyphus happy."

—Albert Camus, *The Myth of Sisyphus*

ZONE ROUGE

PART I

HUGO & THE TOAD

Démineurs

The cows, they suffer in silence.

Once, we were called out to one heifer, sweet old girl, her abdomen so distended it almost touched the packed dirt of the threshing floor. She had eaten an entire bellyful of the shrapnel that had shredded her digestive tract to confetti. They called us because they had no idea what to do. But we couldn't do anything. We are démineurs. We dismantle bombs, not cows. She died right there in front of us without a single sound.

Gaston Odin plunges each of his cows daily to avoid such catastrophes. He has a small dairy farm on the outskirts of Samogneux, a scratch of a commune ten minutes outside of Verdun. He takes a magnet—it's a heavy little cylinder, you can almost wrap a hand around it—and he uses it to get every piece of shrapnel out that they've swallowed.

"What? What was that? You have to speak up. *Speak* up," he says, deaf in one ear from the time a German hand grenade rolled up into his plow and blew the turbine to pieces. We know it was German because we found another seven grenades in the following weeks.

It's a Tuesday and unseasonably warm for February. We've stripped off our winter coats and opened our coveralls. Gaston tosses the magnet from one hand to the other. He's donned his leather apron over a fraying collared shirt and heavy rubber boots caked with God knows what. His face is all jowls and sweat, a receded hairline holding ground at the sides of his scalp. In the barn, he locks the magnet on to one end of a long metal rod. The cow waits with its head stuck through a gate. Then Gaston braces himself near the cow's head. We lean against the other stalls, cross our arms. A shock of pale blue sky frames the open barn door. A sneeze. A cough. Gaston wraps one arm around her snout and slides his bare hand into her mouth.

"She never enjoys this part," he says, shoulders braced and ready for a fight.

Gaston inserts the magnet between her teeth and forcefully plunges it down her throat and into her stomach. He shoves it with the same force of a man loading a cannon with a ramrod. It's not a single motion but a series of forceful jams. Again and again and again. The cow flinches and shudders, but not as much as you might expect.

"Almost there, almost there, I know," Gaston says.

Long, thick strands of mucus drip onto the lap of his apron. She tolerates the procedure surprisingly well. Aside from a few light grunts, she barely moves. Her hooves remain planted on the dirt floor the entire time. When he knows it is placed deep enough, Gaston hits the release latch on the end of the rod.

"Getting it in is the easy part," Gaston says, and wipes his hands down the front of his apron. "It's when I need to bring it back out in a few days that it gets tricky."

Is it really necessary? Is there any other easier way?

"I've taken to doing it to every beast just to be safe," he says. "Sometimes I get a bunch, other times I get nothing at all. But I just can't risk it anymore. I don't have the money to have the vet out—endoscopies every week—and I can't afford the tools myself. This is the only method

I can manage. If I could, I would just open them all up and take out every little bit of shrapnel with my fingers. It would be much easier, to tell the truth. I mean, if it didn't kill them."

The following Friday we make our way back out, and the weather is feeling much more itself. We pull our knit caps over our ears, and each breath hangs before us in the barn. The retrieval is somewhat similar to the placement, only in reverse. Again, Gaston positions himself beside her head, braces himself against the gate, and then plunges the rod. To our dismay, he appears to be wearing the exact same shirt as several days before, and his brow glistens as ever. No gloves. There is a fair amount of jostling and fishing that is more unpleasant than the placement. He needs to find it somewhere in her gastric tract.

"It can't get far," he says. "It is too heavy to move all the way through. Gravity does the work. I just need to aim for the lowest place."

When he pulls the magnet out into the mouth and then through the teeth, there's some blood and other fluids. Bile slicks the rod. The magnet is a raging hive teeming with shrapnel. The cow's eyes don't change: docile as anything, utterly unfazed.

*

Today, we take the trenches. It's easier than slinking between the trees. Hand-dug fortifications stand sentry, eroded to calf height and eternally crumbling, but there, nonetheless, a century later. These cuts in the earth once provided shelter through those many cold nights. To pass the time in late morning, we imagine tiny soldiers running between our feet—us with the footfalls of giants. It's all thick clay underfoot, light in some spots, tar dark in others, and it clumps in the lugs of our boots. Perfect material for building sandcastles during a day at the beach, but a terror to walk over all day.

When we reach an opening, the sun's warmth overtakes the chill of the woods and morning light catches the mist off the freshly plowed fields. Boulder-sized bales of wheat, stacked along the road for pickup, radiate enough steam to generate their own clouds. Rusted ribbons of iron line our path. A warped metal rod supports a thin, curling strand of barbed wire that dances delicately in the wind.

The day wears on as we get farther along, and the old trench shallows until it vanishes altogether. For a moment, it is just normal land. A pasture. A softly babbling creek. A place like any other.

Every week we recover dozens of shells. Every month, hundreds. Every year, tens of thousands. We carry them out of the ground to our trucks by the armfuls. In canvas sacks on our backs. Stack them in lockers lined with sand. Cinch them together with slick cable wire and pack them by the pallet. Put them on trucks and fill them to the ceiling. Store them in steel-lined cellars with thick iron doors that shut with a dull clunk. And when there is no room left, we shove them in the corners of the lot in our depot. Find odd gaps where they can be stacked a dozen high. Every nook and cranny. Loads and loads and loads.

The shells have been at rest so long, and the risks of waking them far outweigh the rewards of retrieving them. It's one thing to dispose of what's worked its way to the surface. But to actively seek them out?

Verdun. Our fortress city of the Meuse. It kept the hordes of invading Germans from ever reaching Paris during the Great War. Twelve million artillery shells still wait. It took less than ten months to fire it all off during the war, and how many lifetimes will be spent picking them all back up in just this one town alone? Beyond these borders, who knows how many more?

Verdun is a quiet town where people drive fast. Old, narrow roads lined with hedges and roundabout after roundabout. It is very easy to get lost. The winding roads, the surrounding farmlands. So much green. It almost swallows us whole. There are whole stretches where it is hard to believe a war ever made its way through here.

Row teams sail up and down the Meuse, and people dock small yachts for days at a time right beneath the old gatehouse of the medieval castle that once encased the city. Scars from the artillery of both World Wars can be seen on its facade, as is the case with many of the older buildings in the area. There are shops and restaurants and bars and discounts at the grocery stores. Petrol is €1.36 per litre. People know one another here. They wave and beep hello at each other. Little dramas occur everywhere.

Most of what they taught us in the Mine Clearing Academy is no good. The academy was all about disarming bombs. Big bombs. Little bombs. Chemistry and electricity. Everything out here is corroded beyond recognition. You might find yourself doing real mine clearing once or twice in an entire career. The rest of it is just babysitting or working in a nursing home. But that doesn't make these foetus avortés any less dangerous.

We work the shells tenderly. Controlled breathing, slowed heart rates, as we patiently brush away the clay. The good news is, even if it does go off, we won't feel a thing.

Never forget what these tortues sinistre were made for.

They're dead for the most part, the artillery shells. Fuses rotted. Ignitors decayed. But the parts are all there—the ingredients for a minor mushroom cloud or shrapnel bath. The sense of danger wears off quicker than one might expect. The thrill of feeling the weight of an unstable explosive that could detonate at any moment is the first thing to go. We handle them like last season's pottery and toss them into piles where they sometimes crack and crumble.

We have all manner of names for them:

Moineaux en colère

Petits crapauds
Foetus avortés
Bébés chauves maléfiques
Tortues sinistre

We tiptoe through the boom-boom graveyard while our directors and supervisors with their fancy made-up titles prefer to sit upstairs, twirling their mustaches and coming up with ways to impress politicians in Paris.

Every month, we take the shells away in trucks to designated locations all over the country. At sea. In woods. In holes. We detonate them, finishing a job that was started lifetimes ago. The caravan leaves in the violet dark before dawn, the unmarked trucks laden with pallets. We move slowly, giant bombs on wheels weaving our way through the countryside. The lumpy craters give way to farmland. All that green. An endless expanse rolling on over the horizon. You need the trees to block the view or you might lose your mind trying to process all that space. Instead, we look at our phones, we nap, we keep our eyes on the road. Every seat taken, not a seat belt strapped on one of us.

Fields of sun-blanched wheat sway in our peripheral vision. When we arrive at the tidal flats of the English Channel, there is no one there to greet the caravan but the wine-blue light of dawn. We get out and stretch—hands over head, craning backward, bent over touching toes—and it's like standing on the edge of the world. The sun will be here soon. The hulk of a long-ago beached wreck, all rust and hollow spaces, is the only silhouette that breaks the straight line of the horizon. The beach town to our rear is silent—darkened shop windows; the lonely, warped planks of the empty boardwalk. A few of the buildings still have their exterior accent lights on, and these beams illuminate the facades of the buildings in a grainy and ambient way that suggests life has only recently departed the streets. There is probably still trash to be cleaned off the sidewalks and evidence of last night's mistakes staining the pavement, but we are out here on the beach with a job to do, and so all we can see is a quaint beach town as picturesque as a postcard. We silently offload the pallets. Cold. Dying for a cigarette. Low tide.

The flats stretch out to the tide, and puddles and rivulets mirror the last remaining stars above. We trudge toward the English Channel, and every step sinks into the sand, the seawater bubbling out around our boots. The wind is in our faces now, and the salt is thick on our skin. Even with our gloves, our fingers go numb as we cram the shells into deep holes that have been dug for us before we arrived. We pack fresh dynamite all around them and then on top.

Back at our trucks, we smoke and wait for the water to rise. When the sea level is high enough, we flip the switch. The explosion shoots half a mile in the sky, and from a distance we watch the cloud linger and dissolve.

*

We find shells in every place imaginable: one underneath a neighbor's porch, another in the wall of Mémé's garden. The soils of Verdun continue to churn. The shells seem to simmer into the floorboards, forever floating upward, trapped beneath the world like bubbles under the surface of a frozen lake. Seven days a week. On four separate shifts. Almost every day of the year. On call on holidays. Some days are boring as hell. Others less so.

We work long hours, but we find ways to enjoy ourselves. We tear one another down and make jokes about wives but never the kids. We laugh and toss equipment at each other, and even with a corroded shell in hand we still joke and shove. We are also careful. We check and re-check and check again our equipment. We sweep the cab of the truck when there is nothing else to do. We smoke cigarettes and watch time drag on. We feel the frenzied tension of the mind after the eighteenth hour of a day has run over. We file pages and pages and pages of reports.

We wear our names on our coveralls. Thick, antistatic blue-gray fabric with our names sewn onto the breast, right above our hearts. And beneath our names, we each wear a circular patch: a skeleton man with arms askew, a German potato masher hand grenade in one hand, a gas canister in the other. Gas spills in a toxic plume above his head with the phrase *Poigne de la Mort* enmeshed in the cloud.

We fear nothing! We dance in the face of certain death! We dance with it in both hands! What a bunch of crap. It's a job. That's it. We don't think of it as anything more. That's how you burn out. This place. Does it give two shits about any of us? It would eat us alive if we let it. *Oh, I'm a démineur, look at me!* The second someone starts living that way, they are done for. Come here. Do the work. Punch out and go home. There's more to life than work. There are no second chances out here. Simple mathematics. You miscalculate, you die. You miscalculate and you don't die? Well, some might wish they had. Surviving something like that, you could be worse off.

We've had a lot come through. Not many stay. It's these young guys. They have no self-awareness. Snotty and disrespectful. Full of confidence, and it comes from where? Nowhere!

We had one guy a few years ago for about a week. Lost puppy with no idea how to do anything with his own ten fingers. Makes you wonder how he made it this far. That kid was in the moon half his waking life. Wound too tight. This job is not for the anxious type. It's all the waiting around. And that anxiety, it spreads like a disease. It's not the anxiety by itself that is even the primary concern. It's that it spreads. Quickly.

The secret to avoiding burnout in a job such as this is treating it exactly for what it is: just a job. We leave it there in the depot. We don't take it home. It will be there tomorrow when we return. Sure as the sun will rise, that depot and those trucks, and all the mysteries the soil holds, will still be there waiting for our return.

It's really the worst-kept secret. We tell everyone who walks through our door this "secret" on their first day. Not much of a secret. No, *secret* is not the correct word. There must be a better word. Something more precise and accurate. What's a good word for a plainly stated fact that no one wants to listen to or acknowledge?

Ignorance?

No, it's more deliberate than that. Ignorance takes away too much of the blame. This word needs to contain more accountability.

Yes, it's something more intentional. Someone is let in on a secret—a very powerful secret—and they choose to ignore it, but in a manner that is both obnoxious and life-threatening.

It's true. He's not just putting himself at risk. It's those around him too. When he chose to take this job home with him and it gradually began to wear him down, he was heading out there to handle these angry sparrows with his head in the moon. It's the guy next to you who takes on the full weight of your mistakes.

It's a form of snubbing. When someone disregards valuable information given to them for free, they've snubbed.

Exactly. It's a choice after a certain point.

We spend our lives watching paint dry while the building might explode at any moment. We hold empty boredom and the possibility of being blown to little bits in each hand at the same time. If we don't learn to let it go, we're really holding them out in front of us, both arms extended, brow furrowed, and furiously analyzing each. We can't hold our arms out forever. Bound to get tired sooner or later. And that's where the rattle comes from. A constant thrum right where a heart should be.

Knuckle cracking. Nose picking. Crotch grabbing. Back stretching. Eye rubbing. Nail biting. Cuticle chewing. Belching. Farting. Singing. Whistling. Humming a tune. All these small gestures of life. One stacked on top of another. These tiny gestures are what make up the majority of our days. And when a shell gets called in, we head to the location and we assess it. Carry it. Load it. Drive it back to the depot. Store it with the others.

The ride back from the flats goes quicker than we expect, and at the end of the shift, we stand in the poorly ventilated locker room, engulfed in steam and mildew. We pull our coveralls down from our shoulders and tie them around our waists. Bare-chested and hairy-backed with tattoos and stretch marks and belly fat and surgical scars and sagging flesh and sinewy muscle and funnel chests and skin freshly moisturized and scabbing and hardened and milky white and honey brown. We laugh and joke and fart and towel snap each other to the creaking clang of locker doors where photos of children and wives hang from barely there bits of Scotch tape.

We call one another by our surnames, never our first, except for Henri, our most cautious démineur (his second child has just arrived), and we always refer to him by his first name, and no one knows why. We bicker. Each one of us knows the roads of the county as intimately as the curves and creases of our own bodies. We scrape the dirt from underneath our fingernails and rub our hands down our coveralls and run our hands through our hair.

And we wait. And wait. Wait to be told what to do. Wait to be told where to go. Wait for the next one.

*

It happens on a Thursday in a place so obvious you have to wonder how it wasn't discovered sooner. Right in the center of the battlefield, no less. Someone has found something, and the forest ranger says it appears to be legitimate.

What do these people think we do all day? Like we are going to drop everything for a single artillery shell that might not even be dangerous. No, if we did that every time someone called one in, nothing would ever get done. Ever.

Half the time, they're not even ordnance. How many times have we hauled ass out to some location to find this bomb they have made a big fuss about is actually just Pepé's old milk jug or a rusted tin can?

The citizens do their part. They find quite a few, actually. But half the time they don't know what they are looking at. Every little lump in the dirt. Why here, right now? It is a question worth asking, but we cannot dwell on it. If we start thinking that way, we'll never be able to sleep, let alone do our job, so we don't think about it at all. You just pause. Stay very still. And look. Just wait. Things begin to emerge. They're right there in front of you. The whole time.

Fleury-devant-Douaumont. Official population: 0.

We are on our way to one of the many Villages That Died for France on the outskirts of Verdun, the city that never fell to the Germans. Little farming communes that were erased in less than a month of fighting. These villages were all abandoned virtually overnight at the start of the fighting. Anything that couldn't be carried out was left behind and lay in the ruins. And unexploded artillery shells. Everywhere.

Fleury-devant-Douaumont is among the villages that were declared too dangerous to return to. But instead of demolishing them, the powers that be left them as monuments to what was lost. It is not difficult to imagine the smoldering ruins of farmhouses and collapsed churches. We place both feet in the village, and it feels like the shelling stopped only a moment before. The foundations of pulverized buildings are still littered about. We stand on the dust of crushed time. The village still elects a mayor, a symbolic position that is considered by many to be a great honor and like all great honors holds no real influence, to maintain its sites. Piles of cut trees line the roads. The bark of the trees is loaded with poison leeched from the ordnance, and there are still shell craters everywhere. This was once a small town. People lived here. People knew one another.

Fleury was at the center of it all. It changed hands fourteen, fifteen, sixteen times? Or was it seventeen?

Does it matter?

We park just past the museum along D913, and there stands Hugo LaFleur, recently elected mayor of Fleury-devant-Douaumont, among the grass-carpeted shell craters of his ghost village. His plain face would blend into a crowd were it not instantly recognizable, plastered across every "For Sale" building in Verdun, his face wearing a smile like a man who was only recently given instructions on how to do so. A unique and somewhat eccentric marketing campaign in some opinions. The mark of a true jackass by all others. He is a one-man real estate agency and has made it publicly known on more than one occasion that he has plans to turn this city around. Not that anyone has asked him to.

1

It is Hugo LaFleur's first year as mayor of Fleury, and he dreads winter. Short days. Frigid weather. The endless ice. He is always cold and tired, and there is never enough light anywhere. Duck hunting season everywhere else in the country. It brings with it a specific kind of cold. Duck cold. Terrible memories. Early mornings setting decoys in waist-deep water and then shivering in the high grass for hours while an uncle he barely knew let out low, methodical mating calls. He stays indoors as much as possible, leaving the warmth and artificial glow of his office or his home only to visit prospective properties.

In Verdun, he sees potential. How long had it taken the city to recover from the Great War? Trick question: it never had. The main city had been rebuilt, but it was not exactly thriving. They never even rebuilt most of the surrounding villages that were all bombed to pieces!

While other realtors launched full-frontal assaults under the banner of revitalization and urban renewal on cities like Paris and Strasbourg, Hugo went the other way. He viewed these one-man attacks as futile and ultimately pointless. Find the quiet towns with a strong sense of heritage and their history, the summer tourist spots and the countryside getaways with their bizarre locals, farmers with faces permanently puckered from a life spent toiling away in the fields, the low-level alertness that comes from having spent a little too much time in the birth canal. These were his people. Here you could unlock real potential. Opportunities abound if you are observant and a little creative. This is going to be an important year: the centennial anniversary of the battle. Many ceremonies, many more opportunities. There's to be a special ceremony commemorating one of the units that fought and lost many men in this area, and he wants to scope the location out since there has been a lot of deforesting activity recently.

Hugo has a newborn son at home as well as a five-year-old daughter who needs to be picked up from school in a few short hours, and there is a whole list of things that need to be finished by close of business and he is already behind schedule. He walks a small circle in the area where he tossed a cigarette only a moment before. Can't be a litterbug when you are the mayor of martyred Fleury. Nowhere to be found. He feels more ridiculous with each step. Hugo scans a bizarre flower budding at his feet.

An artillery shell, un petit crapaud.

A 75mm. French. Fired from one of the thousands of field guns during the battle. The single most fired piece of ordnance on either side. Shot all day and all night at relatively short distances with the goal of reducing whole men to their parts.

But LaFleur doesn't recognize any of that. He thinks, *A light bulb?* The nose cone, with primer attached, looks identical to the base cap of a standard light bulb. It is wedged in the roots of a poplar tree stump, poking through a bed of leaves. Nose up, the body of the missile buried beneath the soil. It was once housed in a brass casing. Shiny and slick. Smelling of oil and cordite. Lifted from a bed of hay in a wooden ammunition crate by the hands of a now forgotten assistant gunner and loaded into the breech of the cannon. And then shot into oblivion, leaving its casing behind.

Now it sits there like an unheard confession. Rusted and caked with soil; harsh and stiff with its corroded edges and rough corners against the natural curves of the tree and fallen leaves. The skin, warped like the flesh of an orange. It might've just fallen from the sky only a moment ago.

Hugo kneels, reaches out a hand, and gently tugs the petit crapaud. Stuck, lodged firmly in the grasp of the roots. Doesn't budge in the slightest. It will need to be cut out. It is not as big as it seemed, though. A little guy. Un nouveau-né. Not much bigger than un ballon. He could carry it out. Certainly. Probably with one hand. Couldn't weigh more than two or three kilos. Drop it off himself. Dust his hands off and be done with it. Simple as that.

But it's not Hugo's first day out in the Rouge. He knows the way these little bombs can be. Sometimes the bomb . . . it does its own thing. It doesn't ask permission. A whole truck exploded years ago a minute after it was loaded. *La vache!* Bad day. Very, very bad day. All anyone could talk about for weeks. The other thing Hugo notices with a slight shiver down his spine is the fuse. It appears to be intact. A live one?

Or, of course, there is another choice. Hugo could just leave it. Pretend like he never saw it. No one would know. This happens all the time. Petit crapauds pop up and go unnoticed for months. The elements have their own disarming effect on the fuses. The rain. The cold. They find them a year later with moss growing on them, completely harmless and benign. And if someone stumbles upon it accidentally before then?

He reaches down to pull it from the roots.

"Maire, s'il vous plaît. Don't. It's not worth it."

Hugo turns to find a woman in a teal-green uniform standing beside him. He releases the shell and stands to greet her. Ranger Elisa Dorsett studies the roots of the poplar stump. Her uniform consists of utility trousers over khaki work boots and a knit sweater with shoulder patches pulled over a mint-green collared shirt. A single khaki stripe runs across the breast of the sweater, the title *Office National des Forêts* stitched into it. In a city of women with cropped hair, she still wears hers in an auburn mess always tumbling out from her cap. She has a reputation. A know-it-all. A bitch. She speaks her mind, and people, they don't like that. She is one of two women in a department of all old men. She crouches to examine the shredded bark and wood chips left behind by the chain saws.

"I am so sorry," says Hugo, "I know we have met before, but—"

"We've never met," she says, cutting him off. "I know who you are. I was at the tree ceremony in September. It's fine, you don't have to pretend."

The tree ceremony. Part of an initiative to combat the large-scale deforestation taking place all around Verdun. Hugo had participated, but every face had been a blur, and the only moment he could recall now was posing hunched over a pile of soil in his best suit, holding a shovel with both hands, a newly planted sapling to his side. There had been many cameras and even more faces, but he was so absorbed in whether he should try to appear stoic or happy that the photos he saw in the local papers later had him with a bizarre expression that somehow contained both emotions in a way that made him cringe.

She picks up a jagged shard from the grass and hands it to Hugo.

"Very light. What's this?" he asks, testing its weight.

Tree bark. The rough and gnarled outer side has clumps of moss and dirt clinging to its ridges, but when he turns it over he finds an unexpected, curious sight. Intricate, looping designs cover the smooth underside. It is the fine line work of a master artist, and it gives him the feeling of looking down on wide-open terrain from high up in a plane, God's view of all the hurrying around his creatures do below.

"This is magnificent. So beautiful. Could it be trench art? Maybe?"

"No. Les scolytes. Bark beetles," Elisa says, and wipes both her hands on her trousers. "Those are the galleries they eat into the wood. It's what's killing everything."

"This? That's it? They are so tiny, though. So thin."

"Would you feel healthy if little insects were eating 'thin' galleries throughout your entire body?"

Hugo turns the piece of bark over. It crumbles at the edges, and some of it flakes onto his shoes—tan oxfords that he is already regretting wearing. Poor choice.

"It's climate change. The direct effect. The heat waves, the repeated droughts, the infestation of these insects. You're witnessing it now in real time. These bugs never used to be able to thrive for extended periods the way they can now. They only went after the spruces. But now they go for every tree in sight."

"I don't mind," he jokes. "Not too bad being able to leave the old coat at home."

Elisa does not laugh. She's examining something in the palm of her hand. She holds it out to Hugo. Several bugs, dead, ugly creatures, alien and bulbous, their many legs up to the sky. The fleshy crevices of her palm, a pyre.

"See? They reproduce under the bark. The larvae feed on the layer underneath the bark. Completely girdles it. Then there is no way for the tree to absorb nutrients or water. Then the tree dies. All these trees, they are suffering. They can't even defend themselves, they are so weakened by the droughts. This is your city. This should concern you."

Not much of a city. Squat cement pillars dot the landscape. Each one has a placard that notes what building once stood there. Here, the butcher. There, the grocer. A blacksmith. A school. Shop after shop after shop. There's a small chapel where descendants of the villagers still come once a year to commemorate their ancestors' sacrifice. Just up the slope, the newly renovated museum and visitor center takes up more of the view than it did two years ago, thanks in no small part to Hugo. A blend of brutalist and modern design, it's all smooth limestone and glass with black retaining walls flanking either side and stone embankments in the foreground. Bold and austere. Symbolic in all the most poignant ways. Mounds of jagged quarried basalt stones evoke the desolate shore of a sea long evaporated. A sublime contrast by all accounts. God, if it didn't take your breath away in that special hour after the sun sets but the night has not yet settled. In fact, much of the reason he stands here as the honorary mayor of a decimated village stems from his contribution to that renovation at the crest of the hill.

"Yes, my beautiful city. Heavy lies the crown," he says to Elisa. "It's all mine to maintain, but I have no authority over any of the actual decisions for the land. What can a single man do?"

She tosses the beetles aside. "Small streams make great rivers, Mayor."

He had made something of a name for himself in commercial real estate in the city, breathing new life into a withering local economy over the last five years. Under his direction, vacant storefronts of rotted wood and crumbling mortar gave way to slick facades and artful exterior lighting that belied a type of rural sophistication.

When the news broke of interest in revitalizing the museum—the first major renovation since it opened in 1967—Hugo slid into those circles of influence as if he had always been there. Using his network in Paris, he brokered a deal that turned heads: a collaboration between Le Conte-Noirot Agency and Brochet Lajus Pueyo, two of the most prominent architecture firms in the country. €12.5 million (from which he took a handsome finder's fee). Nineteen hundred square meters of extensions. Enhanced exhibit spaces with both state-of-the-art audio and interactive visual displays. The battle came to life when you stood in there now. It brought a smile to Hugo's face every time he passed it.

He had done that. He had made it happen. He alone. Yes, yes. Transformation. With a capital "T." If not for him, that museum would still be just a poorly lit cavern of dusty military jackets trapped behind smudged glass and dented handrails rusting along the sidewalks to the parking lot. People were beginning to know him as a guy worth knowing, and it was now only a matter of time until he could begin his true ambition in earnest: luxury villas. There's no better location. Two hours from Paris by car, an hour and a half by train. A walkable city with a fine row of chic shops. Restaurants, bars, cafés. Away from all the pestilence and filth of the city. Verdun is calm and populated by just the right type of people—approachable, congenial—aside from a handful of shady Moroccans who seem to have nothing better to do than stand aimlessly on the same few street corners day in, day out. This might just be his ticket to get more involved with the community and hopefully boost his real estate agency.

Still, it came as somewhat of a surprise when a representative from the office of the Préfet de la Meuse approached him in the months following the reopening. After thirty-five years of faithful service, Maire Pascale Delarue, the grandson of Alain Delarue, cobbler of Fleury, had stepped down from his mayoral duties for Fleury, leaving a vacancy they wanted filled yesterday. Hugo thought they were asking him because he might know somebody who was interested. It didn't occur to him immediately that they might want him. For him, the Battle of Verdun has always just been a half-heard history lesson he dozed through at the back of a classroom in elementary school. Still, he was flattered and agreed to at least hear them out. He had made the hour-long drive to the municipal building, where he met the préfet in a cavernous conference room and sat through the meeting while everyone droned on and on and on about the importance of memory and heritage and legacy. When the meeting concluded, he gladly accepted their offer.

It has been nothing but a headache. Pointless phone calls with officials, reports of vandalism to the various signage around the area, complaints from other descendants about all manner of inconsequential items, and he is expected to host or attend a variety of different ceremonies, the most important being the Armistice Day celebration in November, which he quickly discovered takes months of preparation. How anyone can justify spending months of time in preparation for a single day is beyond him.

His only other obligation so far has been a visit to a local school in which he spent an afternoon going from classroom to classroom espousing the significance of Fleury during the battle and the importance of remembering it to a horde of glassy-eyed children with runny noses and stained blouses. The school officials insisted he wear his ceremonial sash—a simple tricolor piece of fabric donned over one shoulder that corresponds with the colors of the flag—but he had refused. There had to be boundaries. He had never enjoyed school as a youngster and found being back in one, even as an esteemed guest, burdensome. He stood at the front of six classrooms in as many hours and espoused the same speech. The children didn't appear capable of remembering what was due for homework, let alone abstract virtues like liberté, égalité, fraternité.

*

The crews work methodically, felling another tree with a rhythmic ease. The hydraulic arm of a mammoth tree removal machine grips the trunk, lifts it into the air, and deposits it on the stack of other trunks.

"What will they do with it all?" he asks.

"Burn it. Shred it. Blow it up. Who knows? It's all useless now."

"*Quelle horreur!* All of it? But that can't be possible."

"They typically harvest seven thousand cubic meters of softwood trees a year. They will be lucky if they make two thousand at this rate. It's poisoned. You can tell by the color. Once the beetles have had their way, the timber turns blue. And gray. Like a suffocated child. Go have a look."

A week ago, after months of deliberation and debate about the continued onslaught by the scolytes, it was finally decided that they were out of options. The forest service would apply the same emergency measures as in the case of a widespread forest fire: cull as many infected trees as it took to bring the infestation to an end. But there is an immediacy in the success of stopping a fire. It can be seen. The heavy smoke can be felt in the lungs. This is not the case with the scolytes. All they can do is wait and hold their breath to see if their efforts were not in vain as the felled trees pile up across the increasingly open lands of Verdun.

Just several days ago, there was a thick woodland in Fleury. Acres of land were reclaimed by the natural world, which felt like the only type of victory that mattered after four years of war and millions killed in ways no one had ever imagined possible. So many of the bunkers were filled in to prevent the overly curious and the flat-out reckless from constantly trying to get inside and explore.

But on this morning, it looks almost exactly as it would have a week into the fighting. Crews have been working throughout the month: trees cleared, their raw, chain saw–eaten stumps jutting into the sky. Not a trace of humanity anywhere. After the war, the government planted trees to limit views of eternity. The German government was required to send several million trees as part of the armistice. That's why there are so many hanging birch and black alders.

Elisa takes a can of spray paint from her backpack and gives it a few vigorous shakes before removing the cap and marking the shell with a generous cloud from the nozzle. It glows neon orange, a luminous iron flower budding in the center of Fleury. The trees, bare. The silence is absolute. Then, wings flapping overhead. Hugo turns in time to see a sparrow hawk—or maybe a merlin?—glide above the bare branches. He steps back and lights a cigarette.

Mayor Hugo isn't stupid, though. The démineurs don't have a reputation for punctuality. Around the time that Hugo accepted the position of mayor, he was offered a special trip to the depot where all the unexploded la Grand Guerre ordnance is stored. The main depository is an open-air bay affectionately known as the "Bomb Garden." There are old, sunken batteries around the perimeter that are too damp to store anything in, where the darkness just sucks in all the light from a flashlight.

Hugo took a walk through the central bay, open to the sky. "See the way the walls slant?" The démineurs gestured to the walls as they passed the rows of ordnance. "Helps if there's a detonation. It all gets directed sky-high. All by design, all by design." They even opened one of the vaults and let Hugo have a look inside. All the large-caliber ordnance stored and cataloged in orderly rows. The démineurs stood there with the smiles of men showing off their wine cellar to a guest.

A single shell. So much commotion for a single shell. Hugo crouches, exhales a cloud of smoke. Elisa relays the situation to dispatch over the radio. He shivers and scans the hillside. The men drag their saws from tree to tree and organize the piles of raw logs that will be taken away later. Others clad in bright orange shirts and navy-blue helmets straddle felled trunks and lean their chain saws into the bark, spewing a storm of splinters in every direction. The grass doused with a million wood chips. It is a striking scene, certainly. Cratered wasteland once again.

Every dip and rise in the earth a frozen flinch from the impact of an artillery shell.

There's an immense sadness to that land. All the pain, the loss. It swallows you. That's what people said to Hugo when he first started coming out. And in some ways it was true. There is a sense of loss when you walk. The slim footpaths were once main roads for this commune. Ruins are right there in front of you. But the sadness? The truth is when Hugo looked around at the scarred landscape, covered up by grass and German trees, he didn't feel much at all. It might have more to do with the future than the past, he speculates. For all the sorrow and pain associated with this war, for all the impassioned cries of "Never again!" for all the promises to learn and grow, it was less than twenty years before the next war blew through. Many of the same players. Many of the same outcomes. The myths from the first one were still warm. The toys got even bigger. Man had the capacity to wipe himself off the face of the earth for good. Verdun's significance as a natural defensive barrier—and the decades spent bracing the region with fortresses and heavy artillery—became obsolete overnight. They had airplanes. They flew over the commanding views that once made Verdun so unique without firing a single shot. Then the Nazis walked right through. And still, there are more wars.

A gendarmerie officer arrives first to inspect and cordon the area. She emerges from her vehicle, a woman of an immediately commanding presence, and takes one of the footpaths to Elisa and Hugo. If Elisa had been looking at Hugo, she would have noticed a momentary smile cross his face.

"Adjutant Moreau, Mayor LaFleur," Elisa introduces them.

Hugo and Camille, new lovers, both married, just not to each other, shake hands professionally in a moment laced with childish glee and pretend to meet for the first time.

"A pleasure," Camille says with a self-assured handshake.

She holds his grip a moment too long, her fingers pressing into the soft, warm palm of his hand. Hugo's jaw clenches.

"Thank you for coming so quickly," says Hugo in an even tone. "Look at what we have here."

She crouches to examine the shell, her tactical trousers hugging her backside.

"Oh yes, this is one of the bad ones. We'll need to get the démineurs out," she says, and turns to radio the report in.

Hugo watches her go to her patrol car and return with a spool of yellow caution tape. She unravels the tape, one hand through the hub, the other pulling long stretches of it onto the grass. After wrapping it around her hand a few times, she attempts to tear it, but the elastic material only stretches longer, so she bites it and the tape gives way in shriveled tatters. Immediately, he remembers her mouth on his neck, those same hands on his collar, slipping each button open. Everything about her, soft except for her bite.

"Well?" asks Elisa.

"Excuse me?"

"I said I can remain here if you have other things to do," she says.

"Oh, that's very kind of you. But I really should stay. At least until the démineurs arrive."

Camille walks back over, and Hugo feigns interest in the shell with the look of a man inconvenienced by a flat tire.

"It's been months since my last cordon. How exciting," Camille says with a smile.

"Last thing I needed today," says Hugo.

"You've got somewhere more important to be?" Camille asks, tilting her head. "We've got it under control, Maire. It might be a while. I would hate to keep you from your evening plans."

"Madame, I've always got time for my duties," Hugo says, returning the smile.

For about three months, they have been taking Hugo's car on nights they can sneak away from their families and driving, his hand on her inner thigh, to the most remote reaches of Verdun to fuck in places completely untouched in decades. Abandoned mines, quarries, and pillboxes. Time capsules of all kinds. They never go anywhere in public together. They rarely lie down or strip naked. Every encounter leaves them tangled in the restraint of their own clothing. It's the type of sex that's all rush, dirty like emptying a compost bin with one hand.

They park at the end of long, winding roads deep in the woods and wander into cavernous concrete structures that once housed machine guns and recoilless cannon and underground shelters for soldiers from every corner of the globe. They use the walls, stripped of light fixtures and wiring, as guides, allowing their fingertips to drag along the surfaces and tingle with the very real sense that a certain type of vermin life is creeping and crawling everywhere just out of sight. Their only rule: nothing is off-limits. No location. No act. They will take every tunnel, every passage. The darker, the better. She lifts the latches to heavy iron doors deep inside bunkers, and they open inward like they want nothing more than to be wide open forever. They grab rickety banisters and follow stairs into pitch darkness so deep and thick you could almost grab it. They step confidently, without the kind of trepidation that informs their public lives. On their second trip, they went to the decrepit pillboxes surrounding Fort Souville—large, dank cavernous structures, some two stories high, that suck the heat right out of your skin the moment you cross the threshold—and Hugo nearly fell down an open shaft in the 155mm turret, right in the center of the tiled floor. Hugo imagined plummeting into it was like drowning in crude oil. Fully enveloped, kicking and screaming in the abyss, until he hit whatever neck-breaking bottom lay beneath. It gave them both a shock so strong that they made love up against the wall beside the opening, riding the wave of adrenaline in a darkness that goes right through the skin and stains the soul.

She isn't really his type, being almost ten years older than him. He tends toward the younger ones, the young professionals fresh from university. Just enough maturity to hold a conversation but eager to please someone of his authority. Camille's eyes, set close together and pale blue, penetrate the veneer of his outward personality that he shows the world. She's nearly a foot taller than him as well, something he never thought he would find attractive in a woman. But he's been discovering new things about himself with every trip they take together. He wants to get on his knees for her.

Just last night, she took him to a new spot, a place he hadn't even known existed. The Tunnel de Tavannes, a twelve-hundred-meter stretch of abandoned rail tunnel less than ten minutes from Fleury. Blocks of limestone stacked to form high archways with a series of reinforced concrete support beams, riblike in their construction, that run the length of the tunnel. A small guard house forms the left wall, where slim observation windows gave them the impression of being watched. Hugo already likes that place most of anywhere they've been.

Upon entering, the temperature dropped immediately. A cool blanket enveloped them, and the single flashlight they brought became less useful with each step forward. A pulsing thrill ran through his chest. A stirring, fluttery feeling. The chill, the bottomless dark, the quiet, the small but comforting warmth of their hands embraced.

"This was unused at the beginning of the war. They didn't need it for trains anymore, but it was a perfect transportation channel to move men. Safe, secure. The German shells couldn't penetrate it, although they could hit both openings on either end. So the French stopped up all the ventilation shafts and turn it into barracks where soldiers were positioned before they went to the front. Overnight, they filled it with one, sometimes two thousand men. Can you imagine?" she told him.

Loose gravel crunched underfoot, softened only by the surprising amount of trash piled up in drifts along the track bed. Paper items of all sorts, soda cans, glass bottles stripped of labels, unidentifiable items with passing resemblances to plastic and latex. Their hands remained entwined. He felt the pinprick of a cuticle on her ring finger. He noticed, to his surprise, the absence of calluses lining her palms, the kind of smooth pebbles that are found only at the bottom of calm rivers.

"There were no latrines, everyone just pissed and shit along the walls, covering the mess with lime. Rats and lice reigned supreme. Absolute squalor powered by a few generators that probably failed all the time, I'm sure. No vents. Erratic resupply. But it was better than out there. All these men, seeking safety, security. Just a little bit of refuge under weak lamplight."

They passed small alcoves lining the walls, safety niches where one could huddle out of the path of an approaching train. A strong draft blew into their faces.

"Feel that?" she asked, and held up her hand.

Hugo nodded and faced her. Condensation clouds escaped their mouths and mingled together, their faces inches apart.

"Months into the battle, there was an accident. No one really knows what happened. Somehow, a fire got started. An explosion in the ammo reserve, a cooking fire. It started at one end of the tunnel, but this air current propelled the flames along the whole tunnel at once. A fire tornado.

"The fire burned for three days. Hundreds died. Trapped. So many, they couldn't even get a final count. That's how badly the bodies were burned. It turned the place into a crematorium."

Hugo shivered. "Horrible."

"The French government hid the whole thing. Listed the men as missing until after the end of the war," Camille said. "Can you imagine? Burning to death in this rat-infested cesspool?"

Hugo shrugged. "Hard to. Unimaginable, really."

She cradled his face, leaned in, and lightly bit his neck. "All those boys crying for their mothers, trampling each other to get out before it's too late," she said, her breath hot and damp on his skin.

She bit again, harder. Hugo looked up and around at the stained and marred walls, her teeth holding his neck. He expelled another large cloud into the air above. His fingers had gone numb. Seeking warmth, he slipped them into her waistband, but she pulled away suddenly, almost taking a chunk of flesh with her.

"These are the same walls, the exact same walls," she said, and spread her arms against the limestone.

Hugo took a step toward Camille, leaned in, and pinned her hands to the wall. Camille grunted with surprised pleasure. He bit the back of her neck and felt the blood come to the surface, dark and sweet, practically glowing. She warmed like an empty glass filled from a hot faucet. The elastic caught around his fingers in his rush to pull her panties to her ankles. He dropped to his knees, plunging his tongue into all her softest places, digging his tongue inside the way he ate certain types of fruit, looking for the pit.

He slid inside and mushed her face into the limestone. Camille cried out in glee. He leaned his weight into her and increased the pressure, keeping her pinned to the wall. She opened her jacket and then her shirt, exposing her breasts. He grabbed them, pinching her nipples.

Each hastily placed slab hung there, the mortar in between old and crumbly. Writing covered the slabs. It came into focus all at once. The words bled from beneath the stone before his eyes. Names. Names and names and names.

Francois Angles

Henri Artaud

Gaston Conneau

Raymond Estienne

Louis Elby

Louis Dupre

Louis Destot

Felix Foch

In between the names, there were little notes. Declarations of love. Jokes. Letters to loved ones that would never be read by those they were addressed to. He could imagine fine streams of dust spilling from the ceiling and the big bombs walking around overhead and soldier after soldier scribbling away as they moved along.

The walls groaned, and the ribbed concrete arches stretched away into the void, folding over one another down the tunnel. The names crowded his mind as she came. He readjusted his stance to get better leverage and stepped on the flashlight. The lens cracked under his boot. Darkness. Darkness so absolute and infinite, being inside her felt like all there was to feel in the universe. The softness. The hardness beneath the softness. The sense that, contained in that graspable form, there was a shapeless soul. The warmth of a stranger's body. The whispers above them of a few thousand souls inscribed on cool, damp stones.

Hugo groaned and pulled out, spurting his semen onto the blackened wall beside them. He stopped straining his eyes and turned inward to search for a light inside. A series of images:

A lone bird gliding across a crystal blue sky.

A spider mending its web after a heavy rainfall.

Ants in a single file carrying grains of sand.

Endless, endless silent trees.

Afterward, they stumbled their way back without a light. At the opening to the tunnel, clouds of steam escaped the open throats of their jackets, their skin slick and dewy.

They stopped at a late-night food truck on their way home, the closest thing to a public appearance they'd risk, and split a greasy rotisserie chicken in his car. They ate with their hands, splitting the legs off, stripping the oily yellow skin and feeding it to each other, sucking meat from every piece, their tongues slipping between the radius and ulna of the wing bones. When they finished devouring it, they dumped the thin bones out the passenger-side window and sped back to their families, all used up but fulfilled.

*

Camille and Elisa stake out a ten-meter perimeter using the yellow caution tape. Hugo takes a few steps in their direction to help but then stops and crosses his arms. Probably best not to appear too familiar. Instead, he watches them at a distance, taking note of the way they negotiate the decimated terrain, maneuvering around stumps and craters and threading the tape back to the starting point. They tie it to whatever is available in their path—a few tree stumps and the cement pillar marking where the corner of the smelter's building once stood. Yes, he and Camille have had one hell of a time over these last few months. Still, even with the memory of their most recent foray pulsing in his mind, the attraction has already begun to wane. She circumvents the rim of a crater and her steps are all brawn, no grace. Too much time in boots, not enough in heels, he speculates.

He walks over to meet them as they close the loop. Camille severs the final strand and wraps the excess tape on the spool. He notices for the first time her hands are large for a woman, certainly bigger than his.

They are dry, and there's ashy residue in the webbing between her fingers. The bright yellow tape casts her skin in a pale, sickly color. He grimaces. This is the nature of an affair. Out of nowhere, you start noticing all these little things that didn't occur to you at the beginning. The sensation starts to wane. The mystery turns out to be much more shallow than originally gauged. It always goes this way. The settling, the mundanity, the familiarity of it all. Where's the risk? Where's the challenge? The mood feels a little tempered. There's no way to avoid it, no way to predict when it will occur. It just happens.

Sure, everyone has a few tricks up their sleeve to keep the carnal pleasure going. Camille's involves a very particular technique she has with her tongue during fellatio. But even so, it's not enough to keep the edge of the affair itself.

Elisa kneels and loops the end of the tape through the anchored knot to complete the cordon. Hugo watches the practiced, graceful way she ties it off, taut and secure. She stands and the two of them are there before him, side by side. He realizes it's not even close. The pair strike a stark contrast to each other, Camille, the ravished, and Elisa, the unexplored. The decimated village where they stand only heightens the difference. Elisa is the lone building left untouched after a violent storm. She is the miracle structure that withstood the destruction against all odds. Hugo wants to open the front door and seek shelter inside.

Ferrand Martin, the supervisor for Verdun's démineurs, arrives with his crew. He has a goose neck whose length adds a certain prominence to his mustache. He's wearing a crushed and wrinkled blue baseball cap with the word *DÉMINAGE* stitched in yellow block letters. The démineurs walk up with a casual air of boredom and mild annoyance. At Martin's side is Antoine Barbeaux, a hulk of a man in thick-framed glasses who drinks like a hole and has the largest beard of the crew. The beard is especially thick under the chin and juts out under his perpetual pout. Yannick Basille trails behind, loaded down with a large pack on his shoulders and a steel claw in his arms he has not yet learned to carry with ease.

"How's Marcel?" Martin asks Barbeaux.

"Walking around, always with his hand buried in his crotch, pants hanging off his ass. I say to him, 'Why do you walk that way? What? Are you afraid someone will steal your balls?'"

They arrive at the site, and Basille drops the gear.

"Salut, Ferrand," Camille greets him warmly. "Say, have you lost weight?"

Martin grunts appreciatively. He crouches down and examines the shell. "Hey, Basille. Come here. Looks like we got a live one."

Basille crouches beside him. Whereas the others are all comfort and ease, Basille is quiet and serious. His coveralls still have that just-out-of-the-package sheen and fit him stiffly. He's zippered and buttoned up to the collar. Under a mop of brown hair, his face scrunches in concentration. If the ground were to suddenly open and swallow Barbeaux whole, Basille would be none the wiser. Martin takes care to point out the various parts of the ancient ordnance. Barbeaux kneels as well and tilts his head back and forth. He's unimpressed.

"Agh, I slap my balls on it. That's nothing. We can have it out of here in twenty. Basille, give me a hand with this."

Whenever Barbeaux says "give me a hand with this," what he really means is "take care of this for me."

"Non, better radio dispatch and let them know we are going to be delayed here a little while. This one looks a little temperamental. Don't see these very often," says Martin.

He pulls on it and feels resistance.

"Basille," Martin commands, "bring me the extraction bag."

Hugo shifts his weight and rocks in place. "While he's doing that, I'm going to check in to see how the clearing is going," he says, and walks toward the crew going to work on a stand of fresh spruces a few hundred meters in the distance.

Basille returns after a few minutes, lugging the canvas bag on his shoulder. Hugo lights his last cigarette and watches the pair get to work. Basille drops the bag beside Martin and unclips the straps. It rolls out like an artist's brush case. A series of pockets contain all manner of tools. Standard screwdrivers and scissors. A few fine picks with curved edges remind him of the same tools he has seen at the dentist. But there are also brushes that would be more at home with a painter and locking forceps that appear surgical in design.

Martin examines the nose of the round and then selects a brush and one of the scythe-shaped picks from the bag. He carves out decades' worth of crud from the rim of the ignitor and delicately brushes it away. This device was made for one purpose: to destroy. It was made for this singular reason and this reason alone. This fact must never be forgotten. The amount of dirt that he brings out is surprising given the small space. He diligently and efficiently works around the rim several times. Scoop. Brush. Scoop. Brush. He hooks his pick in and digs around.

Hugo saunters up from the opposite side of the field, and from his new vantage point, he has a clearer view of the crew. Martin, the older, wiry fellow, and Basille, the younger one, clearly following Martin's lead. Barbeaux busies himself organizing some tools. Camille relays a message to headquarters over her radio. Elisa seems at ease as well. For the first time, Hugo notes the way her utility pants hug her waistline. They are fitted to her form, whereas every other ranger he has interacted with wears formless trousers that sag in all the worst places. She looks over at him, and he glances away, pretending to take interest in a family walking from their car to the museum at the crest of the slope.

While Camille is preoccupied with her radio traffic, Hugo sidles up beside Elisa.

“Not the most cordial bunch, those clearing crews,” he says.

“Impervious to your charm?” asks Elisa.

Might that be just the slightest hint of flirtation?

“Like taking one of their chain saws to a steel column. I cut my losses and scampered. Any plans for the weekend?”

“Sleep. Catch up on a few episodes of *The Bureau*. Maybe go for a run. Nothing crazy.”

“You’re a runner? Me too. I’m about to start training for a marathon in a few weeks. It will be my fifth. Do you have any races coming up?”

“Oh, I’m nothing special. I just do it for exercise. Easier than going to the gym. And cheaper.”

“It’s a way of life! I started a running group here in town. You should come sometime.”

“I don’t know. I never run with other people. I’d probably just get in the way.”

“No, no. It’s really not that serious. We have people of all experience levels. It’s a great way to spend a morning. We run, we grab lunch. It’s always a good time.”

“Yeah, I’ll think about it,” she says.

Metal grinds against iron, and Hugo’s skin crawls. Hugo turns from Elisa and takes another few subtle steps away. The key is to focus on something over there, something that seems more interesting. The last thing he wants is for the démineurs to think he’s scared. Each step he takes is slow. Not in a straight path. Almost as if he’s just restless and bored. Which he is, sure. It’s been over four hours. Martin lathers the area around the nose cone in a substance from a small can.

“That’s going to need to sit for a little while and settle in. Break up some of the corrosion,” he says.

Hugo buries his hands in his pockets again. To hide the gleaming wedding band on his finger? "Can this go any faster? I'm starving."

The démineurs try at first to placate him. Basille even offers him part of his lunch: "Bacon, lettuce, and brie on a baguette. Can't go wrong."

Hugo considers it for a moment, thinking of a polite way to decline. "I can't have soft cheese. Dietary restrictions."

"You can't be that hungry then," Barbeaux grumbles.

Nothing in their appearance suggests they are anxious or experiencing any type of unease standing over the unstable explosive. Martin and Basille are both so engrossed in the work that they seem to have forgotten Hugo's even there. Their true faces have emerged. Uninterested. Inconvenienced by having to do their jobs. It's cold and wet. Both of them would probably much rather be seated in their truck with the heat turned way up and the radio on or endlessly scrolling through their phones.

"You may want to take a step or two back," Basille says.

In his attempt to identify the tools, Hugo has unknowingly drifted much closer and now practically leans over Martin's shoulder.

"Of course, my apologies." Hugo backs up a respectable distance.

Martin doesn't appear to notice the transgression, completely absorbed in his work. He has the steadiest hands in the district. He has "the feel," they say. Not everyone has it. Either you have it or you don't. You don't always know right away who has it and who doesn't. It takes time. Others would have called for backup. Waited for one of the army units to come from several hours away. Not Martin.

There is a gritty click.

"I hate that sound," Martin says, and chuckles. "Still makes me flinch."

The ignitor edges upward from its seat in the shell's nose. Martin pauses and takes a look at his fingernail. He grimaces and shakes it out.

Hugo resists the urge to shout, *No, seriously, take your time! Nothing urgent going on right now!* He positions himself behind one of the few trees.

Martin shakes his hand once more and resumes the removal. He is careful but quick. His movements, smooth. He has the gentle, firm touch of a father who has raised several children. Basille hunches over his shoulder, and the two of them inspect the extracted ignitor.

"Surprisingly good condition!" says Martin. "Haven't seen one like this in years. Give this one a good wash and it will be like new."

He looks up and around, expecting to find Hugo beside them. Hugo quickly steps out from behind the tree and tries to shorten his distance before Martin sees him.

"I'd love to see it!"

Martin turns to the sound of his voice. If he's noticed the great distance Hugo put between them as they dismantled the bomb, he doesn't show it.

"Of course, of course. Take a look here."

Martin shows Hugo the finer points of a 75mm artillery round. But it's Basille who is about to steal the show. He's digging deeper into the earth surrounding the ordnance and pulling out various debris—rocks, twigs, all the solid junk that gets in the way—when he yanks out something a little different from the rest: a slim, curved thing, fine as a fingernail clipping. Clots of dirt cling to it, and he almost whisks it away into a crater behind him. He pauses. He wipes away the dirt and examines it. The others take notice, and everyone stops what they are doing. Silence.

A human rib.

Excerpts from the Field Journal of Hans Kraemer, Field Director and Lead Archaeologist

FEBRUARY 19, 2016

WORD'S OUT. Bones in Verdun. First time this has happened in a few years, and no one wastes the opportunity. There's a reason the Direction Régionale des Affaires Culturelles leaves me at the top of their contact list for moments such as this one. Sure, in my twenty-year career I've led excavation projects all across Europe, including at Ypres and Passchendaele. Yes, I'm considered an expert in forensic archaeology and the recovery of human remains. But there are experts everywhere. You can't walk through the Sorbonne without tripping over one. More so than anything else, they trust me, which is a consideration I do not take for granted.

With remains, I'm all details, details, details. Minimal disturbance. Preserve the evidence. My teams work like silent, cloaked specters under the crimson banner of science. One develops a reputation in time. People forget, it wasn't until 1984 that French President François Mitterrand and German Chancellor Helmut Kohl stood hand in hand at the Douaumont Ossuary and committed openly to a more peaceful future. When someone discovers bones in Verdun, they know whom to call.

Other than myself, DRAC reached out to a few other specialists and excavators they keep on contract for this exact purpose, as well as all the various partnerships we have with nearby universities so we can borrow a few PhD candidates. There's been a slight delay—the excavator teams are all tied up, so we will have to make do with the PhD candidates—which has put us a day or so behind schedule. Not a big deal, this is a small site. We meet the late arrivals along with two gendarmes at the train station and load everyone into vans. They take us right out to la cicatrice, luggage and all. A general sense of excitement pervades the ride, the same buzz that percolates the nerves when the doors of Élysée Montmartre yawn open on a Saturday night, the headlining act about to take the stage.

We go from the train station through the city, right past the old castle gate and the Meuse, and straight out to the battlefields. Everything about the land feels so quaint and bucolic, mesmerizing pastures. Behold, we turn a bend in the road and the next field in view is nothing but overgrown shell holes. The light hits the ridges of the grass-covered shell holes at a low angle and creates shadows that look like the hollows of vacant eye sockets.

Is there any other way to see the battlefields of Verdun than in the rain? A low fog hangs over the land and obscures the tops of the trees against a matte, flinty sky. Despite all the impact craters and the remaining rubble, there is a profound sense of peace among the wooded hills. Thick stretches of forest so dense it's hard to believe it was all wasteland a couple of decades ago. The symbolism is obvious: rebirth, regeneration, the ability to heal. But the bug has destroyed that illusion. We can see evidence of its handiwork in the crumbling parapets of the old forts, Vaux and Douaumont. When we scan the horizon with care, there are gaps. Odd holes in the fabric. Lo, the scars, exposed anew. It took generations to reclaim this earth, and now it is all being lost again in an instant.

The ride continues, and we pass the big monuments, the ossuary and its cemetery. Now, a low-hanging sky. Raw stumps and churned clay. The bug has ravaged this land. It is as bad as they say—no, worse. Where are all the trees? Where are the many forests that crowded the ravaged village of Fleury? I swear, for a brief moment, we are right back in 1916. I'm the only one who has spent any time in this area, so for the rest of the crew, they have no idea, it's all new.

It's difficult to understate the importance of this battle, this city, in the mind of a certain kind of Frenchman. Verdun forms the core of a national pride that becomes scarcer with each new generation. The connections run deep. Charles de Gaulle was wounded and captured here, at Douaumont, and spent the rest of the war a prisoner. And he was just one of over a million soldiers who held the line against the invading Germans. Ask any French person you meet about Verdun, and they will gesture to some half-remembered name of a great-uncle or some other who they think spent some time here during that terrible year. *Ils ne passeront pas!* Nearly every single regiment in the French army spent time in Verdun during the battle. It is everyone's; it is no one's. Which is another way of saying almost everyone has a piece of Verdun, but there's no one individual who knows everything about this battle.

Ferrand Martin and his crew of démineurs greet us with an attitude that can only be described as cool and bristly, but the way they joke with one another, it seems they might warm to us given some time. They stand around the site, hands in pockets, a foot out front, cocked at an angle, while we carefully examine the exposed earth. This pose they strike over and over says, *I've seen a thing or two in my time in these boots.* Barbeaux leans back on his heels, one hand rubbing his belly, the crust of this place all over his coveralls. They all have this look to some degree, as if they were all pulled from the soil by their ancestors.

They wear the same drab coveralls made of static-dissipative fabric, varying shades of faded blue. Barbeaux wears a heavy knit sweater under his coveralls, which are always open. Henri sports a dark blue linen scarf. None of them wear the gloves they were issued. According to all of them, the issued ones are trash, as is much of the equipment provided. Instead, they've bought thick lumber gloves with their own money.

Every excavation is the same. Cordons and pink ribbons. We take our time conducting the initial survey of the area. Our photographer takes photo after photo from every angle imaginable, his flash jolting the site with the spontaneity of lightning. The surveyor sketches a rough map of the spot. Our PhD students, Juliette and Clémence, move quickly, taking notes and rearranging our gear. I swear, people drop what they're doing and board the first train out of town just for a chance to be a part of it. For what? I've got two decades in this line of work and I still don't have a good answer to that question. Closure? To heal? To say you were part of something much larger and significant than yourself? Methinks the sentiment rings a bit hollow, the conviction wooden.

They remove the petit crapaud, as they call it, and carry the relic off with nonchalance soon after we arrive. I can't help but see the humor in such a situation. All the factors that have to come together for this shell to have arrived *here* at this precise location. The lore of invention: Fritz Haber in his lab in Munich fiddled with his flasks and test tubes and accidentally knocked one containing his most recent experiment to the floor. As he gasped for air, scrambling to escape the poisonous vapors that clung to his skin and worked their way into his lungs, it is not difficult to imagine a look of awe beneath his pain, and then a realization bloomed in his mind that he had just changed the course of modern warfare.

An old woman bent over a table in a factory, her trembling fingers loading the poison into its compartment in the partially assembled shell before passing it farther down the line, where a man began fixing the (faulty) blasting cap to the shell's body like he did to the one hundred shells before with no way of knowing this one would be one of the 15 percent that would fail to detonate in battle.

The French gunner, all covered in mud and who knows what else, daydreamed of the last time he felt a woman's touch at a brothel, where he waited in line for two hours for twelve minutes with a red-haired woman twice his age, as he lifted the defective shell from the stockpile, a couple hundred spent casings beside his steaming cannon. His eyes, empty; his ears, plugged with cotton as the barrage of a soul-rattling caliber rolled on around him. He loaded the defective shell into the chamber, a soggy half of a cigar lodged between his teeth, as his assistant gunner slammed the breech closed.

And then feet. Thousands and thousands of feet walked over the spot where the projectile lay slowly working its way up and then down and then back up like a piece of errant driftwood momentarily submerged beneath the rolling swells of a great blue ocean before poking back up above the surface.

Verdun's land is no longer the wasteland but a fresh scab—gooey platelets beneath churned rock and stone. German POWs armed with baskets and black-robed missionaries once scattered seeds here to reclaim the wasteland. Black pines and firs, sent by the German government, lined the roads, waiting to root. But all the same, the vast expanse of the countryside was just the idea of what the place used to be. Now a desert, but a healthy desert.

It all seems so likely, and yet at the same time implausible, that a shell could have traveled almost one hundred years through the shifting soil of this earth just to pop up at our feet. It's been more than a lifetime since that war, and still, more death. In just this one town. That's not even counting the rest of the country. The farmlands of the Somme.

The beaches of Normandy. The River Marne. The whole country is one giant booby trap. And the French, victorious, could erect their monuments. Tell their stories. Honor their dead. And if you met a man who was around during those four horrible years and you asked, *Did you serve?* he only had to say, *Oui, j'*étais *à Verdun.*

Upon entering the city limits of Hiroshima, after the mushroom cloud dissipated, American forces found a most peculiar phenomenon among the burning rubble, the liquefied glass and molten iron: dark gray shadows staining the marble exteriors of some buildings. Human-shaped shadows, on closer inspection. Legs and torsos and the vague outline of where a mind once existed, erased in an instant. The solemn echo of a life snuffed out from several thousand meters above as if the hand of God had forced it out. It could not be worse than the physical evidence to come: the radiation burns, the tumors, and the birth defects. But the shadows linger in the mind. The absence is what sticks in the memory. The knowledge that an entire being can be disappeared into thin air.

When the Germans first approached and the shelling began, the trees cried. They wept tears of sap and trembled. The buildings flinched with each impact. It continued until they were all gone. Erased. Welcome to the necropolis, God's own acres. At the end of the war, France cordoned off sixteen million acres of uninhabitable land. Twelve thousand miles of trenches, where entire armies had lived and died, now quiet as tombs. A barren landscape dotted with rifles plunged bayonet-down into the soil with a helmet atop to mark the location of a buried body.

*

On a soiled tarp, our démineurs have placed the discovery: a single rib bone, along with a humerus and several knotty vertebrae. Small orange flags dot the area beside it like toothpicks in a plate of gougères. I slip on a pair of gloves and inspect the rib bone first. One of twenty-four in the human body. A funny-looking thing when separated from its cage. The protector of our most precious organs. Great indicator of sex as well as age. Flat and robust at the sternal end, clearly a male. A minor callus along the shaft indicating a fully healed fracture long before whatever caused his death. No other deformities, pitting, projections, or ossification. Dense and smooth. A young man.

So, a soldier. Big mystery solved.

If only it were that simple. Even as we stand there, the démineurs pull more of the vertebrae from the pit in the earth. There are 206 bones in the human body, and it looks like we might just find every last one of them. Time to get to work. We grid the area with twine and label each section by letter and number. Out come the hand shovels and the mesh screens. We go until the sun sets.

After our first day walking the site, we find our pockets laden with lead and iron. It's impossible to resist picking the bits and pieces of shrapnel off the ground; they are everywhere. All you have to do is look down, study the soil. What might first appear to be a rock or a pebble actually is a shard of shell upon closer examination. If you look across the open, sodden ground of Fleury, the bits glow in the sunlight piercing the fog. Titian red, oxidized rust, glittering in our palms. Some are as tiny as baby teeth, and others are so large, they can barely be held in one hand. No wonder so many bodies will never be found. If chunks of iron this large were flying around, all it would take was one to remove a person from this world entirely. There is no better proof of how tenuous the thread between body and soul is than the misshapen hills of Verdun.

Some tree bark looks like shrapnel until you pick it up and it crumbles to pieces in your fingers. You can tell the difference from the weight alone. The shrapnel is heavier than the rocks, and the rocks are heavier than the bones, lightest of all and yet the most important. If weight is any indication of permanence, the weapons used in the war will outlast even our memories of just how horrible the whole affair was for the human race. Even so, the conclusion feels counterintuitive.

Human bones are fascinating. They are incredibly strong despite being somewhat porous on the inside. Many of the larger ones are quite spongy in the center, trabecular and cancellous. These spongy places contain the production sites of our white and red blood cells as well as our platelets, the defenders of our body. And yet, bones can bear more weight, ounce for ounce, than steel. They can repair and realign themselves without our guidance. Our skeletons completely renew themselves every ten years. Imagine that. An entirely new set of bones every decade. They can withstand the pressure of a century interred beneath the surface of the earth and reemerge in an instant. All by design.

That night, we settle into our lodgings, Les Jardins Du Mess, a nice, quiet hotel in the center of the city, and I unload my pockets. What to do with them now? All these pieces that seemed so valuable and important only a few hours ago are now unsettling and out of place beside my bed. Twisted, jagged pieces of iron slowly sink their teeth into the hides of the leather chairs, until I lift them off for fear they might do some damage and I will lose my deposit. What to do with them now? I stuff them into my luggage, where they remain for the rest of the trip until I leave—whereupon packing my bags, I will rediscover these forgotten pieces of shrapnel and, realizing there is no room in my suitcases, will shove them in the backs of the dresser cabinets for the next guest to discover.

Démineurs

It isn't that this hasn't happened before.

There were a couple hundred thousand deaths in that battle over the course of a single year. Many of those bodies were never recovered, swallowed whole by the earth. Don't have to look too hard in Verdun to find the odd bone.

Most times we just slip it in a bag and send it off to the lab, where it remains as much an artifact as any weapon or piece of gear, unless they can identify the bones, but what's more likely is they catalog it and then toss it into some vault up in the Douaumont Ossuary, a giant, mass catacomb made of granite and feldspar that dominates the landscape a few miles down the road from Fleury. Its bell tower rises above the land, and the only way to view the full scale of its necropolis is to climb the many flights of stairs to the belfry and look out over the manicured landscape. Everyone has been there. Every president lights the eternal flame when they take office.

But every once in a while, after the rains fall long and hard and the earth shifts in just the right way, we dig a hole like any of the millions of other holes we have dug before, not there, or there, but *there*, and when we reach a hand down, something else comes back with it.

What's different about this site is once we find this first bone, we find more.

And it isn't that we find another bone, but the way that the second bone and then the third and fourth are in relation to one another.

All one on top of the next.

Yes, almost anatomically.

Which means?

A body.

A whole body. Buried.

This isn't just a simple hole in the ground anymore.

No, it transforms into an archaeological dig site overnight. An investigation is in order. The proper authorities need to be alerted. Certain protocols need to be followed.

Oh mon Dieu, the protocols.

The academics start dropping right out of the sky.

The anthropologists, the archaeologists, the sociologists, all the 'gists! They arrive the same way: off the first train from the city, laminated passes around their necks, dragging their theories and research behind them. Bodies shriveled and saggy from years spent hunched in poorly lit archives. They inject their opinions into everything—every conversation, every decision.

Oh oui, they love to hear themselves talk.

Hans is okay, though.

Yes, we all love Hans. No one has ever had an issue with him. He always looks a little out of place with his colleagues, like he might've stumbled upon the site by accident. His entire wardrobe consists of Black Sabbath and Motörhead T-shirts. And what a mustache. His boots have seen more concert venue floors than academic halls.

Hans is pretty quiet for the most part, but every once in a while he says the strangest things. One time he turned around and, out of nowhere, said, "This is our territory. This"—and he gestured widely—"France's disowned soil. It's a forgotten wasteland and it is ours now. All you need to know about humanity can be found out here between these trees. Embrace it."

Yeah, Hans is the man. The rest?

As much as they want to take the whole thing off our hands and send us on our way, the academics can't dig for shit.

Excerpts from the Field Journal of Hans Kraemer, Field Director and Lead Archaeologist

February 22, 2016

THE FOLLOWING WEEK proceeds at the same pace. We meticulously scrape and sweep every centimeter of la cicatrice until the sun dips beneath the horizon and twilight gives way to night. We go layer by layer through the soil and catalog every bone we find. Our excavators phone us on the second day to let us know they will be unable to make it in time, so we enlist the démineurs to assist with the excavation. They need to remain on-site anyway, in case we discover another piece of ordnance. Part of the team digs under our supervision while the others sift buckets of soil through mesh screens for teeth and other small bones. We find more shrapnel than anything else. The days drag on and on. During our breaks, we huddle in a truck with a broken heater and measure our warmth with each exhaled breath. An ongoing debate begins with the démineurs as to whether the heat is malfunctioning or whether it just takes a little while before the cab heats up. We stand firm that it needs to be taken in and looked at. Beyond a shadow of a doubt. Ferrand thinks otherwise.

"There's nothing to fix. That's the way it is. The way it's always been," Ferrand says, craning his neck into the cab.

"It shouldn't take this long to heat up," Juliette insists.

It's always worse in the early morning. Like trying to warm the body with the flame of a lighter in a blizzard. We recoil from the cracked leather seats any time our exposed skin touches them.

Barbeaux takes a cursory look at it but sides with Ferrand. "There's nothing wrong with it," he says. "It's just old."

That is that. We have gone as far up the chain as is possible and will just have to deal with the circumstances. I suspect the simple reason is that Martin doesn't want to have to pay for the repairs. It all comes out of the budget for their depot. They don't get any help from the district, and their budget shrinks a little every year. Nine times out of ten, it is best to make do.

The frosted clouds that escape our lungs hang in the air before us and then dissipate into nothing. Each one lingers for a little bit less, while the frail heater rattles away. When we can no longer stand it, we huddle in our rented van and blast the heat while the engine runs and eats up the gas we will have to replace ourselves since we were allotted only a certain amount for fuel in our expenses.

The seats do nothing to support our backs, but we seem to be the only ones bothered by it. The démineurs come by to take a break and plop right down as if it is the most comfortable vehicle imaginable. There is just enough of a lip on the edge to keep a passenger from slipping onto the floor of the cab. And then we return to the site, don our gloves, and drop to our knees, a council of fools laboring in the shadow of eternity. I do not trust memory; I have little faith in history. Instead, I watch my team.

I watch their faces, how they hold this experience, soft and insistent solemnity emanating outward. Juliette and Clémence take their responsibilities seriously, recording the position and orientation of every bone as discovered. The démineurs, roughnecks transformed into careful, gentle pairs of hands, move with the kind of reverence used to prepare a pyre. Their fingers twist through the loose clay and limestone fragments, the crushed snail shells and shrapnel, and more bones emerge. Piece by piece, the remains return to the world. And then—can you believe it?—when we finish and stand above the bones, they all remove their hats.

We spend the final minutes of the day scrambling to use the dying half-light to capture whatever we can before darkness consumes us again. We continue every night until it reaches a point where we are no longer making any progress but just fumbling in the dark, tripping over one another, and cursing.

Night. Velvet darkness. The cats take back the streets, and motorists cut right through the center of the roundabouts without any regard for traffic. Narrow streets force people to park on the sidewalks. Windows still have wooden covers, and at night, you might catch a glimpse of the interior and find rooms lit with ambient blue light, or papered in vintage London Underground prints. Other windows have modern automatic metal coverings that slide down and block out the sun and any unwanted voyeurs. The roofs slope at casual angles and are made of slate tiles. Scooters and crotch rocket motorbikes are popular alternatives and get around much quicker. The poles that line the city streets are almost all dented and scuffed. The démineurs call them "Barbeaux's bumpers" because he rarely ever makes a trip without swiping one or two. He uses them like guides to propel him to his destination.

We return to the depot with them at the end of the shift; the vehicles enter the open gate and the headlights illuminate the Bomb Garden. Basille closes the gate behind us. Barbeaux and Henri's vehicle slows to a stop, and Henri exits the passenger side and walks ahead to guide Barbeaux through the stacks. The vehicle rolls forward under his direction. The beams spread over the artifacts, the shadows behind them warping at once from small to gigantic and then vanishing into darkness once more as the vehicle passes.

Henri weaves between the neat piles of collected ordnance, hands in pockets. Barbeaux follows. A pallet has already been prepared for them, clean and empty. Basille meets them there and helps offload the truck. Another day. Their hands move through the motions, fumbling the many bébés chauves maléfiques into place and packing them tight. No one talks. Everyone is tired. Henri cinches the pallet together with cable wire, the slick metal grasping the lot with balanced, uniform tension.

The job is just work like anyone else's job. And who wants to talk about that?

I never expected this job to become my career. It was supposed to pay the bills while my band Eisensturm got its footing. The record deal never came, and I'm still here, on speed dial for every préfet with an acre touched by war. I still play the odd open mic at L'Antirouille when I have the time, mostly medieval and Breton folk these days.

I discovered the human skeletal system in a drawing class of all places. Professor Chavanel's Fundamentals of Figure Drawing during my L2 studies at *École* Nationale Supérieure des Beaux-Arts de Lyon. A lecture on Tuesday followed by a studio session with a live nude model on Thursday. Early in the semester, we arrived to find the studio lights dimmed and the projector screen lit with a diagram unlike anything hanging on the walls.

"This is an anatomy program for premed students," she said, "but it will work for us as well. You *will* learn how the body is assembled if you want to learn how to draw. How can you create on the page what you do not understand in your mind?"

She actually assigned quizzes from the program and made us take them. For a grade.

In that darkened studio, illuminated on her jaundiced projector screen, the divine magnificence of the human body came to life. I could not unsee it. I would never look at another human the same way again. By the end of the semester, I could identify the nub of a stapes from the middle ear at a glance. There was no going back.

My brain had been rewired. The body was no longer just a person but a whole system, a structure of interlocking parts where every piece serves a function. The skeleton supports it all. Even from the stage, on a night when we drew a solid crowd, the bodies loomed incandescent in the void below us. Chalky faces glowed back at me, floating ghostly through the scorching stage lights. I could see everything underneath, all the parts, the stony calcium holding them together. I followed that fascination from undergrad through a master's program and into the field, quiet battlefields overgrown and tempered, waiting to reveal their secrets.

If you find something you're good at *and* someone will pay you for it, you better stick with it.

Démineurs

THE DIG CONTINUES—more carefully now. Appearances to keep up. We walk a fifteen-meter perimeter around the hole and place stakes at each corner. We tie them together with string and hang strips of bright pink ribbon that dance in the breeze.

So festive, we say, like a crime scene.

Any given day we could be standing on a few hundred skeletons of lost soldiers. This is a fact. But the second we actually see one? Well, now we need to act on ceremony. We put down the large shovels in favor of handpicks and scrapers that resemble our mothers' gardening tools. We spend the daylight on our hands and knees scraping away moss and dirt.

We sit around the site those first few days speculating the cause and circumstances, removing the dirt handfuls at a time.

Handfuls!

We scoop out the area around it and find more shells too. It is like draining a swamp one drop of water at a time. Things just begin to emerge. Bits of barbed wire and twisted horseshoes mostly. But then his clavicle, the rest of his rib cage. We label it all with paper tags tied to more pink ribbons.

We come in on our days off and bitch and moan and wear the plastic ribbons around our waists like a sash and mark every item that presents itself.

We sing songs to make time pass.

Back bone's connected to the shoulder bone,
Shoulder bone's connected to the neck bone,
Neck bone's connected to the head bone . . .

Funny. A single bone can be cataloged away in a day or two. An entire body requires answers.

A soldier killed in the worst war in human history. Mystery solved. Why the need to drag everyone out? When you go digging, you're bound to find dirt.

It's only natural to wonder who. And how. And why.

Couldn't have been artillery fire. Not one of the big ones, at least. We wouldn't be finding all the bones together if it had been a big one. Every time we find a large chunk of shrapnel, all it takes is one casual toss of the piece, to feel that weight, and realize why so many bodies were never recovered. Take one of these directly in the chest? Forget it. Pink mist.

What about a sneak attack? Dead of night. Someone crawled in there while he was on post and slit his throat before he knew what hit him.

Never underestimate the elements. Could have frozen to death. Some of them, they were just left out there for too long. Caught cold, pneumonia. Hypothermia. Those have killed more in war than any bullet or bomb could hope to.

You know you get really warm right before you die of hypothermia? Saw it once. We had a job clearing trails out in the Alps. Awful time. Out of nowhere, guy just started ripping all his clothes off. Right there in the snow. Below zero, and he was stripping naked, he felt so hot. That was what he kept saying—"I'm burning up! I'm burning up!"—while he was up to his waist in snow.

What if it isn't a soldier? What if it is some random person who was murdered and dumped there? Genius, really. No one would ever suspect a thing. We could be sifting through some serial killer's dumping ground, and they're going to spend the next couple of months going through archives from the Great War. It's true, the Ogre of the Ardennes once lived nearby. He killed at least twelve people and disposed of them all over. They think there are more. Somewhere.

Maybe not a human at all. A cow. Or a pet dog. The bones all look the same jumbled up in the dirt.

That would be embarrassing, wouldn't it? They came all the way out to Verdun from Paris for someone's pet Chihuahua.

But then we find the jawbone, every tooth still in its place. A smile seen from the inside.

Undoubtedly human.

They instruct us to spread a tarp over the ground and to arrange the rib bone along with several others found over the course of that first week. Slowly, they try to put him back together. All of them on their hands and knees, silent and focused. They have before them the greatest jigsaw puzzle. From the earth, against all odds, he becomes whole again on the tarp under their meticulous placement. Right before our eyes. These anonymous pieces make the outline of a man.

We have all seen dead bodies. But not like this. You think differently of your own body once you have watched one assembled piece by piece on a tarp stretched over cold earth in the fading, gauzy light of a February evening.

Of course, right after we tell them the odds of ever being able to locate the man's identity are slim to none, what does one of the snivelly little turds do? Reaches right down at our feet and pulls up the tiniest sliver of aluminum.

Eyes like hawks, those academics.

Half a bottle of water is all it needs, though. Rinse and rub. And there it is.

A name. Barely readable, but a name.

They whisk it off to the lab to douse it with chemicals to take off the rust.

Augustin Caledec.

Excerpts from the Field Journal of Hans Kraemer, Field Director and Lead Archaeologist

February 26, 2016

Our final day at the depot, and it looks like rain. Marbled clouds churn outside the windows. A layer of film coats each pane and the world appears out of focus. Rain yesterday. And the day before. Of course it will rain again today. Another shift begins in the break room. The lounge, longer than it is wide, gives off a compressed, corset feeling. Not exactly a place where a person can relax. An unleveled table surrounded by orphaned chairs, none of which match, takes up the middle of the room. Against one wall a lumpy sofa sags into the floor. A kitchenette and a counter occupy the far wall. Basille fumbles around at the counter. Henri sits at the table, arms crossed, and watches the room with tiger eyes. Ferrand is out sick. Baptiste Leclerc, a temporary replacement from another shift, studies a water stain on the ceiling. There's the unmistakable smell of singed insulation, possibly from being installed too close to the heating unit. The lights overhead whine, and a few of the bulbs are dark, their glass blackened from having been left in the socket. Stale cigarette smoke lingers in the air even though smoking in the depot is against regulations. The carpet is so worn that, with a little effort, it is easier to glide across it than step.

The last week has been one of early mornings and late nights. Days spent combing the soil and handling bulky, cavernous gear bags with straps that left oily residue on our hands. By now, our site is fully recovered. The bones and the ID tag have been collected, labeled, and stored for transportation and transfer to the lab. The twine and flags, all removed. Fleury is a resting place for a martyred village once more.

There's a grease board on one wall that none of us have been able to figure out the purpose of in the week we've been here. Some mornings there are notes or a part of a schedule, perhaps last-minute changes. But other times the notes bear little rhyme or reason to any of the démineurs' tasks or responsibilities.

Yesterday morning, there was a motivational quote (*Everyone has a plan until they get hit. —Mike Tyson*), and later in the day it was replaced with a single phrase: *No Boring Days!* Another morning, someone had scribbled the heading *Morning Coffee Thoughts* and then followed it with an interesting sentence: *The unexploded shells have a smell to them.* No further elaboration or follow-up. It stayed there for the entire day, and its enduring existence seemed to serve as agreement from every person who passed it. The handwriting, always different from the last, provides a space for anyone to leave a comment or thought. A type of virtual town square, so to speak.

On this morning, there is a salutation: *Good Morning Fritz Haber!* A joke of some kind? Possibly. And underneath the salutation, the phrase *12,000,000 LEFT TO GO* is scrawled across the board. Later in the day, right before we leave for good, I will notice someone has drawn a line through *12,000,000* and put *11,999,999* beneath it.

The drone off the generator makes the counter vibrate and sends ripples through our coffee. Leclerc blows his nose in a hand towel and tosses it on the table. Between the generator and the light bulbs, there's something of an electronic symphony: the soundtrack of their days. You can get used to almost anything if you allow it for long enough.

*

We all make our way outside. In the vestibule of the depot, the first thing one sees is a grand plaque of cast bronze mounted on a brick wall. Etched on its surface are the names of every démineur killed in the line of duty since 1965: 406 in total. The bronze names shine bold against the rough brick. Even though it is waxed once a week, the hazy glare of the fluorescent bulbs above reveal faint scratches across its surface.

There is little, if any, logical construction to the building, aside from the open bay at the center around which the rest of the building is formed. It was built inside the husk of an old fort constructed in the late seventeenth century. The layout has been quartered and then quartered again to fit within the existing space.

Henri sighs and opens the rear hatch of their truck. He checks off the gear, a worn clipboard in one hand. Barbeaux opens the driver's-side door and yawns wide enough to swallow the truck. He checks the fuel level, writes down the mileage in a logbook. They will spend the morning riding through the county, making rounds at various places and waiting for any calls that might come through. The roads around Verdun are dotted with signs—a simple drawing of an artillery shell cracked in half with a skull above it—where one can leave discovered munitions. These spots aren't usually overflowing. Most people are too cautious to handle the munitions themselves. Most people. But there's usually one or two, leaning on the post or standing straight up like a miniature obelisk, a memorial to some small truth on the shoulder of the road.

The Bomb Garden is a perfect circle stretching thirty meters across and contained by concrete walls almost two meters thick and three and a half meters high. The floor slopes downward at a slight angle toward the center. The only way in or out is through a set of double cast-iron doors on its south end. They open when a vehicle deposits ordnance in the Garden and for no one else.

A cradle.

When glanced at from the entrance it is unmistakably craterlike in appearance. A crater to store crater makers. All by design. The idea, the hope, is that if any one of these sleeping devils were to wake suddenly, the resulting explosion of several tons of unstable ordnance will shoot straight into the sky instead of laterally.

The Bomb Garden doesn't feel like a museum so much as it does a zoo. The exhibits in a museum don't threaten to kill you in a split second the way they do in a zoo. The exhibits at the museums we've all worked in lack the same vitality of these.

Basille starts the other truck and logs the fuel level. Leclerc picks up each piece of equipment, every item, and gives it a look over. Hammers, picks, shovels, and other tools. A quad-claw, mechanical steel grappler originally made for lumber workers to carry logs that could be clamped onto a larger shell. Slim tongs that could be clamped onto the body of a projectile to help with leverage if a shell was in a particularly stuck place. A small kit for disarming and removing fuses: small clippers and picks similar to the ones that come in a personal grooming kit.

Before they arrived at the Département du Déminage, each man was another thing: ex-navy divers, mineral miners, deep-sea welders, oil refinery foremen. They are almost all veterans. Each man ended up here for different reasons.

They all have children except for Basille. Barbeaux's daughter moved to Spain three years ago, but he still talks as if she's moved to Mars. He's always on his son's case. Henri has a two-year-old boy whose photo is the first thing you see when he opens his wallet. They all avoid talking with their families about their work. They never mention the job because then come the questions. The worries. The concerns. So, they stay silent on the subject, turning their focus away to leave it sitting in the corner of the room where everyone knows it is sitting but chooses not to speak about it. Like shining a flashlight in one corner of a dark room and not another to avoid it.

There's a certain phase during the decomposition of a human body when the eyes have rotted away and the flesh tightens around the skull with a dull shine like a dried apple. At that point, the body is not yet a skeleton but rather something entirely different and altogether unnamable. We have seen the photos. They are not too difficult to find. A body in a supine position in the mud, the crown of the head resting on the earth. The arms, tangled. One of however many hundred thousand casualties at Verdun. What is this in-between phase? The action of decomposition, frozen. Caught like a rodent in the misty cone of a flashlight beam. A state that escapes description, resists classification.

It's difficult to comprehend just exactly how horrible this place was for so many in the span of a few years. It's probably an evolutionary defense mechanism. How could anyone ever leave bed if they truly understood the pain and suffering one group of humans is capable of causing another? We found a ghastly sight on one of our excursions through the city streets of Verdun. A rat huddled against the corner of a building, where the wall met the street. Dead and beginning to rot. Middle of the day, the sun is out, cold but no wind. There's the rat, decaying. Covered in flies. They're feasting. Right as we pass it, the thing moves. Dear God, it's not dead. We couldn't help but stop. The sight was too horrific not to take in. The rat squirmed and wriggled pathetically, without success, without relief. The flies leaped and dived back on top of it, eating its eyes, which were mostly consumed at this point, leaving partially empty sockets from which the rat could no longer view the world. It felt like a moment from the battle somehow punctured our reality and returned to torment us.

That was your existence if you fought here. Not the rat. Not the fly. But rather the space in the socket. The hollow part. The act of consumption. It is what became of them all. And those who survived this battle were born again from that consumption. They, on some level, needed to indulge in the feast. They needed to become that feast, even if for just a short time. Because those who could not were destroyed by it. Those who could not allow some part of themselves to become that all-consuming horror could not survive, in body or mind. Imagine nightmares that have burst from your skull and you awake in some water-filled dugout to find the land all around you painted with them, in every direction you can see.

No more early-morning rides out to la cicatrice before the rest of the city has risen. No more narrow, winding roads through the dark, long after the sun has set, with only the glow of light from Verdun to guide us. No more following the démineurs' trucks in a rented van and desperately trying to keep up. No more watching Henri endlessly floss his teeth, a habit he seems fixated on no matter the time or location. No more watching Antoine Barbeaux nap his way through the day with beads of perspiration perpetually forming on his brow because even sleeping made that brute sweat. The rolls of his bearded chin seem to have hardened over the years into a permanent platform for his head to rest upon. Almost as if God designed him this way, with a perfect, built-in nap perch. He doesn't even need to lower his head. It just settles there and then he snores softly. No more endless days spent huddled in the frigid cabs of the démineurs' trucks with our hands buried in our armpits and bags of saltines in our laps while they smirk and ask if we are cold. Of course we are cold.

ÉDUL—Éditions de l'Université de Lorraine, Official Blog

Submission: "My Week in Verdun" by Clémence Durand, Anthropology and Forensic Archaeology, PhD Candidate at Université de Lorraine

Status: Rejected. After an initial review, we have determined that your submission lacks the necessary theoretical framework and methodological rigor required for publication.

Our last night in town, and we all could use a drink. This trip could not have come at a worse time. The chance to excavate freshly discovered human remains as a PhD candidate is, yes, rare as they come. But life has other plans. The evening before we left, I got the type of call from my fiancé every woman dreads. Things have been strained between us, doing the long-distance thing, with Mathieu at Université Catholique de Louvain and me here in Lorraine, but we were working on it. Antwerp. Field research. There had been an indiscretion with another candidate. An American woman he had mentioned more than once. I knew who it was before he even admitted it. You always know. Combine that with a week of living out of a suitcase as well as ten-hour days on your knees in the mud putting a man back together one bone at a time, and you get a group of people ready to foutre le bordel.

We want a dark place where you can't see the walls. A place so loud it resets your heartbeat every song and your feet stick to the floor. But Verdun is very much a vacation town for summer tourists, families passing through to some other place, and it takes a little while to find anything open after five in the evening this time of year. We settle on a local bar, one of the few still open in the offseason. Low lit, quiet. Unlikely to water down the drinks, which is more than we can ask for at this late an hour. It will do.

Juliette and I arrive earlier than the rest for a heart-to-heart, this serious matter I need guidance on. We push two tables together and drop ourselves in the walnut side chairs. Shallow pools of warm light from table lamps give everything a champagne hue. We manage to get to the discussion, but the guidance leaves me wanting.

"You're still wearing that?" Juliette points to my ring.

"It's not the ring I'm upset about," I say.

We open the first bottle and the cork gets stuck in the neck. Too tired to care, we shove the cork down into the bottle. She listens and sips while I tell her everything I have been holding in since we got off the train last week.

"Break it off. Take that ring and toss it in the Meuse," she says when I finish.

"He didn't hide it, though. People make mistakes, and he was honest with me. I think that counts for something, no?"

"God, Clémence! Use your brain! They are still together there. You know the way these 'fieldwork operations' go."

I swirl the wine in my glass and try not to think about it.

"Antwerp is three and a half hours away. If we leave right now, we can surprise him and that slut first thing in the morning. We can make it in less than three hours if you let me drive," she says. "People don't change, my dear. Once a cheater, always a cheater."

"I think—"

The rest of our party arrives at the table and scuttles our road trip plans. They pull up seats for a moment and then scatter to the bar. Our surveyor and photographer have already left town, leaving us with Monsieur Kraemer and two of the démineurs, Barbeaux and Henri. If it weren't for us, everyone might be in bed by now. Monsieur Kraemer, squinty and lean, nurses an absinthe sour and lingers on the outer edge of the barroom, half in darkness and shadow, watching everyone enjoy themselves. Neither of us can surmise the clue to his character aside from his infatuation with heavy metal music, which he forced on us, the stereo cranked full volume, every morning ride out to la cicatrice. He treated us like two giddy schoolgirls when we first stepped from the van and walked down the slope to the cordoned area, pink banners fluttering with our arrival. But we've noticed a burgeoning sense of trust from him over the last several days. Henri orders a sidecar; Barbeaux, a Picon bière. They remain at the bar while Monsieur Kraemer exchanges a few pleasantries.

They are a very secretive breed, these démineurs. Driving us around in their little Land Rover trucks here and there. Polite, respectful when addressed. But that's all we got. They stayed with us all week and helped quite a lot, but we barely spoke.

What a bizarre existence, to live in a state of constant reversal. A démineur. A minesweeper, or explosive ordnance disposal tech, as some refer to it. *Dé*minage. To de-mine. A plumber plumbs. An electrician conducts electricity. But a démineur? It's a life spent in a deficit. A life spent extracting and removing. A life spent disposing as opposed to creating. To say nothing of the constant risk of vaporizing oneself with a false move or an unstable munition. But perhaps one grows used to it, the same way a person grows used to the various sounds of their house: the clinking pipes, the whirring ventilation, the regular workings that go unnoticed day in and day out.

Dé.

From Latin, no? *De.* "Off." Or "from"? Existing in the absence as opposed to the present. The here and now.

One thing that surprised us all was the lack of knowledge all the démineurs possessed when it came to the actual history of the battle. Such interests seem beyond their intellectual horizons. Despite the fact that we agreed tonight was for fun, no work talk allowed, I pull my head from the clouds to find Henri and Barbeaux back at our table discussing the function of trench works during the battle.

"They hardly fought in the trenches here," Juliette tells them.

"No?" Barbeaux responds.

"Hardly at all. Too much artillery. It was really more of an artillery duel than a conventional infantry battle. The artillery fire destroyed everything they built. The only trenches here were for communication, between posts. The real fighting was done out there in those holes, clambering from one to the next. Stuck in them for days at a time. Unable to stand, no room to lay out. You might drown in the mud. Couldn't even risk going to the bathroom. It was all done in those holes," she says.

For the démineurs, the war is counted in the tonnage of ordnance removed each year or the weight of a single spent artillery round carried out of Zone Rouge on their back. For us, the war is global consequences and personal interest stories. We read the letters home and imagine what it was like to have crouched in some rat-infested dugout with all those explosions above and watch the earth tremble in pain from the impacts.

It must have been horrible beyond anything we can comprehend. A short lifetime of jaundiced eyes overlooking the battlefield. Watching from hidden places. Marveling at the waste. Picking at scabs and sores. Scratching lice and infected cuts and wounds. And then you get liquefied by a bomb you never see coming.

Numbers have such a bizarre power to them. One man killed in a car wreck on his way home from work? An unimaginable tragedy. Make it five people killed in that same wreck. The families affected won't ever be the same. Three hundred thousand soldiers were killed over the ten months of the Battle of Verdun. Eighty thousand bodies were never recovered at all. That's the Stade de France filled to capacity. Imagine standing at the midfield line and looking at all those faces. Not an empty seat in sight.

France lost over a million in the four years of the war. We can hardly keep that number in our heads. What is a hundred thousand? A million? Means next to nothing to us. How do you quantify such a figure? If you lined those bodies up from head to toe, would they reach to the moon and back? Farther? What a ghastly image. But what other way do we have? When you blow those numbers up, somewhere along the way they lose meaning. Which number is the tipping point? No idea. They have no idea how many artillery shells were even shot during the battle. Only guesses.

Well, figure one cannon could shoot, what, three, four rounds in a minute? Multiply that by sixty, so you're looking at anywhere from 200 to 240 in an hour if they are really cooking. And then multiply that by an entire battery, and then multiply *that* by an entire regiment and then a battalion, and *then* multiply that by 306, since that's how many days the battle lasted. That is a hell of a lot of artillery.

A missile for every star in the sky. One for one. Above our heads and beneath our feet. Yes, a star for every missile, but don't forget, they are quite different. The light from those stars? Quite weak. It has traveled so far to get here, so far across the vast, cold, dead space. Frail light. The light from the ones under our feet? That light is still very much alive. Sure, many of them are dead, corrupted by the churning earth, the effects of time. But not all of them. No, not all of them. How can we redeem ourselves in the gaze of this poisoned land? How can we restore ourselves in the view of this traumatized space? We will be paying interest on these sins for generations to come.

The figures are ultimately useless, too difficult to hold in the mind. But what else is there? A mother's pain of loss for her only son who vanished into the mud of Verdun. How can you quantify a mother's love? Maybe that's the true loss of war, not what can be counted but what remains unquantified, forever uncounted. A little more than a week ago, we descended on Verdun with the same swiftness of the invading Germans a century before, converging rapidly from multiple directions on this doomed fortress city, the gateway to the French hinterland. Now, just like the kaiser's army, we leave empty-handed, neither victorious nor defeated, but somewhere in between.

The conversation takes on a different tone from that of the previous few days. The alcohol flows. We are meeting these men for the first time in many ways. Work of any kind has a stultifying effect on most people's personalities, whether they're excavating human remains or working the register at the local corner shop. They've not even finished their first drinks, and already, Henri lets out a bawdy joke, and to everyone's surprise, Monsieur Kraemer laughs heartily. This night threatens to blossom into something other than forced camaraderie.

Henri and Barbeaux correct each other and argue over the finer details of a story about a time they got called out to a man who had inserted a live artillery round in his anus. It wasn't discovered on the battlefield but purchased from a collector. Nonetheless, they were placed on standby while the operation to remove the offending ordnance was completed in the cordoned parking lot of the hospital.

I go to the bar to order another round, and when I return, I find someone in my seat. It takes a moment to place him, then it all comes back. The mayor. He's with one of the forest rangers who came to the site as well, a sharp-faced woman who looks ready to leave.

"It's been a *week*! I probably shouldn't be telling you all this, it's not quite finalized yet . . . Well, what the hell. What's a few words between new friends?" he says, and notices me standing above him. "I am so sorry, is this your seat? Allow me to grab another."

Before I can say a word, he's up and about. He's in quite the chipper mood.

"The beetles may have won the battle, but we are certain to win the war. All that wood they ate through? We have rescued it from the incinerator."

He gives a lengthy explanation that puts almost everyone to sleep. We know this mayor figure is involved with real estate, and it seems he's reappropriating all the unusable wood for a variety of different revitalization projects in the newer neighborhoods outside the main city. Monsieur Kraemer redirects the conversation back to our site.

"I'd love to be involved. Is there anything you might need help with?" Hugo asks.

"Our work is all done. Everything has been sent off to the lab, the mortuary here at Saint-Nicolas," says Monsieur Kraemer. "Now begins the work of trying to figure out just who he was."

"Honestly, don't take this the wrong way, but I hope they can't figure it out."

"There will be a big ceremony either way," I say. "Whether here or whatever village he came from."

"Yes, but think about that. An unknown soldier? It's romantic and tragic and unnerving and profound. If we figure out who exactly he was, it loses all the magic," says Hugo.

He's a little goofy, but he seems to know it. Self-awareness will take you far. I imagine he is one of those guys with a large bush of wild, frizzy pubic hair like steel wool and a crooked dick. Gross.

"I'm a sucker for tragedy," I say.

"Aren't we all?" he says, and smiles.

Another round. Things are feeling a little looser now. We are all much more chummy. But exhaustion tugs at the edges of my mind. I cannot wait to be home, tit-deep in my tub, toes curled around the rim, glass of prosecco in hand.

Barbeaux complains they don't offer any food here, all they have are bags of overpriced potato chips. Juliette turns to say something and knocks a glass from the table that shatters on the floor. Everyone boos her and laughs. We are entering the sweet spot of the night. Time moves quickly, and the conversations move in short, distracted bursts. This little bar is turning out to be a lot more fun than any of us expected. Half-finished thoughts plummet off the table in every direction. The attention turns increasingly toward Juliette and myself. We excuse ourselves to the ladies' room for a break.

"What do you think of the mayor?" she asks me while she touches up her lipstick in the mirror.

"What a doofus," I respond.

"I might fuck him," she says.

I slap her on the shoulder.

"Why not?" she exclaims.

Back at the table, Monsieur Kraemer, lost in some explanation about the nuances between traditional Breton folk and the revivalist movement of the seventies, spills a drink all down his lap. More booing erupts. Barbeaux drops to the floor, and for a moment we believe he's collapsed. But then he crawls and howls and barks like a dog. For what reason? Who cares. It is hilarious. We continue on this way, drinking, flirting. Hugo keeps saying he has to leave, but all he does is get closer to me. He squeezes my shoulder and leaves his hand there for just a moment longer than one should. Then the bartender flicks the light and it's over, time to get out. The happiness fades fast, and we will do nearly anything to hold on for even one more drop of pleasure, which means the quarrels and fists are mere moments away.

Hugo insists on walking us back to the hotel. He holds our hands in the empty streets; a light drizzle glistens on the stones, the lamplight illuminating our steps. We swing our hands in great arcs, singing then shouting the words of decade-old pop songs. The champagne hue follows us from the bar all the way to the front door, where we reach for the handle but Hugo will not let go. He will not say good night so easily. Despite everything, every way we try, he will not leave. "Good night, good night," we say. We keep saying it, even after we allow him to walk us up to our room, up the staircase to our very door. And then, of course, there's no other way it can end. He enters behind me and the door shuts. Juliette busies herself in the bathroom.

He shuts the light off, and I'm immediately taken back to the day they took us beneath the city. A rare chance to get away from la cicatrice for an afternoon, we went there to examine the foundation of the old citadel where the French command staged its headquarters for the entire battle. The cool darkness welcomed us. We placed our hands on the stones, and we could feel them breathing.

There are so many ways to disappear. Into the earth, swallowed whole by the soil that was churned to soup from months of relentless artillery fire. Into the body. Many remains were so badly disfigured that even though they were returned, no one could identify who they had been. Bodies upon bodies. Mostly pieces, rarely entirely whole. These were the ones that were laid to rest in the ossuary. The carcass evidence of something more than just cells divinely organized into organs and systems but no longer identifiable as anything other than a maybe somebody at one point or another. Into thin air. There were artillery shells so powerful that upon exploding they vaporized anyone at the impact site. This kind of disappearing seemed to terrify the majority of people the most. There is something in the permanent vanishing of the human body that unnerves people. It's understandable. It is incredibly humiliating and demonstrates how pathetically delicate humanity's existence actually is.

Being down beneath the citadel, our hands on the cold, damp stone, was all we needed to understand. An ancient city. Older than any one of us. And it pays no mind to the bombs and bullets and petty wars. It will go on breathing. Quietly. Steadily. Calmly moving forward to the next dawn.

He strips my clothing, and then we are in bed, the room spinning, just two lonely people taking their loneliness out on each other.

*

Weak light from an ash-and-pearl sky wakes us in the morning. Hugo is gone, and I'm lying in a wet spot on the bed. The scorched remnants of my brain throb inside my skull. It's ready to break free any way it can. I have several missed calls from Mathieu. Juliette vomits in the toilet. We are late for our train.

Démineurs

CLOSE TO FIVE METRIC TONS of displaced soil later, it is over. After the identification tag is whisked away to the lab, things slow considerably at the site. We return the soil to the hole from which it came. The bones, taken to the lab to do whatever it is the 'gists do with bones.

It's easy to forget that the shells fell everywhere: on land and water, on heads and vacant open spaces alike. There's only so much one can do to direct the trajectory. Bijoux, who spends many hours sitting outside his front door, a pail by his side from which he draws turnips and onions and cuts the heads off and drops them in a pile behind him? His family was one of the last to flee and the first to return. If you catch him during a good time and he's willing to talk, he will tell you all about it. "They stayed as long as they could. This place was everything they had," he reminds us every now and again. "My grandmother spoke of how they hid in the barn—what was left of it—right before they fled for good, after the house was destroyed. She said it was the most miserable time of her life. She came down with a fever. Her throat was on fire. Could hardly breathe. Imagine waking up with a cold on the last day of the world. And how at night there were always more bombardments. They were mostly out of the path of it all, but they could see the bombs falling, tumbling out of the sky, and disappearing into the lake. Hellfire. All these silent stones dropping into the water. No explosions. Hardly even a splash. Just hundreds of missiles falling from the heavens into a black lake in the dead of night while the rest of the world came apart all around them."

Everyone knows you don't drink the water in Verdun.

2

That's why Martin first took the job out here. They needed experienced divers at the time. Martin did deep-sea welding for nearly a decade before he came to Verdun to tinker with crusty old bombs. Taking a dip in a river to dredge up a few slug-covered bébés chauves maléfique was nothing compared to what he did before. Practically an early retirement.

He wants to stay close to the water. The rivers and lakes, they make him think of Charisse, even though she's no longer here. He doesn't talk about that part. He talks about the water. That's where he met her, where all true love begins: suspended between the earth and the sky.

Martin and Henri arrive at Hugo's house in Woël in the morning, scuba gear in the trunk. They park out front on a quiet street while Hugo waits at the front door. He checks his watch with a look of mild frustration. He should be handsome. Not quite thirty-five, piercing blue eyes, a strong jaw, clear skin—but the parts just don't line up the way they should, and he dresses like a man eager for middle age: boxy suit and a hastily done tie with a knot like a cancerous knuckle.

"Very nice to see you again! How long do you think this will take?" he asks, his tie swinging loosely. "I've got a few properties I need to check out today."

Henri tries his best to hide a smile. *Oh, only a few hundred more years.*

Martin is tempted in the moment to explain to him that he is actually incredibly fortunate they are able to be here at all. He wants to tell Monsieur LaFleur that had he called a week ago, they still would have been stuck out at la cicatrice with the bones, and he probably would still be hiding in his house where they found him, waiting for someone to be available to come out and pick his little river clean of hand grenades.

"Don't worry, chef. In the blink of an eye. We will have you on your way in no time at all."

"Parfait. Let me show you around," he says, and waves them along enthusiastically.

He leads them down the length of the house, a traditional master farmhouse with plastered rubble walls, flower-adorned wooden shutters, and a gently sloping tiled roof. Small, symmetrical windows line the front, along with a front door as well as a broad carriage door on the far end facing directly onto the street. The doors and the shutters are painted a brilliant, deep red. There's a child's bike with training wheels off to one side.

"Built in the eighteenth century, three-bay design with a living space, stable, and barn. Converted to a three-bedroom with a garage. I'm told at one point it was a functioning dairy farm with a bakery."

"It looks cozy," says Henri.

"The place is a miracle, really," Hugo says. "Hardly any damage at all despite a fair amount of fighting in the area during the war. A rare find. It still has the original masonry."

They round the house and find the side to be in a state of renovation. One entire wall has been demolished, replaced with a few thick sheets of plastic that hang from the roof and distort the exposed rooms beyond them. He stops to show them the work.

"Listen to this. Léa and I, we wanted to add an extension. Take down that wall, push it out a bit, and add another room. A family room most likely, maybe an office. Nothing major, easy work. It goes without saying, the place was listed as a historical monument. God, what a headache. The favors I had to call in to get around that obstacle. They make it so difficult, you know?"

Martin and Henri observe the gash in the side of the house with the vague dismay of watching someone guzzle a fine bottle of wine.

"We finally get the approval to make the modification only to discover there are loads—*loads*—of issues with the structure. It's all irregular stone coated with lime plaster. Timber framing. They only hold up if you really take care of them. It's almost a full-time job. So we're going to gut it and demo the whole place. Start over."

"Must cost a fortune," Martin wonders aloud.

"I can afford it, don't you worry," Hugo says, and winks, clapping Martin on the shoulder. "We will go in phases," he continues, and dissects the house with chops of his hand. "This way we can stay in the house the whole time. It will be a little cramped, but we will make it work. I've got tons of ideas. We will keep some of the foundation, but everything else will be brand-new. I've got a flare for the modern."

"Wouldn't it make more sense to move out for a few months?" asks Henri.

"Eh. Maybe. But then I'd have to rent some drab condo in a shithole neighborhood like Anthouard-Pré l'*Évêque* or something. Put a bunch of our stuff in storage. No, sounds like more work than it is worth."

Henri nods. He lives in Anthouard-Pré l'*Évêque*.

"The river?" asks Henri.

"Of course. Allow me to show you the spot," Hugo says with an air of solemnity.

"I left the city to get away from all the crime and violence. I thought it would be safer out here," he tells them as they arrive at the water. "The quiet country life."

But they had lived here less than a year when his daughter, Éloïse, came running to him after playing down on the bank of the river cradling something against her chest.

"Papa! Patate, Papa, Papa!"

And he smiled and opened his arms to receive her, until he noticed the "potato" she was hugging was in fact a French hand grenade, swollen like an over-ripened piece of fruit and caked in mud.

Hugo's property touches a bend in the river where it is low and wide, almost hard to tell it is a river. The current is slow and hardly appears to move at all. After a major storm, it swells and overflows the banks, and when it recedes, it leaves behind whatever it has dredged from its bottom.

"All right, I'll leave you to it," says Hugo, and walks back to the house.

They set down their gear and wait until Hugo is out of earshot.

"Can you believe what they have done to that house? They're ruining it! What a travesty," says Henri.

"Wealth is wasted on the rich," Martin replies.

He slips off his coveralls and dons his scuba gear—a slick black wetsuit and an oxygen tank with a mask and goggles as well as a pair of open-heel fins he can slip over a pair of dive boots—while Henri unloads a coil of rope and a pail of scrub brushes. This particular section of water functions as a type of net and catches many of the ordnances lost to the meandering path of the river. It is actually quite beautiful, aside from all the little French toads that continue to pop up. Martin checks his oxygen and places the demand valve in his mouth. Henri uncoils the rope and hands one end to Martin, who takes it and wades out into the river. The water, almost completely still, captures a perfect reflection of the trees in the sky above, everything soaked with light. The only thing that disturbs the precise symmetry of the reflection is Martin's movements through the wake.

Henri stands at the edge of the river and lets out the line. Hugo watches with crossed arms from a farther distance behind Henri.

Martin dives, scans the riverbed, and finds bébés chauves maléfique, but of course, there are more than just hand grenades. Of course, of course. 155mm rounds from a glance. And so the day begins. He descends and pulls them from the riverbed. He ties the rope around the larger ones, and Henri assists him in pulling them ashore. A labor-intensive and time-consuming process for everyone involved. A small pile of ordnance accumulates beside Henri. Four grenades, a lone 75mm shell, and two 155mm. When Martin goes underwater, Henri scrubs them with a small, stiff-bristled brush. They will all need to be cleaned before they can be logged in the depot and later detonated. It is one of those bizarre rules that no one has ever come up with a completely sound explanation for. They will be blown to pieces at some point in the next few weeks, so what's the use of cleaning them? Questions not worth asking.

Martin breaks the surface and removes the mouthpiece. Water drips from his mustache, and he spits it out.

"Reel her in!" he yells to Henri on the shore.

Henri picks up the cord. Even though it is a chilly day, he sweats. He opens his coveralls at the collar, and now his cap comes off too. He plants both feet shoulder-width apart and leans back while pulling the cord hand over hand, exerting all his strength. Henri gives the line one final tug, and another 155mm shell emerges from the river.

"Ah, tortue sinistre," he bellows, and reaches down to grab it by the rim and roll it to the growing pile.

Martin tries to take a few deep breaths. He's having a difficult time drawing a full lung of air. There's a tightness in his chest that he cannot get past. It wasn't there when he woke early this morning, not that he can remember at least. It may have started when he donned the oxygen tank and slipped into the river. He's in the shallow part where his flippers graze the bottom, but he's having trouble staying steady. His vision darkens with a flutter of gray and then black splotches.

"Need a break?" asks Henri. "We can switch if you want."

The splotches recede just as quickly as they began. Color bleeds back into Martin's surroundings. Everything becomes pronounced and vivid.

"No, no. I am fine. I'll be all right."

Martin takes a few breaths before placing the demand valve back in his mouth. He sinks back under the surface, and a cloud of silt envelopes him. The light dims and, with it, almost all sound. It's like falling into his own head, both the darkness and the silence. His chest loosens and his shoulders drop.

Hugo watches the pair work from his patio. Almost an hour late. Without so much as an apology. Démineurs are known to keep their own time, but an hour? It's inconsiderate. But what can you do when dealing with les prolos? Typical.

They're making quick work of the river, though. He watches them pull out several pieces of ordnance in quick succession. You have to admire their efficiency. They have it down pat. Martin dives again and again. Henri wastes no time while he's submerged. A cigarette dangling from his lip, he scrubs the ugly things and marks them with chalk.

They didn't even seem interested in the renovations. It's a mystery to him how some people just go through life oblivious to the wider world. It's not every day you get to see an eighteenth-century farmhouse under renovation. And yet they stood there mute and unimpressed. The polite thing—the very bare minimum—would be to feign interest. Ask a question. This is why so few of these guys ever get ahead in life. They end their lives right back where they started.

Besides, today has not gotten off to a great start. He awoke to a text message from Camille canceling their plans for the evening. The first time she has done this. Although admittedly his persistence has diminished somewhat since he has shifted his focus to Elisa, this upsets him nonetheless. Apparently, Gabriel, her husband, surprised her with tickets to a play in Metz last night. He got a babysitter and everything. Her last message simply read, "sry, tomorrow?" *We will see about that,* he thinks.

She has no idea about Elisa. But then again, Elisa has no idea about Elisa. Nothing has happened between the two of them aside from some casual flirting. She's so difficult to read. There's more laughter now and she always replies to his texts, both of which are good signs, but he still hasn't sensed a real moment to make a move. For the last week they have been getting coffee to discuss some ideas he's had about this tainted blue wood. There seems to be an opportunity to rescue it from destruction. Elisa is fully invested in the project and wants to help. What worries him is that might be exactly the beginning, middle, and end of why she is reciprocating his attention.

He takes his phone out and texts Camille: "I need u. Tell him u got called in. Easy excuse."

The back door opens and Léa walks out with Éloïse close behind. Hugo shuts his phone and immediately goes into husband and father mode, a switch he is so used to making he doesn't even realize he does it anymore.

"Papa, what are they doing?" Éloïse asks as she grabs his leg.

Hugo picks her up and looks to the river. Henri, hands on his hips, and Martin, his mask atop his head, talk to each other at the river's edge.

"They're Papa's friends, mon coeur. They're here to clean the river of all the potatoes," he tells her.

Éloïse watches them as they continue to talk.

"Apparently it's break time," he adds, his tone flat.

"Let them do their work, Hug," says Léa, playful and wry. "We're about to leave. Do you need anything at the grocer?"

He tells her no and tells her he might not be home until late again tonight, depending on whether some plans to meet a prospective buyer for a property hold up.

"They're swimming! Look!" Éloïse says, and points.

"Yes, yes, they work together—" Hugo begins.

He looks out to see Henri plunging into the water and pulling a lifeless body to shore.

*

"Martin! Martin! Answer!"

The cool air jolts Martin awake. He's overwhelmed by the sensation of his scuba gear being torn from his body. His goggles, his mouthpiece. Somehow, they've all become full of water. Henri and Monsieur LaFleur are soaked through and pulling him from the river. Martin notices, as if from a great distance, Hugo's nipples plastered to the inside of his wet dress shirt. No undershirt. Martin looks up and away and is consumed by the infinite blue sky above him. He starts by wiggling his fingers and then his toes. They move just fine. He doesn't remember losing consciousness. It was more like he nodded off for a second the same way one might, late at night, on a long drive down a dark highway. Lost in thought. Heavy eyelids. The radio drones.

But it was long enough that Henri left the dry comfort of the bank and jumped in to grab him, notebook still in hand. Hugo stood there, mouth hanging agape, until Henri shouted at him to help.

Not that Martin remembers any of it. Martin moves his arms and legs, and to his relief, nothing hurts. A little dizzy, sure. But there is no pain. He props himself onto his elbows to sit up, but Henri forces him back down.

"Stay still! The ambulance is on its way!"

Martin closes his eyes, and Henri's voice crowds his mind.

"Where were you!? Coward!"

"The ambulance should be here by now."

"When I say come, you come! You just stood there. Coward!"

"What's taking them so long?"

Henri shouts at Hugo and then shouts to the sky, and Hugo ignores it and rubs the back of his head while he wonders aloud about the response time of the ambulance. The experience has rattled them both. They talk past each other, their sentences short and rushed. Neither of them listens to Martin.

"I am fine. Really. Listen. I am fine. I just lost my bearings for a moment, is all. Hey. Listen to me."

What a sight they must be. Henri and Hugo pacing in anxious circles, carving trenches into the soft grass with their feet, while Martin sits in the mud between the two of them, his arms propped on his knees, focusing on the individual drops of water running off the tip of each finger.

"I am fine. Really."

But that isn't entirely true. His chest tightens with every attempt to draw a full breath. He didn't feel great that morning, but hell, it was Monday. When was the last time he felt great and ready to take on the world on a Monday morning?

Henri and Hugo pace until the ambulance arrives. That is the extent of the drama. The paramedics emerge from the van, one of them yawning, and walk over with their hands in their trouser pockets to where Martin sits on the riverbank.

Martin refuses to go to the ER.

But Henri insists. And just to prevent another round of pacing and shouting, Martin agrees. Henri hands him his clothing, and Martin walks to the stretcher.

Once the doors slide shut, everything is surprisingly routine during the quiet and maybe even peaceful half-hour ride to the hospital. They prop him up on the stretcher, take some vitals from him. He signs a few forms and watches the world slip away through the back window of the ambulance.

The ER waiting room is mundane, but only in the way emergency rooms can be mundane. They place Martin in the waiting room since there are no beds available. Martin sits in a chair and watches the day creep by. A janitor mops the floor and sets off the sensor for the sliding doors again and again, each time opening with a respiratory sigh. A scent of disinfectant and excrement hangs in the air after he leaves. A young woman cries silently in a chair in the corner of the room for over an hour before abruptly standing and walking out the door. She does not return. A police officer enters through the sliding doors holding a duffel bag.

"Has he arrived?" he asks the nurse at the front desk.

"Who?"

He places the bag on her desk. "The wreck from the highway. Have they brought him in yet?"

"Uh, I have no idea. Let me check," she says, her mouth full. She studies the computer screen. She has blond hair styled in a layered bob that was popular a few years ago, but she's holding on, waiting for it to come back into style. Beside her she has laid out a snack of saltines with a jar of Nutella.

"This is for him. They left it."

"He just arrived. He's been taken to surgery already. They must have been moving," she says, and loads another cracker with Nutella.

"Can you take this up there? It's for him."

She stands and unzips the bag.

"*Oh mon Dieu!* His whole arm?" she asks, peering into the bag.

"Just make sure he gets it," the officer says, and turns to leave.

"Of course. I'll see to it."

She grabs the bag off the counter and leaves for a moment, Nutella cracker in one hand, duffel bag in the other.

Martin admires the nurses and the physicians as they move between rooms and down the halls. Sick and hurt people everywhere. Recycled air that never feels fresh and with the faintest metallic tinge as well—iodine, blood. But what are these people doing? Smiling. Joking. Laughing. Nodding to each other and the patients as well. Many of them walk with a certain lightness in their step. Such ease. It isn't because they don't care. To say they don't care would be to miss the point entirely. These are people who are comfortable around pain and distress. Some are probably calloused, sure. But many are just comfortable. Confident in their abilities to ease pain and correct problems. How many times has Martin's crew arrived to a distressed family that has discovered a decrepit mortar round or artillery shell wedged in the wall of their garden or under a bed of crops, and the démineurs walk up with that same ease, cracking jokes and sporting smiles? If anything, it makes him trust them more.

When they finally take him back, his examination lasts about fifteen minutes. There are more vitals. More paperwork. A young and antsy physician who seems competent and knowledgeable but eager to get out of the ER and on to whatever would come next. The physician proceeds with confidence through his exam, surely the umpteenth one of his shift. The nurse draws blood while he asks all manner of questions, quick and rehearsed.

"What were you doing right before you passed out?"

"I was at work, diving."

"Did it come on suddenly or more gradually?"

"Sudden."

"Did you eat this morning?"

"No."

"Any dizziness?"

"No."

"Vomiting or diarrhea?"

Martin glances at the nurse. "Non."

"Shortness of breath?"

"A little. I was having a hard time catching my breath while I was in the water."

The doctor listens to his lungs, requesting Martin take deep breaths. "Well, lungs sound clear. No water. That's good. Smoker?"

"No, not in years."

His eyes scan Martin's face and his hands roam freely under his jaw where they pause suddenly. "Hmm."

He presses his fingers again under Martin's jaw line. Gently at first, then firmer. He traces his way to the base of his skull, where he repeats the palpation, and then farther down to his underarms.

"Have you been feeling exhausted lately?"

"Doctor, I'm a shift worker for the government. Aren't we all exhausted?"

"More than normal, though. Or any unexplained weight loss? Strange aches or pains?"

Martin has lost about five kilograms in the last few months, but he hasn't been eating nearly as much, no appetite. He didn't think anything of it.

"Here's my concern," the physician says, and folds his hands. "You experienced what sounds like an unprovoked syncopal episode, and from what I can tell right now, everything looks okay. But some of these spots, these are your lymph nodes, and they feel swollen and hard. I don't like that. It could be any number of things, an infection or some other condition. But I think we need to send you for a few more exams. Do you have any other questions for me right now?"

Martin massages the side of his neck and rolls his head side to side, an audible pop coming from somewhere deep in his vertebrae. "Nothing at the moment, thank you."

The physician writes Martin a referral for a specialist, some other 'gist who will run a battery of tests that might offer insight into this episode.

Hugo enters the postage stamp of a room—just enough space for an exam table, a chair, and a standalone sink on the opposite wall with a soap dispenser and boxes of gloves mounted beside it—just as the physician leaves. Martin blinks twice, folds his paperwork and tucks it into his pocket.

"Ready to get back out there? I think you missed one or two," Hugo says, and smiles.

Martin laughs. For all the unflattering things everyone has to say about Hugo, Martin finds him to be kind enough. Hugo takes a seat, and although the room has not changed, it doesn't feel nearly as cramped.

The fluorescent lights hum, and there's enough antiseptic in the air that Hugo sits up a little straighter than normal. Hugo looks at Martin. "Ferrand, are you okay? What happened out there?"

"You know I used to be a diver before all of this? Underwater welder. When I worked on the oil rigs, we used to just get drunk every night and then spend the first half of the shift napping. At the bottom of the gulf. We would sink down there, open up our oxygen, and nap. Supervisor up top had no idea. Job would usually only take a day, but we would make it take three. We slept it off on the ocean floor, while the rest of the world kept turning. Just the silvery circle of Snell's window above us to suggest there was still a world to return to. That's where I felt like I was. Back on that floor. So deep the sun doesn't touch it. No one is looking for you. Most of the world doesn't even know you're there. The silt and sand could easily swallow you up, and no one would even know.

"I swear I've done this a million times by now. A million. You do it so many times you don't even think about it anymore. Check your line. Check your harness. Check your goggles. Take a few deep breaths and then down you go.

"It's a little different down there under the water. Have you ever felt that way? I mean, it's obvious. You're underwater. Of course it is different. But I'm talking about something beyond the obvious. It's the way time moves. There's something about how delicate it feels. It's more giving and easy to manipulate. I was down there poking around at the riverbed. All the silt starts rising, clouding up around me. Everything feels foreign but almost familiar. Maybe that's a rock? Maybe that's some vegetation?

"I found two grenades, and I had them in the pouch, but I could hardly see anything. Which is always the way it goes. You have your eyes for a minute and then you're in darkness—total darkness—so you have to use your hands. All you can do is touch. I'm groping here and there, separating rocks from grenades, but I start feeling other things. Things I can't easily identify. It's a strange sensation. I look up and I can see the sun doing its best to cut through the water and the silt, and it's so high up and wobbling there, barely noticeable.

"I think that might have been when I first noticed the lightheadedness, but maybe not. I skipped breakfast this morning. And honestly it didn't stand out to me. I just kept going. I kept groping, and I found another grenade, but I couldn't shake this feeling that I was touching something else—other objects—and then I kept getting a sensation like I was sinking. It was ridiculous because I had my gauge on me and I could see nothing to suggest this was the case, yet . . . I couldn't ignore that the bottom was coming out. Then I looked up and I saw the hulls of two boats drifting toward each other."

A groan from another room floats into their conversation, and a nurse rolls past the open door with a cart stacked full of food trays, the aroma filling their room for a moment. Something rich and savory but heated in plastic. It's gone before they can guess what it might be, leaving them once again with the recycled air of many sick patients and exhaust fans trying to keep up.

"There weren't any boats out there," says Hugo.

"Water is a strange place. We are mostly made of water, you know? Ninety-something percent. Immerse yourself in it, and you don't totally know what might be getting in or getting out. We think we live in a hard world with hard things. This is simply not the case. Time just feels so flimsy down there. Like I could reach out and poke a finger through it. And I think I might have. I think I've punctured something down there and slipped out somewhere else. I know that sounds ridiculous, but that's exactly how I feel."

Martin removes the gauze the nurse had taped over the catheter site. "Do you love your wife, Hugo?"

Hugo visibly bristles at the question. He has been married to Léa for almost ten years and they have two kids together. He cannot imagine his life without her. Who is he without his family? But almost immediately, Camille's face surfaces in his mind and lingers there until guilt eclipses every other thought. He hasn't felt guilt like this in a long time. But it has never been put to him before in such a blunt way. The way Martin asks the question—direct eye contact, genuinely waiting for an answer—softens his demeanor. "Of course. I love Léa with every ounce of my soul."

"Do you love her, or do you have love for her? Those two are different. Very different. It is so easy to find love but so difficult to hold on to. Have I ever told you about how I met my wife?"

Hugo shifts his weight. "Non, I don't believe you have."

"Late summer. A warm evening. We spent our summer vacation working the docks around Lac d'Éternité, a popular tourist spot with a cheap resort for schoolteachers on summer vacation. A lot of slightly deflated bodies showing everything off before wrapping themselves up in heavy garments for the winter. It was a little run-down, but everyone was so happy. They all tipped. Opportunities for easy employment to fund a carefree teenage existence. It was both dreamlike and unending. Wake up, spend the day boating tourists around the lake, drink all night, and then repeat. Intoxicating. Our boss hated us.

"It would all be over in another day. We were headed home. School was due to start in another week. We were giddy with the realization that our freedom was fleeting. This was it. We were not just returning home for another start to another school year. Sébastien was enlisting. George was leaving for university in a week. There was the sense that this would be the last summer quite like this one. Of course we would try to come back again the following year. I was the youngest of the three and headed into my final year of lycée.

"We had taken one of the boats out. Might be the last opportunity to do so. The evening air had a broken-in feeling to it like well-worn leather. The end of summer. We were all exactly who we wanted to be in that moment. Who we imagined ourselves to be. Who we might never actually be once this moment passed and the drudgery of day-to-day life crashed down on us. It felt like only moments before Sébastien exclaimed, 'Time! Time is on our side. We've got nothing but time!' But that had already been a lifetime ago, the first night, on the first boat we had snuck from the docks.

"We had no destination. No real plan. It was one last chance to take the boat out. One last opportunity to meander freely without a care. We were all young and clueless, but we knew something was coming. Life. Change. We had yet to experience it, but we had seen it on the faces of our parents and grandparents and every other older friend who had left and graduated and returned with that same pinched look of disappointment.

"But we were here. In this boat. Drinking wine and feeling the way our weight shifted with each slipping turn over the dark water. Maybe if we went long enough and far enough, we might outpace whatever phantom claimed all those who had come before us. The stale air of wasted life. The cream beginning to turn. Sébastien twisted the throttle, and the stern dipped a little deeper into the water as our boat gained speed.

"He steered the boat lazily around the lake, and we drifted over the surface, passing a bottle of something awful—was it Salignac? or no, St-Rémy?—between the three of us and enjoying the breeze that lifted our hair from our heads. George had brought his boom box, which he kept on his lap like his child, twisting the volume knob up during the parts of songs that he loved and bobbing his head along, lost to most of the conversation. The faint laughs and cries of families playing on the shore competed with the boom box, and I watched as they ran about like little ants that might as well have been a million miles away.

"'Hey, hey! Over there!' said George, and he pointed off in the distance.

"Sébastien guided the tiller over. The boat abruptly dipped and turned left. 'Let's see what they're up to,' said Sébastien. I looked up. Another boat idled on the water ahead. Sébastien eased off the throttle as we approached. '*Salut!*' he bellowed, pulling alongside the boat in a surge of lake water.

"'*Quoi de nerf?*' asked a slim girl, elbows like stilettoes, from the bow.

"'How's your night going?' asked a shorter girl from behind the wheel.

"'Much better now that we are talking with you three!' said Sébastien.

"I don't remember who spoke first, Sébastien or maybe one of the girls. Whatever words were exchanged are lost to time. There was flirting and dramatic gestures to attract their attention. The typical peacock strutting of teenagers. But I had locked in on Charisse. I saw her and forgot my own body entirely. She was seated on the bench, one arm resting across the gunwale, a slight smile playing on her face. I suspected her skin was typically much paler than it looked in the deepening twilight, but summer on the lake in the sun had turned it to a rosy brown. I could practically feel the warmth radiating from her. My own skin was in a similar state. It had taken all summer to get it that way. The key is to get the first bad burn out of the way early on in the season to allow it to peel and toughen up. And her eyes. A pale, vibrant blue that immediately held me in her gaze. Her voice took me by surprise. Rough and full of attitude, like broken shards of fine china rubbing against one another.

"Un amour d'été. Ces moments là où le temps s'arrête. And when time stops, people are able to open. All the sensations flood the mind. Every detail. The sound of the water against the side of the boat. The aftertaste of the liquor. The way the lungs feel massive and every breath infinite. They rush inside in one great wave, and there's nothing to do but accept it and take it all in. She looked back at me. Smiled.

"My heart soared. Ah, the electric sensation of a pretty girl's interest. The shore was a world away and so was every day to come after this. A million personal tragedies. All there was was this one moment and all the potential it held. We cling to these moments.

"But I didn't take advantage of it. I was so shy back then. Next thing I know, the boats are drifting apart. And that's what I was seeing this afternoon from the bottom of that river. Right before I passed out. The hulls of two ships drifting away from each other in the hazy vibrance of the current. My opportunity was closing. I was about to lose my chance. Coward.

"I wasn't the best swimmer. I wasn't the strongest. I wasn't the most charismatic. I wasn't the best looking. But none of that mattered. No, not that night.

"I stood and stepped to the edge and in one motion dove off the side of the boat. I slipped into the water headfirst, arms outstretched. If my friends had any reaction, it was lost in the rush of water in my ears. It roared like a rocket blasting into space. When I reemerged, their boat was within arm's reach. I reached up and grabbed the gunwale. The boat swayed to one side as I pulled myself up, and one of the girls squealed with delight. But not Charisse. Her mouth was slightly open. Was it amazement? Surprise?

"I smiled and pulled my pocketknife from my waistband. I flipped the slim blade out and went to work on the swollen gunwale. The memory is frayed, but so much of it is still there. Fragments. Singular moments and sensations. The tip of the blade sinking through the varnish and into the gunwale. The way the bloated wood gave under the weight of the blade's edge. The cuts left behind that revealed fresh wood and the beads of lake water that slipped in to form the digits of my phone number that I left inscribed. The flecks of paint that clung to my skin. The way my feet floated in the water, tethered only by my grip on the boat and the clear sky above with its stars just beginning to show, and how it made me feel like I was among those stars, weightless. The squeals of excitement from the girls in the boat. The echoes of shouts from the families on the shore. And Charisse's eyes locked on mine.

"The moment an unfamiliar face becomes familiar. The potential to know more. The distance closing. The sweet rush of mutual attraction, animalistic and yet tender. As old as the water beneath us.

"'In case you get bored later,' I said, and pushed myself off and back into the lake. Along the beach, families were packing it in, drawing down their kites and shaking the sand from the children's toys and blankets. Laughter and happy shouts of joy followed them to their vehicles. And although my hands were empty, inside I felt full. All the air in the world could not fill my lungs.

"We were still talking about my reckless suaveness as we dragged the boat ashore. The moon glowed, and there was dark water in between the pebbles. We lifted the boat back into its rack, and we felt like we could lift a whole cruise liner. But the ride back to town was quiet, and the effects of the wine turned us sullen and lethargic. The sensation of her smile faded with it. By the time I reached home, I wondered whether it had really happened that way at all. The remainder of the night gave me ample time to reinterpret the events from earlier in the evening a million and one different ways. Every smile. Every glance. Every minor expression. They all seemed to have taken on a more sinister appearance. A fool thing to have done. A bit desperate, no?

"How desperate does one have to be for a girl's attention to dive off the side of a boat and carve a phone number into wood? Night was here. The moment, passed. The summer was over. The rest of life would arrive at dawn.

"Sébastien was lost over the Bay of Biscay in a training accident three years later. George died of an aneurysm twelve years after that. It was ours for a moment. Life. We held it and then it was gone. It happened."

Hugo checks his watch subtly and smiles. "We were all kids once. I bet that wasn't the only boat with your phone number carved into it."

"She did call, though. The next day, right as we were getting ready to leave. We had this horrible old phone in the cottage. It had the worst bell that sounded like a steel shaft going through a wood chipper. In some ways, there's a significant part of me that is forever fixed in that moment: hand outstretched, phone ringing loudly, my entire life about to change. It was the beginning of it all.

"It was beautiful for about a month. And then all we did was fight for the next eleven. I was such a little shit. I needed to know everything. Who she had been with. How many, how many times? All that stuff. I didn't like her answers.

"'Don't be like that,' she said. 'Don't be that way.' I could hardly look at her. Childish, I know. But that's what we were. Children. It shouldn't matter. But it did. My friends all told me to forget her. 'If she's out of your life tomorrow, you know where you are? Right where you were before. You've lost nothing. Nothing at all.' But that wasn't true. I knew it wasn't true at all. I was in love. There was everything to lose, everything I had never known was possible to lose.

"Of course, I got over it. You realize how little that stuff actually matters if you hold on for long enough. We experienced so many moments together. All of these moments. Life changing. We went everywhere. We spent all kinds of money we didn't have and we didn't care. We didn't think at all. Love like that, it's like letting go.

"All that summer, before we met, there were mornings I would wake up before anyone else, and I would go out to that lake when it was empty and calm and I would walk into it. I walked until it got too deep, and I would go up on my tiptoes for a bit until I drifted farther out and couldn't touch any ground. I always thought about that when I was a welder. Our final test before we were cleared to work? They just threw us over the side of a ship, and you had to stay afloat for an hour. They would loop around and come get you. Just you. Middle of the ocean. A speck.

"It's important to feel small every now and again, to go somewhere where your feet can't touch the bottom."

"Do you miss her?" Hugo asks. He knows bits and pieces about why she left—some ghastly incident that he imagines is mostly gossip. There's no way what he has heard could be the whole truth.

Martin considers the question. "I'm more comfortable being alone than I thought I would be. Loneliness is knowable. There is safety and comfort in that knowingness. Loneliness is an empty room, but a space where one can know each wall. These walls can be seen. They can be touched. The distance between can be measured. Love is something else. Love is a wide-open plain, and you have no idea what is over the horizon. It is the things we wish we had said and the things we wish we hadn't.

"That's what I saw down there. My own life. And then water began to move. Fast. I tried reaching down to grab hold of something, but it was useless. And the thing is I didn't really mind. I just went with it. Isn't that strange? And then I was going through the riverbed and out to some other side, some other river or body of water entirely. The light was different. Brighter yet softer. I could feel the heat from the sun on my skin."

"Life can be weird like that" is all Hugo can think to say.

Martin holds his eye until Hugo can stand it no longer. Hugo thinks of Léa, he thinks of Éloïse and Emmanuel—his whole world. And yet, he suddenly remembers the face of every woman he's ever been with and he misses each one. Even he realizes the utter ridiculousness of this sentiment, but he can't help it. A flicker of desire for Camille burns beneath it all and he is surprised to feel it again, but it makes sense. It's because she is the one who is there, right in front of him, and he can reach out and grab her almost any time he wants. Who knows what will happen with Elisa? Léa will be there forever. For better or worse. Camille is the possibility of passion untethered from duty and responsibility. He's been through too much with Léa. They've made a life together and, by doing so, exchanged romance for partnership like two associates in a law firm. So much of their relationship is day-to day business. He cares about her, of course. She's the mother of his children. But he couldn't even look down there between her legs in the delivery room to witness them come into the world. Neither time. Some part of him wanted to, but he knew if he did, it was over. If he crossed that line, if he looked down there, there was no way he would ever be able to touch her again. So, he stood by her, he held her hand and whispered to her, and he did everything he could to be there for her, but he did so like a man pressed to the rock face of a sheer cliff, clinging for his life.

The guilt evaporates like rubbing alcohol. There must be a way to have both. He considers the man before him in silence. A wail drifts in through the open door to their room, faint and desperate. Ferrand Martin, the man who cheated death more than once, who lived an entire life before becoming a démineur, who lost his entire family to this job, this land. What is left after everything you love is consumed by fate? Martin's eyes, glassy and round, study a cuticle on the bed of his fingernail. He puts it in his mouth and tears it off with his teeth.

"Let me give you a ride," Hugo says.

The ride home is quiet as neither man speaks. When Hugo drops him off he waits to make sure Martin gets inside, and then he lingers another few minutes, although he's not sure why. He feels like he should have said something but can't figure out what.

He takes out his phone and texts Camille: "I need u. I've had a horrible day."

He waits. No response.

The kitchen light illuminates the window. It goes dark. Hugo loses his nerve, starts the engine, and drives home.

*

All doctors' offices are identical, Martin thinks. It doesn't matter the city. Or the country. Or even the health care system. Every single one looks exactly like the one that came before it.

It's two weeks later, and he sits in a chair beside the counter, arms crossed, and looks around the room. A potted dwarf umbrella tree sits in the far corner. It looks out of place. Possibly left there by accident. The leaves are slightly wilted, and some dirt from its pot has spilled onto the floor.

Martin's neck is sore from the biopsy the previous week. Some kind of issue had arisen with the sample—it wasn't enough or they couldn't get enough from it, he hadn't understood which—so he is back again. His muscles ache deeply in places he didn't know existed. *Is this what getting old feels like?* he thinks. Not yet fifty-five, and he feels twice that old. It's a thought he has almost every morning, and every morning the thought feels new. *Is this what it feels like?* But in some ways, he should consider himself lucky. They considered removing the nearest lymph node out of caution. They had decided against it at the last moment. It could be worse. It could always be worse.

Dr. Corbin, his surgical oncologist, enters the room, an open file in hand.

"Boom, boom!" says the physician with a smile. Everything about him looks clean and crisp, from his mane of blond hair to his clear, smooth complexion. His demeanor suggests he's never felt so much as a papercut in his life.

"Tell me something good, Doctor," Martin says, brushing off the doctor's greeting.

The doctor grins and opens up Martin's file. "Who's winning the war? Any good ones lately?"

It's the same joke he leads with at each appointment. Dr. Corbin possesses the type of fascination with Martin's line of work that many people outside of his profession do.

"Eh. Found some bones a few weeks back."

"Bones! Human bones?" he says with curiosity.

Martin nods.

"Mon Dieu, that's amazing!" he says as his eyes narrow with all the possibilities of whose bones they could be.

"It happens every now and again. Not often. At least not anymore. But it happens."

The young doctor places one hand on the counter, his focus homing in on every word, and waits for Martin to continue. Martin drops the subject and does not add anything more. Dr. Corbin recomposes himself by opening the file again and reexamining the first page.

"You really have the most interesting job in the world, I have to say."

Martin laughs a low huff of a laugh. "Yeah, sure. Most days I feel like a glorified garbage man. You actually save lives."

"Human bones," Dr. Corbin says, and shakes his head.

"Just another pain in my ass," says Martin. "We had to call everyone else out. The archaeologists. The anthropologists. All the 'gists."

Dr. Corbin looks off, lost in thought.

Martin sees the doctor transported to another world with a brief glimpse of the actions he will have to take in the coming days. A world of small pickaxes and brushes, careful gestures over bones encased in earth's dusty crust, and life-changing discoveries that end up in widely read publications. "But never mind all that. Why am I here again, Doctor?"

Dr. Corbin's eyebrows raise for a second, and it appears he has forgotten why they are sitting in his office in the first place. He quickly reassumes the posture of a serious man, a total transformation he executes from his facial expression down to his arms. He closes the file.

"Of course, pardon my fascination," he says. "Listen, I am going to give it to you straight. The results of the biopsy, the fine needle aspiration we performed, provided us with some initial insights, but it is not enough to make a definitive diagnosis. This happens, it's not a big deal. Especially if we are looking for some of the ugly boys—lymphoma and the like. We need a larger sample of tissue for analysis."

Martin sighs and sinks lower into the chair. Dr. Corbin calmly rolls a stool over and sits in a single, unbroken motion. It brings him down below Martin's height.

"Look, I know that's not what you want to hear. It might sound like the worst news. But we discussed that this next step might be a possibility. And here's the thing: It's not as bad as it sounds. It's really not. What I'm recommending now is a core needle biopsy. It's a little more intense than the FNA we took the other day, but not much. This time, instead of just removing cells, we are going to take a sample of core tissue from the lymph node. This tissue will provide our pathologists with more to work with so they can get a clearer picture of what's going on."

Martin rubs a hand through his mustache. How quickly life can change. "I was hoping this might be the last time we'd have to see each other. No offense."

Dr. Corbin places a hand on his shoulder. "Hey, you've been through a lot. I understand. One thing at a time. Seriously, this is the right move. Trust me. We lay you down, numb you up, get in, get out, and you're done. Minimally invasive and no need for general anesthesia, you go home the same day. I can even squeeze you in today if you have the time."

Martin nods.

An hour later, he changes into a paper gown in a dressing room. The cool air sends a shiver through him as he slips off his sweater and then his pants. A nurse quietly knocks to see if he is ready, and then they make their way down to the procedure room, where Dr. Corbin is waiting. Martin moves to the examination table and mounts. The loose, airy gown gives little peace of mind, and he crosses his legs in fear of exposing himself.

"Lie facing that way," Dr. Corbin instructs as he gestures toward one end of the table.

Dr. Corbin slips on a pair of gloves, and the sound of latex stretching over skin fills the room. He places the transducer against Martin's neck and probes the area. The sonogram monitor's screen churns in a gradient of gray and white from which oblong shapes appear. None appear ill or cancerous, but Martin has no idea what he is looking at. The inside of his body, a foreign land. It occurs to him the last time he watched a sonogram screen, Charisse was eight weeks pregnant. Similar shapes, identical confusion. The faint flicker of a heartbeat.

"There's our landing pad," says the doctor.

Next comes the unfamiliar chill of Betadine on his skin. Dr. Corbin thoroughly rubs it over the site. Martin watches the doctor prepare a syringe of lidocaine. The doctor reaches over him, and he feels a sharp pinch as the needle enters. Martin focuses on a spot on the ceiling, and at the same time, his skin goes numb, a quieting of the nerves that feels as strange as the first time.

Despite having just done this last week, everything about this experience, from the gown to the procedure, still feels foreign. Martin derives a sense of pride from this lack of comfort. Up until this point, his interactions with the medical world have been brief and almost nonexistent. He's never even broken a bone. In all his life, he's had only one other procedure similar to this one. When he was twenty-three, he had a mole removed. Charisse found it and insisted he get it checked out.

Sure enough, it roused enough suspicion that the doctor wanted to do a shave biopsy of the site. He could still see the mole: a lopsided brown nub jutting from the barren expanse of his naked back like a projectile crash-landed on its surface.

A tray of tools sat on the counter. A nurse spaced them out evenly, lining them up in a neat row. One in particular looked like a miniature crosscut saw—a slim, flexible blade that could be held between a thumb and pointer finger with ease.

Martin arched his back in surprise each time he was touched during the procedure. He didn't feel the blade begin to scrape, or at least he didn't feel pain. The doctor bent the miniature crosscut razor between his thumb and forefinger and employed a dull, rhythmic scooping motion. A distinct nudging sensation, the kind when someone tries to wake you from a deep sleep.

After what felt like a lifetime, he looked over at the doctor's mess on the examination table. Bloody patches of gauze and Q-tips stained with Betadine. But no mole. The doctor scraped and shaved until there was nothing left. Strangest of all, Martin wished there were something to see. A pulpy tumor. A parasite expunged. An object he could grimace at. Good riddance.

There was no feeling either, when the doctor cauterized the incision. But Martin smelled it. There's no way to ever forget how your own burning flesh smells.

*

"You're definitely my toughest patient," says Dr. Corbin. "Of that, I have no doubt."

Martin forces another smile. "I can hardly stand the sight of blood, Doctor."

"You could have fooled me. Here we go, almost there."

A slight pulling sensation in his neck.

"That's it, there it is. A little more."

The pressure increases. Just like the mole, he feels everything absent any pain. His dulled nerves do not protest as the small mass of cells leaves his neck through the needle. They were once his, yes. They were a part of him as much as any other cell in his body. Not anymore.

"Perfect, done!"

After Corbin finishes dressing the site, Martin slowly sits up and gets off the table. The doctor whistles a tune and strips off his gloves.

"You know the drill. Keep it clean. Pay attention for the next few days. We should have results within a week. Let us know if you have any issues. Nanani nanana."

"Oui, nanani nanana."

*

The ride home takes longer than expected. There is substantial construction along D112, adding another twenty-five minutes to Martin's trip. The construction crews mill about in fluorescent-yellow vests and scuffed white hard hats. Fresh mounds of dirt line the roadway. At the end of the roadwork, right as the cars begin to pick up speed, he notices another pile, this one different. Twisted metal, all corroded and oxidized. Splinters pulled from the thumb of a giant and discarded.

Those are whole rifles, he recognizes, and strands of barbed wire, fortification materials pulled from the earth. The wood stocks rotted. The thin iron warped and twisted like petrified dental floss or the bark of an alien tree species. *Ten euros says we get a call from them in the next few days,* he thinks. Any time anyone so much as lifts the corner of a rug in this town, some rusted artillery shell or grenade tumbles out. Martin notices his tank is slightly below a quarter full—he never lets it go below half a tank. *It's been a busy week*. He pulls off to get gas.

By the time he gets back on the road, the sun has set, and the sky is on fire. It matches the stabbing pain pulsing in his back. Martin readjusts his seat, yet it does little to alleviate his discomfort. The seat belt feels too tight. The driver's seat does not feel designed for a human body. Outside, the world seems to be going by too fast all at once and, at the same time, frozen in a blurred snapshot. His house is ten minutes away, a small bungalow on a corner tucked away in one of the outer neighborhoods, and it is dark and quiet and waiting to consume him. Some frozen leftovers sit in the freezer. Setting them out to thaw is all he has to look forward to for the rest of the evening.

Martin turns into the parking lot of the Douaumont Ossuary, the memorial to the Battle of Verdun's dead. It's near closing time; small groups of tourists make their way to their vehicles, and only a few cars remain in the lot. The final bus from town idles at its stop as a line of passengers enters one by one. Martin cuts the engine and sits for a moment.

To his left, the ossuary, a strange building at the top of a hill above town: a single enclosed corridor from end to end with a bell tower looming skyward at its center. The hilt of a sword, its blade plunged deep in the earth. To his right, a field of bone-white crosses stretches outward. Some sixteen thousand graves altogether. Uniform and impossibly precise in their alignment. The grass is immaculately manicured. The rows they form become lines, and it is possible to make shapes and patterns from them at a distance. A sense of order reclaimed from all the waste of life.

In the months after his daughter died, Martin briefly saw a therapist who stressed the importance of remaining present. They did this through breathing exercises and meditation. In truth, Martin found the silence of his mind terrifying. His mind is a dangerous neighborhood to be in after a certain hour. Instead, he began coming to the ossuary at dusk because it had the type of quiet the therapist claimed was helpful.

The woman in the ossuary's doorway holds the A-frame welcome sign under her arm, ready to close for the evening. However, when she notices Martin, she waves. He returns the gesture. He likes her. She takes her job, a minor role, seriously. When guests enter the ossuary, she makes sure each one takes off their hat. Assertive and direct. They close in less than ten minutes, but she lets him inside. He only needs a few moments.

Copper light pours through the thick stained glass. Cool air, silence. Martin takes his time walking the corridor. One door leads to a small chapel that houses the tomb of Monsignor Charles Ginisty, bishop of Verdun, who campaigned all over France as well as Canada and the United States to raise the funds to build the structure. At one end is a stand of twenty votive candles. The walls and ceilings are lined with plaques engraved with the names of French soldiers killed in the battle. The space glows with grainy red light. The rays feel essential, cleansing, and full, something other than holy.

Everyone at command was incredibly understanding and told him he could take however much time he needed after she passed. A kind gesture. A strange one. Why did they encourage him to remain by himself at home when he felt most lonely? Charisse had left by that point too. They didn't know that part at the time. It was just him.

He told them merci but absolutely not, and returned to work a day after the funeral.

Martin wanders out the door and wraps around the rear of the building. A row of knee-high windows lines the exterior wall. In the ossuary's shadow, Martin crouches. He rests on one knee and peers into the low portal. His dusty reflection meets his gaze. He strains his eyes and looks deeper. Bones. Piles of bones. No organization, no design. An alcove stacked to the ceiling. Orphaned ribs scattered like wood shavings. Pelvis bones and skulls discarded like forgotten chipped mugs in a sink.

The ossuary is a memorial to all the ways one could die—16,000 out front and an estimated 130,000 tossed into the vaults below. Imagine the mess. Imagine the job. The sheer magnitude of it. Bodies dangling from the arms of the few trees left standing. There was no telling how many more they would find. Too many to count. His reflection is a contour on the pane, but his features are obscured. *The eternal anonymity of it all.*

At some point, someone looked around the slaughter field after all the armies went home, after all the treaties were signed, and stared out over that lunar landscape so quiet you could hear the earth turn and realized they'd had enough and didn't want to deal with the rest. Just dump the remaining bodies. Pile them up. They built a place that captured the similitude of the waste, the devastation, and the sheer helplessness of it all. Soon, those bones they discovered will be placed here as well unless someone can confirm his identity. Another nameless soldier stripped of every unique feature, every piece that made him *him*.

He surveys the surrounding area. Rolling fields of green. Thick woods of shadowland, with sundry species of trees, their limbs softly waving in the twilight. So quaint and peaceful. Hard to believe it is all poisoned. Over time the shells have leached chemicals into the earth so that even though they might not pose any risk of detonation, the ground is useless. The land is poisoned. It is all poisoned for centuries to come.

*

Less than a week later, Martin returns to Dr. Corbin's office to receive the results. No one has cleaned the dirt beside the dwarf umbrella plant in the corner, making it feel like he never left, as if the days between this appointment and the last were only a dream. As for the results, he will definitely be seeing Dr. Corbin again, as well as many other doctors.

"There's clear evidence of lymphoma, which means it is affecting your lymphatic system. Now, there are different types of lymphoma, so the next step is further testing to figure out which beast we are dealing with here. I can tell you this, lymphoma is treatable. The things we can do nowadays, unbelievable. Many people respond quite well," says Dr. Corbin.

"What sort of testing?"

"I won't lie to you. Quite a few. There will be several blood tests, LDH, CBC, and we will also want to test your liver and kidney function. We might want to do a CT scan of your chest, probably a PET scan as well. There's also a bone marrow biopsy. It is critical we act fast at this stage. Lucky for you, all of this can be handled at Saint-Nicolas, so you won't have to travel far."

"I hate hospitals."

"Me too! Come on! Who likes hospitals? They're terrible places. Ferrand, you are a lucky man. That ER doctor probably saved your life. They're not all equal, you know? Scary to say, but it's luck of the draw in those places. They miss things all the time. Easy mistake to make.

"And you? Of all people? You're out there playing with bombs all day. This is nothing compared to that."

I'd rather disarm a seventy-five-millimeter artillery shell with my bare feet than go through treatment, Martin thinks, and forces a smile. He lets the doctor think he has done his job in disarming his unease.

Within days Martin sits in another procedure room. The television is tuned to a game show, the volume too low to hear. The dissonant beeps of various machines and equipment make the unit more spaceship than hospital. He looks over an IV setup on a tray. Neat, precise rows. Evenly spaced and aligned. The nurse ties a tourniquet around his biceps and cleans the inside crook of his elbow. She taps around to find a vein. Then the needle slips in with a pinch.

"First try," she says. "You have such lovely veins."

His blood fills vial after vial. He goes from one part of the hospital to another doing test after test. He spends a whole day inside its walls being poked, prodded, and scanned. Martin finishes the day with the bone marrow biopsy. He lies on his side and waits for the doctor.

A nurse enters with a warm expression. "Are you comfortable?" she asks.

A laughable question.

"Oui," he says.

"The doctor will be in momentarily to administer the anesthesia," she says with a kind smile as she sanitizes the back of his hand with an alcohol wipe. "Then we will begin with the bone marrow aspiration, followed quickly with the core biopsy. You're almost done."

He waits. Another disposal day is approaching. Henri is in charge now, and this will be his first disposal day. It's not just any other day. A lot of moving parts. But he will be all right, he will figure it out. Martin believes in his abilities to pick up where he left off. That's the mark of true leadership. They carry on as if you were never there in the first place.

Martin takes his mind off it all with thoughts of the ossuary. What it must have looked like on the day of its dedication. He could imagine speeches with poetic intonations of eternal sleep and rest. Large crowds. Bright balloons all around the building and observation balloons dotting the horizon. Binoculared eyes peering from their baskets suspended beneath the taut canvas skin. The ceremony might have provided some relief at the moment. But after the crowds had dispersed and wandered home, after the speeches concluded and the stages with their draperies were all dismantled, the bones were still there. For all to see. A puzzle impossible to solve. One that didn't ask to be solved in the first place. It is a quintessentially human quality to create a mess and then feel the need to make it somehow better. He's thinking about balloons as the doctor inserts the needle into the back of his hip bone. The pain is immediate. His vision clouds, a flurry of black balloons obscuring his sight.

When it passes, his eyes feel like two pinballs, dense and metallic and rolling free in the sockets for which they are a size too small. Everything around him feels too far away.

*

There is comfort in routine and structure. A certain sense of safety can be gleaned from repetition. Habits with purpose. A guiding principle that suggests that if you stick to these habits, you are guaranteed a particular result. You have a chance. This is largely the reason Martin returns to work despite some lingering soreness and goes with the crew to the field a day after he finishes his tests at the hospital.

A gray mossy dawn. New site, same routine. A local farmer has found a couple of 75mm shells on the edge of his property. They're here to disarm and remove them. In another week, Martin will get a call saying the cancer has spread to his bone marrow. They must begin aggressive treatment immediately.

That's still a week away. Instead, he watches Basille struggle with a shell half embedded in the earth, the nub of its fuse exposed to the air. Martin steps forward to help, inculcating him with techniques and tips so that maybe he can do it on his own next time. He shows him how to scrape the dirt away and which side to start with so that it's easier to wriggle the thing free. He shows him that it's okay to be rough with this one since the fuse is ruptured and therefore the shell is in no danger of detonating. After enough soil has been cleared, he cracks it from its place. From around the vessel, he gently claws the loose dirt away. They scan for any leaks or fissures. Some could be so fine they are impossible to see until you try to lift it out of the hole. The hair on the back of Martin's neck stands up from the pain as he lifts the shell.

Not a bead of sweat, not the slightest tremor in his hands. He could be in a warm bath on a lazy evening in. He rubs the grubby skin of le manqué with a kindly affection like he is bathing a little piglet.

At this moment, the exact moment it breaks free and into his grasp, he looks at the artillery shell and sees it anew. Martin lifts it from the soil, revealing the mold of where the bomb had been, its curve and shape still perfect. Something about the cavity in the earth is grotesque, and although he would never admit it, the sight makes him uneasy.

Martin senses what it all really means. Progress. Control. Time is constant. The war never ended. It is here. Right now, in his hands. He wants to smash all the shells like clay pots. Crush them in his hands. He runs his finger along the shell's arsenic-encrusted rim; the texture is the same as the soil they pulled it from. Some German gunner's fingerprints are on the skin of this shell, right beneath the clots of soil that still cling to it. It is all right here.

He holds the shell up to the sun. It shrivels in the light.

*

In the steam-choked locker room of the depot that night, Martin sits on a bench, elbows resting on his thighs, and studies his hands. The calluses have a crimped look to them tonight. They have been reshaped yet again, another layer added, re-formed by another ninety-kilogram shell carried out of Zone Rouge. The oppressive smell of male body odor, masked with deodorant and cologne, fills the room, and they fit together like two feet in one shoe. This will be his last day. There are no more moments like this one in his future. He received the news at the start of the shift, but he kept it to himself and went about the day like normal. *Normal.* A word he knows will become foreign to him in the near future.

This last day has been particularly long. He can't say why. Nothing unusual happened. Actually, it was an ordinary day. Ordinary in every sense of the word. Some days were like this, though. Long. Longer than the day before. Heavier. Some days Martin had looked out over the cratered landscape and counted the endless trees that stretch in every direction and thought, *What the hell is the point?*

One hundred years. That is the number they give on the annual reports. Every year, after all the numbers from all the districts involved in the cleanup have been calculated and compared with the numbers from the previous years, the primary office, headquartered in Paris, publishes an updated projection on the progress of the operation. And every year, the number stays at one hundred. Another century of cleansing before the countryside can be renewed. A lifetime and then some.

One hundred years. A century. At least. At most? Who knows? Barbeaux sings in the shower, a warbling, out-of-tune melody that Martin cannot identify. The sound echoes off the tiles. One hundred years. The steam makes it difficult to breathe. Martin leans his head back and looks up at the ceiling. He draws a deep breath. The echoes from the shower bounce around in his mind.

Even the streets of Verdun. How many years since it ended? And still, always so quiet. Like the lobby of a funeral home. A certain weariness overtakes Martin every now and again, something deeper than exhaustion. Something that sleep cannot solve. Something that isn't just a matter of needing a break or a vacation. That something is the recognition that there is a very good chance this job will never be finished. One hundred years. And after that? Even if they somehow managed to pull every splinter of shrapnel out of the ground, the chemicals leeched will last centuries. It's the echoes in the trees between the moss-covered craters and the way the trees begin to look like broken teeth in a gaping smile. A smile for a joke that he is only beginning to realize is on him.

A wrinkled Band-Aid hangs by one end from the side of the last locker. Martin can't stop staring at it. The fleshy tab clings to the hard, rusted patina of the locker surface. A piece that does not belong and makes the nose crinkle just at the thought of how it had gotten there and from where it had come. The shower stops. Martin stands. He grabs his bag and walks to the door. He hears Barbeaux grab his towel and step out. He does not want to talk tonight.

On nights like this, he always takes the long way home and stops off for an espresso by himself at a café where they know him by name. A local spot with tile floors and tables along plate glass windows. It's tucked away on one of the thin, twisty backstreets in the city's oldest quarter. Outside the dust-coated café windows, Verdun turns without pause as the clouds thicken with the threat of snow. The wind picks up, and little bits of trash swirl about in the doorway of the small café, bouncing off the windows like grains of sand. Most people wouldn't even be able to tell you there is a café on this street, it is so rarely visited. Those who know about it couldn't tell you how they know about it. It isn't a place people discover—it's either known or forever overlooked.

Martin likes it here because it is usually very quiet and no one bothers him. Always the same bartender, a burly, bearded middle-aged guy with a pinkie ring and a single hoop earring. He is always dressed just younger than he should be, cuffed blue jeans and brown leather boots, a red plaid shirt with rolled sleeves. A very congenial guy. Martin can enjoy a cup of coffee after his shift and not have to worry about bumping into someone from the job. The bartender pours his coffee without a word. If Martin isn't at the bar, there is a table in the back corner tucked into the shadows where he can keep a good view of the room and slip into his thoughts. Martin exchanges some casual pleasantries with the bartender and then, with coffee in hand, makes his way to the back.

It is one of those nights. He takes the table.

Martin sips the espresso. Looks at nothing. Thinks nothing. Feels only a vague sense of relaxation. All the heaviness of the Rouge leaves him. A single candle on the table illuminates his back corner table, and he can feel himself slipping into the darkness behind him. Less himself and a little more a part of the physical place around him. Another few minutes and it will be difficult to say exactly where he ends and the wall begins.

Hugo sees him before he can get up to leave.

"Ferrand!" Hugo claps him on the shoulder. "Perfect timing! You're the first person I get to tell. I've got great news. All that wood they're trying to get rid of? The ones the beetles ravaged? I have just worked out a deal to salvage it. For pennies on the dollar!"

"Oh yeah? How's that?"

"It's all quite simple. It's not actually rotted, not in the least. People just don't like the way it looks. It's a style thing. But the wood itself is sturdy as anything. This is going to be huge, you just wait," he says, his face humming with excitement.

Martin bows and gestures outward in deference. "Congratulations. I'm sure you'll put it to good use."

"I'm surprised to see you here. I heard the news. I'm so sorry."

Of course he already knows.

"Just one of those things, Mayor," Martin says, and shrugs.

"I mean, all those chemicals you're exposed to out there. You think you got it from the ordnance?"

"Could be. What does it matter? There's no way to know for certain."

Hugo slides into the seat opposite him. "What have they told you so far? Have they given you an idea of what you're up against?"

"Official diagnosis is non-Hodgkin lymphoma. Stage four. It's in my bone marrow."

"I'd kill myself," Hugo blurts out, his face flushing. "I mean, only if it got really bad. Really, really bad. You're brave for the way you're taking it."

Martin sips his espresso, his expression unreadable.

"You look great, all things considered. I just . . . What keeps you going?" Hugo asks.

"Thirty years—merde, thirty years—ago. The Piper Echo Platform in the Gulf of Mexico. A ghost city on stilts above the swells sucking oil up through the ocean floor. The boys with flash burn cream spread over their faces, thick and chalky, all clown smiles and dangling cigarettes.

"Management replaced a pressure safety valve on one of the backup condensate pumps with a blind flange. Typical maintenance upkeep, but no one told us when we changed over. So, a little while later, one of the pumps tripped and the control room ordered the backup pump—the one with the flange—to be restarted. Can't do that. It was leaking gas for half an hour. All it took was a spark. Set off a massive explosion."

He leans forward, gently swipes a few crumbs off the table.

"It was chaos. Everyone scrambled to secure the lines. A total mess. The flames engulfed five men. Sixteen others were seriously injured. It was a bad day. Very bad day. The coveralls melted to their bodies. They had to use dental records to tell who was who afterward. I can't remember much of what they looked like anymore, but the smell."

Hugo exhales sharply, unable to meet Martin's gaze. "Christ."

"You don't forget the smells," Martin adds, almost to himself.

"I can't imagine." Hugo grimaces and looks away.

Martin fixes him with a tired, but resolute, stare. "You don't know how bad life can get. Trust me. Every day is a gift. It's another chance. It's all we have. There's nothing in this life I've seen that really makes sense. Someone decides to change a piece of a pipe and forgets to tell someone else and people die. You can do everything right and still get crushed by a meteor falling from the sky."

"Of course. Carpe diem. YOLO. The here and now. All the clichés."

"They only become clichés if you don't practice them."

Outside the café window, Martin notices a woman and a little girl. They hold hands, swinging them back and forth, smiles all around. The glare on the windowpane obscures their features and renders them familiar. The little girl breaks away and leans to the window, cupping her hands around her eyes to look in at them. Recognition triggers deep in his mind. But then the woman steps to the glass as well, and he remembers them from the day on the river all those weeks ago.

Hugo watches surprise flash across Martin's face before he regains his composure. He follows his gaze and hesitates.

"A rare night out with the family. Crepes. Babysitter has the littlest one," Hugo says.

"For a second, I thought . . ." Martin says, but leaves the thought unfinished.

Léa waves politely and gestures to Hugo that it is time to go.

Martin gets up to leave. "You won't see much of me after tonight. Medical leave. I start treatment next week."

"Ferrand," Hugo says, and grabs his arm. "Just, if you need anything, don't hesitate to reach out."

Martin nods, offering the faintest hint of a smile. "Take care of yourself, Mayor."

Martin walks away, his movements a little slower than they were a few short weeks ago, and Hugo sits for a moment longer, the ambient clatter of chairs sliding and glasses clinking all around him. Hugo looks at Martin's empty espresso cup. Along the rim, a faint grease stain is already drying. He rises and turns to greet Léa and Éloïse, putting on a smile that doesn't sit quite right. They leave together, passing under the flickering sign above the café, and their laughter blends with the drone of a passing car that winds into the deepening night.

Démineurs

We might as well be on the opposite side of the world from Martin at this point. An entire career spent out here pruning these lead-saturated farmlands just for it all to end in a lumpy hospital bed with a chemo IV stuck in his arm. News that arrives like a hair in the soup. Martin has left. We are still here. Our job keeps going. It is time for us to get back to our sheep, gars. The last time we see Martin is the day before, just as we return from our shift. He wants to say goodbye. We offer encouragement and luck. *Courage, tu vas y arriver!* He tells us he likes his doctors, they seem confident in his treatment. But guarantees are for contracts and deeds. All they can do is promise to do no harm.

He watches us deposit the payload for the day with the others. As we line the shells on the pallets, we wrap the others with the wire coil line, clipping the bundles and tightening each pallet until they feel nearly solid. A lifetime chipping away, chipping away, chipping away. How easily one can grow comfortable around these unpredictable devils. They are safe and quiet. Until they are not.

Late night and everyone just wants to get home. We have to be back at five again tomorrow to head to the flats. He is still there when we leave.

*

Disposal days are all the same. We half expect to see Martin when we show up at the depot—that same serious expression, his rumpled cap cocked back on the crown of his head—but he isn't here. Predawn chill on our skin. Blue tobacco smoke hangs heavy in the cabs. A full moon is the only fixture in the sky. The stars fade and morning encroaches. The loaded Land Rovers rattle through the front gate of the depot with the same timbre of cabinets filled with fine china. All those shells clinking together in the back. The cabs rock with every bump as we take the turns away from the depot.

We take the back roads to the autoroute and ride through leaf-speckled puddles as the woods grow thinner around us before they vanish entirely to reveal the vast expanse of Verdun's hills stretching as far as we can see—lumpy and brilliant ancient impact craters like rogue waves of a sea caught in a storm.

Who gets the final word in a war we haven't finished picking up after? The wakeful and the downtrodden. The ambitious and the hopelessly bored. Verdun is a quiet little town. The old buildings with their drab colors. Most were here before the war. The shadows of the passing armies once fell on their walls. It is easy to feel like a ghost in Verdun. We are all ghosts in the Rouge. This job. There are enough ghosts out there that a person might mistake one for their own if they are not careful.

We attract death. We welcome it in. We wear it. It becomes us. French dead. German dead. Canadian dead. Moroccan dead. Senegalese dead. Indian dead. It is more difficult to believe that something hasn't stuck around. How could there not be some type of residual waste? Think of it as a smearing of the soul. Three hundred thousand deaths in the space of a single year. Violent deaths. Slow deaths. Disease deaths. Quiet deaths. How could there not be something left over?

In the early days, those who were left to clean up just walked around picking them up off the ground. The shells were everywhere and much deadlier. We find one poking out of the ground now and it's a big event. Immediately after the war? That was just reality. They took prisoners and put them to work out here collecting and disposing. Black-robed Christian missionaries. Migrant workers. Gypsies. Former military. We have all these tools and trinkets at our disposal. Back then? They shouldered rifles and walked around shooting them at a distance. Set them off right where they found them if they could help it. One at a time.

Mon Dieu. How big the job must have seemed.

*

When we arrive, we have beaten the sun. The tidal flats are as unimpressed as usual. The boardwalks, vacant. Doors creak and sand crunches under our boots when we step from our trucks. We make our way out over the fresh clay, and it feels like we are walking over the hide of some slumbering beast. Dig a hole with the mini tractor at first and then our hands. Lower the pallet. Repeat.

We work opposite each other, cigarettes between our lips, the gray clumps of sand coming up crumbly and chalky. We blow smoke out the sides of our mouths and work steadily. The hole we dig has fine, clean walls cut down at a sheer angle.

We wipe our hands on our trousers, but it does no good. The sand! The harder we try, the more the grains seem to stick. We hate the beach.

Every pallet looks the same. The toxic shells go on the very bottom with layers of explosive and incendiary shells on top. We top it off with anti-tank mines or maybe plastic explosives. The explosion starts from the top, incinerating the toxic gas.

Disposing of toxic chemicals at sea doesn't make any friends with the environmentalists in the area. At least once a year there is a demonstration of some sort. There is always some political bill moving its way through the government to make it illegal to detonate them under the ocean. But what will we do with them? They don't want to leave them in the ground. But they also don't want us leaving them stockpiled in their neighborhoods. And then they don't want us destroying them at sea. They can't be persuaded.

The flats cannot support the full weight of a forklift, so we move the pallets of munitions from the trucks to the hole with pallet jacks. It is a strange combination of pulling, shoving, and shimmying that looks both manic and, somehow, strangely spiritual. Our band of pilgrims dragging our load one step at a time out to the hole, only to begin again.

We maneuver the pallets down to the lip of the hole one by one. From there, we unpack the loads so they can be rearranged at the bottom of the hole, returned to the underground one more time. We start with a single empty pallet to keep the floor level. Then we stack the shelves according to size and disposition. They feel breakable, the shells. So fragile. We handle them with care, not because they might explode in our arms but because they might crumble to dust without a trace. And then what would all our work be for? What would we have to show for our efforts?

Pedestrians on their early-morning walks whistle and shout from the boardwalk. The tide returns. Every once in a while, one of us looks up and notices the water much closer than the last time we looked up.

The guys from the Le Crotoy division handle the detonator cables. They carry out a large spool of narrow-gauge wire and test it to make sure it works before attaching it to the top layer of the pallet sunk down in the hole. We leave a gap in the center, and the demolition team lowers themselves into the hole with their charges and cables. These two are a serious pair. Sleeves rolled halfway up their forearms to keep them from catching on any loose bits and pieces. They slip the plastic explosive into the center of the pile and then a few other strategic places. They twist fuses into the putty, molded together to make the final charge. Monsieur Plastique is no longer our friend.

Spectators line the boardwalk, the crowd already almost twice the size it was twenty minutes ago. They gawk, their elbows perched on the top rail, several feet hiked up on the middle rail. A strong breeze wreaks havoc on every head of hair. Small children straddle their fathers' shoulders. A man in sunglasses kneels beside his son and explains what we are doing with dramatic hand gestures. One woman in a salt-stiffened windbreaker props herself up on the middle rail and focuses her camera lens on us, twisting the adjuster to get the shot just right. They know it's coming. They follow this impulse the same way they crane their necks when they pass a car wreck. Curiosity. They're too far away to hear, but we don't need to. Every smile, every pair of lips, every wide-open mouth says the same thing: *This is going to be something.* When we detonate the pallets, they'll gleefully walk away, the ringing in their ears a souvenir, a small badge of honor.

We run the line out a safe distance and shelter behind an outcropping of boulders more than three hundred meters away. The tide creeps in, and we all watch it fill the hole. Slowly, and then all at once. In the meantime, we smoke another cigarette and doze against the warm surface of the rocks.

*

Remember the day Gaston lost his mind?

Nearly blew us all to bits.

We pulled up to his farm on the outskirts of Samogneux just before sunset and found Monsieur Gaston pitching 75mm artillery shells at his own house. The same man who used to drop off the vegetables he couldn't use at our depot once a month. Such a kind guy. His cows. His magnet and rod. The 75s were scattered all over, like a child's marbles in the dust. In the flashing blue lights of the emergency vehicles, he appeared possessed, fully absorbed by some malignant force. Gaunt and skeletal. Foaming from the mouth. At any moment, one of those rounds could have exploded and killed us all. And his voice. Remember his voice?

How could we forget? Ranting so incoherently that no one could understand a word.

It's the lead in the water. We all know it's there. Been leeching into the water tables for almost a century. That same lead is in each and every one of us. We could all end up like that. Easily.

They don't pay us enough for this shit.

He kept picking the shells up one at a time and launching them from his shoulder with the motion of a shot-putter. Unbelievable strength for a man who looked so fragile. Each one hit the side of his home with a solid thud and fell immediately to the ground. One shell took out a window and went right through the kitchen and into the sitting room. They found it later resting under the couch like a kitten hidden away for an afternoon nap.

His clothing hung from him like tattered sails.

But that's the thing. Came out later. The clothing he had on wasn't his. Wasn't even his size. No one knows where he got it from. When they took him away, they changed him out because the rags he was wearing were completely soiled. They came to find everything he was wearing was two sizes larger than anything else he had in his closet and there were someone else's initials sewn in the collar of the shirt.

Another one of those mysteries.

But where did he get all those artillery shells?

He was a collector. Descended from a long line of collectors. A surprise to us all. How many trips had we made out there around the time of the iron harvest? How many times had we watched him plunge his cows and roll shrapnel around in the palm of his hand like a fistful of dice. We never knew. All those moineaux en colère. He had been storing them for years in his barn, many of them passed down to him by family. Heirlooms? Perhaps. A private museum of sorts. He had displayed all of them according to caliber and size. Tagged and organized, growing black mold in the shadows. A few rare eighteen-pounders at the center of the display.

But why? Who would collect such bizarre artifacts?

This city is filled with weirdos.

No, it's easy to understand. There's an undeniable attraction to the moineau en colère. Every shell we pull from this earth has a secret. Powder. Ball. Chlorine. Mustard. Arsenic. It's hard to tell exactly what might still be inside. That's the appeal. At least part of it. They come up to the surface in all variety of conditions. Some in pieces like shards of seashells along a shoreline at low tide. Others intact and perfectly preserved as if they were left there only yesterday. We find them orphaned and alone, and then we find whole fields of them. When many of them surface, they are rusted and corroded beyond recognition. An entire lifetime spent worming their way upward through the churning banks of sod that have encased them since before any of us were born. Some even still have the paint clinging to their jackets, these thin white bands denoting a poisonous gas type from a phosphorous type from a high-explosive type, flaking off on our gloved fingers. The bad ones ooze. You can taste it. Like the mouth of every sewer in Paris. They ooze their gas, and the second you taste it, you run. Don't think. Run.

And the smell. Death's own odor.

Brings to mind all the dark corners of seldom-used rooms in an old house or a windowless cellar where no one has bothered to replace an extinguished blackened light bulb from years before. A staleness that lets you know this thing had once been very much alive. Makes you wonder whether a dead thing might be just as deadly as when it was alive. Usually there's more underneath. Pull one up from the dirt, there can be another five or six right beneath it. Or wrapped up in the roots of a tree. Most of the vegetation grows right around them. Absorbs them.

The ones that work themselves to the surface on their own don't have a smell. They're found lounging on the ground in the shade under a tree like miscreant hobos or baked in the sun like a brick, and they are odorless. But much of the time there's only a small portion protruding from the earth, and we have to gingerly brush the loose soil away and then carefully carve the thicker clumps of dirt from their skin. When we bring one up into our arms, holding it close to our bodies in our antistatic coveralls, you know this is the first time this projectile is seeing the sun since it exited the muzzle of some German or French artillery piece decades before.

The gendarmes were already staged at a safe distance when we got out to the dairy farmer. They'd set up a few wooden barriers near the entrance—for what reason, no one knows. It's not like he was going to escape any of us anytime soon. Everyone was looking around, wondering what could be done. We stood far enough away that we could not understand a word he said but could see patches on his scalp where he had torn out large tufts of his hair. The wooden pallets stacked up against the stone wall of the yard. A few empty oil drums beside them. The tractor under its overhang with the wheels just past its coverage. Manure turned the air sweet and pungent. Everything in the countryside is covered in shit. Aside from the man's mumbled ramblings, it was so quiet. All that could be heard was the worried cries from a single cow in a pen. Church bells floated over the hum of the running engines of our vehicles. Empty sky. Nightfall rapidly approaching. They switched on their high beams to keep the space illuminated, and it cast kaleidoscopic shadows with his movements all across the yard. Eyes from neighboring windows watched from behind drawn curtains. We couldn't see them, but we could feel them.

"He's all yours," one of the cops said.

What do we look like? Therapists? We are démineurs. We dismantle bombs, not people.

Just a game of passing the bullshit around that no one wants to deal with.

But what did Ferrand Martin do? Without a word, he crossed through the barricade and walked right over to the man. Martin with his bushy mustache and glasses. He just walked right out to him and crossed that open ground in no time. Hands in pockets. A calm, soft gait that Frenchmen of a certain age develop. Didn't pause once. That lunatic was still holding one of the 75mm shells when Martin got to him. Cradling it in his arms and looking around wildly. Seemed just as surprised as the rest of us.

No one could say a word. Every individual held their breath, waiting for whatever might come next. You just don't know with a person like that, what they will do next.

Absolute silence, save for the perpetual ringing in our ears. Light was fading. A cool breeze blew through the courtyard, and off in the distance, the headlights of passing vehicles could be seen making their way back to the city.

But then?

They just talked. Martin reached out and put a hand on the farmer's shoulder. We could hear their voices. Not the words. Just their voices.

Less than a minute.

Felt like a lifetime.

What were we expecting? Something more than a chat.

And then Martin took the shell from him. Gaston just handed it over and crumbled to the ground where he stood. The officers rushed the man, and Martin turned and walked back toward us, up the slope, the shell perched on his right shoulder.

He climbed so steadily, and he walked right past us, back to the ridge where we had parked the trucks. Something more than a shadow but not quite a ghost. He crested the ridge and stood there a moment, a defiant charcoal splinter stuck in the amber sky.

What did he say to him? What did he say?

It's not the words that matter. It was the action. A lot can be learned about a man by what he runs to when he's afraid. But you find what he's actually made of by what he's willing to lose in order to do the right thing. There are actions and then consequences. That's it. Actions. Consequences.

It wasn't a waste. Life isn't just about chasing whatever moves you every waking second of your life. There is something to be said for someone who can show up to the same place, the same building, the same *room* with the same people, more or less, for almost twenty years. And do it well too.

What is it that we miss about the past? What do we fear in the future?

Maybe you meet someone. Maybe you settle down and decide to make a life together. Maybe you have kids. Grow old together, it's all very nice. It sounds beautiful. And it is beautiful. But those are all maybes. So many maybes and no guarantees. And even if it did happen, if all of that happened, there's still the fact that the majority of your life, the actual number of minutes piled up on top of one another, is spent doing the mundane, the numbingly boring. Getting from here to there. Just moving through space. You have to cook the food before you can eat it, right? And then someone has to clean it up.

Yeah, you might say, *Oh, and at the end of it all, all he got was a wristwatch.* That's because there's nothing they could have given him! Nothing could have compensated. It's intangible. And after everything he went through with his daughter? His wife? That horrible mess. Any one of us would drink ourselves to death if we had been through what he had been through. We can't bring ourselves to talk about it. So there won't be any monuments to him. You won't find his name in a history book. But they're going to feel that loss after he leaves. Even after they forget his name, they will have a difficult time filling that gap. He mattered. His efforts mattered. Guaranteed.

Well, he who lives shall see.

Oui.

*

Once the tide fills the hole, we are ready to set off the charge. We hook a slim black box to the charging cables. We perform one last check, and the demo man gets the all clear.

"Let's see if anyone over there is still paying us any attention," he says, his thumb on the switch.

He clicks it.

We always expect the explosion to be bigger than it is. There's a delay. A great bubble rises to the surface with a sudden, intense flash of silver before a thick foam column shoots upward. The smoke rises, first blue, then flinty gray. The ocean fuses to the sky without a discernible seam. Starbursts hang there like blossoms. After, a cloud of mist hovers above the surf. The crowd cheers with amazement.

We wait until the tide goes out. The boardwalk empties again. We wait so we can see the hole again. We walk out over the slick clay and look into it.

Nothing left. No casings, no shrapnel, no blasting caps. Just a gray hole in the clay that we remember being much deeper a few hours before.

As we walk back to the trucks, Henri announces he's enrolled in night classes for a degree in civil engineering. He plans to pursue a career at an infrastructure agency or in government construction, maybe even become a contractor if he's lucky. You can do pretty much anything once you've spent a few years tilling the iron harvest in Verdun. We all agree. This job opens so many other doors.

We answer all manner of calls. We educate and we offer relief. We reassure and we joke. We have seen it all. Our job is huge. Endless. None of us, not one, will see the end of this mission in our own lifetimes. It will be carried on by the next generation. By our children. And then our children's children. Each new generation with their hand on the valve, waiting and waiting and waiting for the flow of remnants from an ancient war to slow. We will be back again tomorrow. There is no other solution. Step by step, friends, step by step.

PART II

LA CICATRICE

3

The chambre mortuaire is the smallest building of six on the property of Hópital Saint-Nicolas, the central campus for the Centre Hospitalier de Verdun Saint-Mihiel. It feels hidden in its location, tucked away at the farthest point from the entrance of the campus. The main building houses the surgical ward, the ICU, Endoscopy, Labor and Delivery, as well as the Emergency Department, and it is the largest at five stories with rows of parallelogram-shaped windows set in a low-angle geometric sandstone facade. It sits squarely in the center surrounded by the other buildings, and from the gated entrance, they resemble a large hive nestled among wispy, dangling leaves. The roads are studded with squat bollards that are colored the type of red found only on the keels of large freighters. The city continues on outside the hospital gates. On the other side, kids play basketball, and an old man buys a lotto ticket at the tabac and smokes a cigarette outside before going back in to have a drink at the bar.

Hugo and Hans wind around the various other facilities, pass the paramedics on a smoke break in the bay outside the emergency room, and weave in between the nurses and staff coming on and off shift with their bags hoisted on their sagging shoulders until they reach a small parking lot with a narrow footpath.

Dr. Alain Perrault meets them at the door. Unlike the other buildings, with their honeycomb windows and sprawling hallways, the mortuary is housed in the basement of a red building in the style of a barn. The front door is all frosted glass but is often propped open. It's only after Dr. Perrault hits a button labeled *B* in the elevator, which takes them down from the first floor to the basement, that Hugo realizes he never knew they had a mortuary in this hospital.

Hugo has Camille on his mind. A second wind has surged through their tryst in the previous weeks. The day after the incident at the river, after she didn't answer a single text or call all day, Hugo had driven out to her house in the middle of the night in a pouring rain and texted her one more time, threatening to come through the front door and blow the whole thing up. Dramatic, sure, he can admit that now. But it worked. She had answered quickly. She had snuck out and found him in his car, and they had an argument that very nearly came to blows in his front seat. Just when everything felt hopeless, something in the air between them cracked open and then, before he knew what was happening, they were fucking again with a renewed vigor almost identical to their first time. Right there in his car, outside her house, so close that the light from the kitchen windows shimmered through the raindrops on his windshield and bathed the cab in shifting prisms of light. It had been a great few weeks since then.

He's still thinking about his rendezvous with her from the night before. They had driven way out to Haumont, one of the first villages to fall to the German advance. The hilly commune is still studded with German pillboxes, and they were on a mission to fuck in every one of them. Yet the renewed tryst seemed predestined to be short-lived. It was already beginning to feel more chore than pleasure. The sex was still great; in some ways they were hitting their stride. They both know each other's bodies and kinks better than either of their spouses. But the price for that knowledge was the thrill and spontaneity that had driven the early days of this affair with such reckless abandon. Hugo, as much as it disappointed him to admit it, found himself laboring under the weight of Camille's body in a manner similar to trudging uphill under a nearly unbearable load. How much longer could he endure? He had no idea. This is the natural shape of an affair in his experience: a series of propulsive, manic spikes oscillating between passion and apathy, each spike shorter than the one before it until it diminishes to an uneven roll like a rubber ball carelessly tossed down an empty street.

Dr. Perrault dresses like his wife has just surprised him with the news that the in-laws are coming over for dinner: a rumpled, patterned gingham button-down shirt with slightly less rumpled khakis and his white lab coat, which hangs open and trails behind him as they make their way from the elevator down the hall.

"Almost twenty-five thousand bodies in my career," Dr. Perrault says, "everything from motor vehicle accidents to murders to burn victims. Every age, every race, every size and shape you can imagine."

"Jesus. I hit four hundred last year and I thought that was a lot," says Hans.

"Ah, coronaries and casualties of the autoroute will always beat the excavation sites, my friend," he replies.

Dr. Perrault is a forensic pathologist hired by the local prosecutor who took accountability of the remains once they were removed from the site. Since being removed from la cicatrice, the bones have become enmeshed in a curious web. They have changed several sets of hands from the démineurs to the 'gists and then on to the local authorities, who gave them over to the prosecutor, an attorney named Luc Chevalier who always seemed a little out of breath and frustrated every time Hugo spoke with him.

Exposed pipes run the length of a low ceiling in the examination room. There's just enough space for everyone to fit. Light boxes line the far wall, on which several printed X-rays glow with an inky luster. Hugo notices a set of tools—scalpels, various different scissors, a couple of fine-toothed picks—all in a precise row on the counter. A set of egress windows on the wall to their left allows a certain amount of light into the room, and there is a small sticker of a cartoon duck—like the kind they give out to the children for being good at the pediatrician—in the top corner of one of the windows. It looks completely out of place.

In the center of the room, the bones are laid out in near-perfect anatomical symmetry on a white sheet draped over the metal examination table. His boots are at the very end, the bones of his feet still inside, encased in the warped leather. A system of easily maneuverable overhead spotlights illuminates the remains.

Dr. Perrault and his assistant, Léon, a stout, dark-haired man with a thick mustache, don green gowns that run to their feet and paper surgical caps and pull purple latex gloves from a tightly packed cardboard box on the counter.

Léon shuts off the overhead lights, and the table becomes a stage. Dr. Perrault lowers one of the spotlights to give the skull a closer examination. The doctor leans in to scrutinize the skull before picking it up. He holds it in a delicate fashion, suspended between his fingers—one set at the crown, the other under the teeth. He holds it in the beam of light so that the bone glows and the dirt, compacted in the tiny ridges and crevices, sparkles.

"Almost Shakespearean," Hans whispers.

Léon sets up a recording. Dr. Perrault begins his oral examination. "No obvious sign of injury. No indications of osteoporosis. Examination of vertebral column reveals signs consistent with repetitive axial loading, including early-onset vertebral compression changes. We can see it in the spine. Here and here. Suggests chronic mechanical stress, heavy load-bearing activity during developmental years. Common for the time."

He draws his pen from under his gown and points to each spot. He then points to corresponding places on the X-ray, and Hugo nods his head even though it all looks the same to him.

"Beginning with the skull, the cranial cultures are partially fused, consistent with an individual in their late teens to early twenties. One of the third molars has erupted but shows minimal wear, further supporting an age estimate of approximately seventeen to twenty years."

He makes his way down the remains, examining each bone and its current state. The clavicles, ribs, vertebrae, pelvis, iliac crest, sacroiliac joint, each demonstrating little wear. Dr. Perrault remarks on various states of fusion in the clavicles as well as the lack of degenerative changes in the vertebrae. The long bones get measured in quick flicks of a tape measure so practiced it appears rehearsed. He finishes back at the skull with some remarks about the teeth, heavy wear with no evidence of restoration, also common for the time. All indicators point to a young man.

"Overall condition, excellent. Slight soil staining as well as some minor erosion indicative of prolonged burial in a stable, protected environment. No evidence of perimortem trauma or any skeletal indicators of cause of death. Given the circumstances surrounding age, sex, and condition of remains, further historical research or contextual investigation should be conducted to identify this individual or provide additional insights into their life," he concludes.

Léon stops recording.

"Each one of us looks like that on the inside. Little bit crazy to think about, eh?" Dr. Perrault says.

Hugo considers the bones on the table before him. "I thought it would bother me more, to be honest. I was expecting them to smell."

"Oh yes. Everyone thinks they smell. Just on their own, the bones do not exude any odor. Only in the immediate aftermath of decomposition. It's all the muscle and tendon and vascular bits that smell. Once those are gone, there's not much left to cause a smell."

A thin, earthy scent hangs in the room.

"All teeth intact. I still find that miraculous whenever I see it, especially given the level of care—or lack thereof—they had at the time. But they didn't keep dental records back then, so it's a bit of a waste. We have very little to go on here."

"But we have a tag. Doesn't that make things simpler?" asks Hugo.

"We have a tag, yes. A possible identification. But we don't have a way of connecting the two. Therein lies our challenge. This could be Monsieur Caledec. But it just as easily could be some other soldier who happened to have Caledec's tag dropped near his body. You know the way it is out there. Better than any of us. It's one big blender. When I was a boy, I spent hours out there collecting everything I could find. Bullet casings, mostly. Those were my favorite. Goofy kid, you know? All about the boom sticks. But I found everything one could imagine," says Dr. Perrault.

He takes one glove off and then the other with a whip-snap intensity and tosses them into the open bin in the corner of the room.

"Tens of thousands of bodies went into that earth. Many of them have crumbled to dust, but not all. All you have to do to find bits and pieces is walk around out there. Imagine what you would find if you really started digging. But what do we have? A coin purse with two French coins. Boots still strapped to his feet. The head of a clay pipe. And an identification tag. That's what we have to work with."

"So he must be French then?" Hugo crosses his arms and leans on the counter, studies the way the light illuminates the bones. They're glowing.

"Not necessarily. It certainly seems that way. And personally, I believe he was. But we can't be certain. Any number of explanations could account for his possessions. It's not that far-fetched to think that a German soldier could end up with a poilu's coin purse and his boots. We don't even have a clear indicator of traumatic injury. It's all speculation at this point," says Hans.

Hugo points to a deep gash about three centimeters long on the forehead of the skull. It reveals a narrow, dark opening to the cranium. "And that?"

"Great eye! Yes, that was the first thing we examined. In fact . . ." The doctor shuffles through the stack of printed X-rays on the counter and then secures one of the skull to the light board. "We paid close attention to that laceration to see if it shows signs of occurring before or after death. You see, we look for indications of micro-hemorrhaging, which would've occurred if this man were still alive. We found none. I speculated it probably occurred after death. Maybe the result of a shovel? During burial? Or perhaps a spade or some other entrenching tool. Won't know for certain. If we can't find a way to connect that tag to those bones, if we can't find a family, then he goes with the others into the ossuary. Simple as that."

Hugo thinks about the many windows lining the base of the ossuary he has peered through every now and again. Beneath the cobwebs and the bones, there is evidence of grit and flakes and shapeless little pieces. The bones crumble to dust, slowly weakening and disintegrating. They are disappearing before their eyes. The bones on the examination table certainly seem out of place, but it's their very out-of-placeness that illuminates the vast task that still lies in the hills surrounding Verdun. The bodies yet to be found. The ordnance that will continue to rise to the surface. All the unanswered questions that will remain unanswered despite the continued work of everyone in this room and beyond.

"How long might this take?" he asks.

"Could be months. There's really no way to know until they begin looking through the archives."

"Months? That's absurd. We are already behind schedule by a month."

"That was out of our control, Mayor. We are on excavation time. It always moves a little slower," says Hans.

"Unacceptable. These are human remains we are dealing with. This is a soldier, gentlemen. Need I remind you, I am the mayor of the village he was found—no, *died* in. I bear a burden of responsibility—"

"We are all working as hard as we can, Maire. This isn't McDonald's," says Hans in a tone both defensive and barbed.

"Well, we need to work *harder* then," Hugo doubles down.

"Gentlemen, gentlemen," says Dr. Perrault. "I know this has been a trying time. These projects are always a little arduous. But let's not let it get the better of us. We are all invested in the same goal, no? There's no need to raise voices."

Hugo nods, smiles. "Of course! Who am I kidding? I'm the mayor of a village with no people and no buildings. What's another couple of months? There's no rush."

Hans stares at him, frowning, but does not say anything in reply.

"I will send all my findings along with the recordings to Château de Vincennes before the end of the week. I just need to finish a few odds and ends. Once they have everything, the archival team can proceed with the rest of the investigation."

Hans and Hugo thank the doctor, and they all shake hands.

"A word?" Hugo asks Hans, and gestures to the hallway.

They step out and wait for a few passersby to round the corner. Hans crosses his arms and leans on the wall.

"Shooting in all directions today, eh?" he asks.

Hugo shakes him off. "That was all theatrics, my friend. Please, do not take it personal. I'm trying to make a point. I want people to realize how important this is. We all win here, regardless."

Hans has an expressionless gaze that makes Hugo squirm. He decides it best to elaborate.

"Listen, the centennial anniversary of the battle is a few months away. This is a big one. It would be very good for the city to have something like this. If they are able to identify him, then what? They take him away to some village where no one was even looking for him. People will forget his name before dinner. An anonymous soldier can be *anyone*. There's a lot of power there. Instead of it being about one man—a boy, really—it becomes about this nation. *Our* nation."

Hans offers only a nod. Probably best just to drop it.

"Here's the thing, I was actually wondering if you might be able to find a spot for another researcher on this next phase."

"A little strange to be asking for a favor from me after putting me at the foot of the wall back there."

"It's Ferrand Martin."

"The démineur?" Hans asks, and gives him an exasperated sigh. "What use will he be?"

"They'll find something for him! Printing things or organizing paper clips, I don't know. He's had a rough go of it. The illness, the treatment, he needs something. He's already in Paris; he received treatment at Gustave Roussy. He's losing his mind there apparently, recovering," Hugo says, and hesitates. "And . . . to be honest, I feel bad for him. He has no one. I just keep thinking about him in that hospital all by himself. It's sad."

"You can't take responsibility for the health of every person you meet, Mayor. You're not that powerful," says Hans with just a trace of condescension.

"Do it for the city then. It would be nice to have some representation there. He seems to be doing well, all things considered. Besides, I only know him a little, but he does not seem the type to sit around. They're not letting him return to the department. What's he to do? Languish in some tabac, elbows propped on a dented zinc countertop over a scratch-off and bottomless glasses of Heineken until he keels over? A man's got to have a purpose," Hugo says.

Hans considers it and stares unblinking at Hugo for what feels like an inappropriate amount of time before something softens.

"No guarantees, but I'll see what I can do. Don't say anything to him just yet."

They pass the room on their way out of the building, and a pair of technicians are carefully placing the bones in plastic bags. These bags are labeled and will be stored in a large plastic box, which will then be carried to a climate-controlled chamber where one of the technicians will close the door, lock it, and shut the light off without another thought, the remains resting in darkness as well as silence—the same silence that pervades their car ride back to the hotel.

*

After dropping Hans off at his hotel, Hugo heads to his only other meeting for the day. He arrives at the Office National des Forêts regional office late and hurries inside. The proposal meeting is already under way, and although he feels somewhat bad about it, in truth, he's here to support Elisa. She's done almost all the work since they began meeting about the blue wood and what could be done about it. He takes a seat at the back of the room as quietly as possible. He counts a total of twelve people in the audience. Like everything else in the world, this was a matter of who you know.

He sees representatives from the Direction Régionale de l'Environnement, Ministère des Armées, Service Territorial de l'Architecture et du Patrimoine, as well as the entire municipal council. All of them men, and not a single one under the age of forty-five. Some might say a tough crowd. You're looking at over three hundred years of experience combined gazing out over the expanse of balding heads and receding hairlines. Not Elisa.

She has a commanding presence at the podium. Not much humor in her approach, she couldn't be said to be having fun. Hugo can't tell if it is the lighting, but she looks a little ragged, like the only thing that will suit her is a few days' worth of sleep. It gives her an ironclad poise—defiant and unshakable. For what she lacks in charisma, she makes up in confidence. Every statement she makes is said directly to the audience with constant scanning eye contact. From the time he enters the room, she doesn't look down at her notes once. She is a woman in full control.

Martin suddenly comes to mind. Hugo thinks back to that first day when he discovered the artillery shell. Martin bore the same level of confidence while he was crouched over the munition. Every movement controlled and precise. Steady, intentional hands disarming an unstable artillery shell that could have erased his existence in a split second.

He doesn't want to admit it, but both of them have something he wants. He can't quite put his finger on it. It's not their jobs or the skills or the unlimited knowledge they seem to possess over their subject matter. It's definitely not the status, because theirs is fairly low in the grand hierarchy of their society. He admires the way they approach these inconsequential jobs with such presence. They don't waste a moment. Hugo smiles. This could all fall apart, sure. In the long run, if this project doesn't work out, oh well. He will move on to other things. And quickly. One cannot get too attached. Yet, watching Elisa at the front of this room, her proposal illuminated on the screen behind her, he has a strong sense she would not take it very well. She is fully committed. Where does that come from? What secret are she and Martin in on that has passed him by? He wants to know.

She finishes her proposal and takes questions. One after another, there's not a single item that stumps her. She doesn't even have to pause to consider an answer or meander her way through one of those non-answers so many public speakers become deftly skilled at providing.

They're not afraid to be alone, he thinks. That's it. Elisa nods along to one question and then answers it without missing a beat. There she is. Completely by herself in front of a room of men, many of whom probably spent the majority of her talk undressing her in their minds. There's no way she doesn't realize this about them. All women know this about these kinds of men. Yet, she got up there anyway. By herself. All eyes on her. Martin, in his own way, did the same thing. He crouched over that artillery shell and never faltered once. Hugo leans forward in his seat. So much of life is spent alone in some way or another, physically or emotionally. In many ways, loneliness is a core part of the human experience. It terrifies him. He will do almost anything to avoid those moments. People like Elisa and Martin don't seem to mind.

The smell of cheap coffee and idle chitchat fill the conference room when they bring the lights on. He makes his way around to show face. Shake hands, nod with approval. The mayor of Fleury is in the building. They won't have the decision until later, but he has a good feeling. There's very little pushback from anyone, a rarity in the bureaucratic myopia of a small municipality.

Hugo waits until the room clears out to approach her. She's packing her materials.

"Oh, great. I didn't see you in there. I thought you probably couldn't make it," she says.

"Wouldn't miss it! Just ran late with my last meeting. You crushed it. How do you feel?"

"Eh, we will see," she says. "You know how these things go."

Strange. She still has yet to loosen up to him. He's not used to this. Typically, after a little bit of time, even the toughest facades begin to crack and let their guard down. Not Elisa. She's basically the same as she was the day they met over the artillery shell in Fleury. Not standoffish necessarily, not unfriendly, just professional. Impervious to charm, ambivalent to humor. It's all very odd to him.

"I have been to quite a few of these kinds of meetings, and I can tell you, there's typically more questions, more sticklers. When are we going to go for a run together?" he asks.

"Whenever I find time to get a day off," she says. "Don't hold your breath."

"Too late. My life is on the line."

He gets a smile from her. That is a start.

Later that night, he gets word. The proposal received unanimous approval. This almost never happens. He immediately texts Elisa as well as the developer he plans on selling the blue wood to at a hefty markup.

4

Hospital time moves differently. Slowly. The night hours warp and stretch, and the waxed hallways calcify into sterile passages where the only suggestions of an outer world come in the silent footsteps of the odd nurse walking from one room to another. Dawn approaches. Martin, PICC line in place and a bag of fluids draining into his body, wanders the oncology ward of Gustave Roussy using his wheeled IV pole to guide his steps. He's supposed to be resting. But there's no use in lying in bed. He's gotten all the sleep he can, given the circumstances. He comes to the window at the end of the hall. He first noticed it early in his stay on his way back to his room. The view gave him a generous perspective of the Paris skyline.

"See something?" asked a passing tech.

Martin turned and shrugged. "Oh no, just getting away for a moment. What a view."

If Martin waits long enough, he witnesses things. Occurrences that he might've missed sitting in his bed. Even at this late hour. Outside the window, birds fly. Trucks move. Vehicles arrive in town. Inside each one, a life. A life with a job or a purpose or pain or happiness or all of the above. Yesterday, he watched two birds tussle mid-sky over something, and then, talons interlocked, they plummeted into the brush never to reemerge. He saw two separate car accidents in one day. Neither serious. Both parties stepped out to wait for the police, waving their arms about in frustration, making calls on their cell phones. Through the window, life plays out in real time. The world is out there. Beyond the walls of the building. He has felt it and seen it and experienced it with his body. The real world is coated in grease and has dirt in its cracks and a weight that can be felt when he tries to move it and it simply says no.

Life.

It is out there. It is happening out there.

The previous few weeks have been blood work, transfusions, chemotherapy sessions, isolation, observation, and nutritional support. The experience has been equal parts enlightening and disorienting. Like, for instance, how he can taste many of the drugs they administer through his PICC line. The salty, coppery taste of magnesium sulfate and potassium infusions administered to prevent an electrolyte imbalance. The chemo agents, even stronger, taste metallic and bitter to their very core. When he commented on this phenomenon, the nurse nodded and said, "Get used to that. Perfectly normal." *Normal* seemed like the wrong word to use. Nothing about anything they have done since he arrived, from the blood draws to the endless checking of vitals at all hours, has felt anywhere near normal.

He probes his gum line for infection with his tongue one tooth at a time. The last thing he had to do before they would give him approval to begin treatment was undergo a routine dental exam. His body needed to be in tip-top shape to withstand the beating chemotherapy would give him. According to one of the nurses, oral infections are often overlooked and cause a devastating amount of damage in a person with a weakened immune system. In these strange night hours, he finds his tongue probing his gums while he wonders about the slim barriers that protect from all sorts of pathogens and bacteria waiting to invade.

A wave of dizziness overtakes him, and he closes his eyes. It is always accompanied by a shudder through his entire body and a vague sense of nausea, the same kind he gets from reading in the car for too long.

Martin reaches out and touches the glass, which sends a bolt of blue electricity through his nerves. His whole body feels not his own, as if it belongs to someone else far more delicate. Every time he changes, he can't help but stare at the bunches and folds of skin around the catheter site. Like a turkey for Christmas dinner. He notices the first sign of morning, a softening of the sky, the suggestion of a horizon. He makes his way back to his room.

*

A surprise visitor arrives the next afternoon. Martin rests in bed after the morning chemo session, riding the wave of aftereffects that comes with unceasing regularity, when the nurse enters his room to tell him a man is waiting for him in the lobby.

"But I wasn't expecting anyone today," he tells her.

"Do you feel up to it? I can turn him away, no problem."

"Who is it?"

She looks at her clipboard where the man filled out his information. "Hugo LaFleur. He's listed himself as a colleague."

Martin sighs. The last thing he wants to do after letting them pump him full of poisons so toxic they could kill a small animal is make small talk with Hugo. His stomach turns. Martin adjusts himself. He has spent so much time in this awful bed, he can feel every little lump and ridge. He longs for a bed without hinges and motors and more buttons than he knows what to do with. Then again, he hasn't had a single visitor besides Henri since he was admitted. He doesn't blame any of them; it's over two hours' drive from Verdun. Can't expect everyone to put their lives on pause when yours comes to a screeching halt. Still. It has been bizarre going in a loop through the same three rooms day after day, while every person you know goes about their lives as if nothing happened. His only deviation has been those walks to the window late at night. He can feel it growing every day. The creeping sensation he is being left behind.

"No, it's fine. He drove all the way out here. It will be nice to break up the routine. Send him up."

As a preventative measure, the hospital requires they both wear surgical masks. Hugo walks in, and even though he already has his mask on, Martin can tell he's smiling.

"Ferrand! Look at you! You look great."

Martin lost all his hair, mustache included, a week and a half ago; his eyes have shrunken into his head; and his general complexion is that of a hairless mole rat. "You are an awful liar, Maire. It does not suit you."

Hugo laughs and takes a seat by the bed. The two of them catch up. Martin is surprised by how easy it is to talk to Hugo. He's never particularly enjoyed Hugo's company, but after all this time spent mostly by himself or with strangers, he's a welcome sight. It's unbelievably nice just to talk about anything at all. They avoid the topic of his treatment and instead discuss everything from Hugo's day at the mortuary to his house renovations.

"The first phase is completely finished, but now all four of us are crammed into a third of the house. I think of it as an opportunity to test the strength of my marriage."

Other than his various side projects and mayoral duties for the centennial, the thing he talks the most about is his progress with the blue wood. Apparently, he's grown quite close to Elisa.

"She's something, eh?" says Hugo.

"She cares about her work. She's serious."

Hugo can't stop playing with his mask. He adjusts it, fiddles with the straps around his ears. Despite only being able to see his eyes over the mask, Martin can tell Hugo has taken some kind of liking to Elisa. He's always been that way around women. A little strange, a little too interested for a married man with children. Something about the way he talks about them turns him off.

"Ferrand, I've wanted to check in. What do you plan on doing when they send you on your way?"

Run as fast as I can away from this place, Martin thinks.

"I haven't thought that far ahead, to be honest. Doubt I'll be able to go back to the depot anytime soon."

"Well, you know they're still sorting out those bones we found back in February. There's a team at Vincennes that's about to start the search for his identity in earnest. What do you think? I can put in a good word."

"What would they do with me?" Martin asks.

"Oh, I'm sure they need you more than you need them. This is a big job, and another pair of hands would be appreciated. I am almost certain."

The idea strikes him as odd and unappealing from the moment Hugo says it. Leave the fluorescent glare of a hospital ward for the dank caverns of some musty archive? He might as well just stay on here at the Gustave Roussy to see if the janitorial crews need any help.

"My friend, thank you for the offer. But I am going to pass."

Hugo leans forward in his chair, elbows on knees. Martin imagines this is the type of posture he assumes when he's digging in for a tough negotiation over one of his properties.

"Ferrand, let me help you. You have had a rough go of it. I think it would be good for you. Stay active."

"Maire, I'm tired," he says. "I am so tired. And this?" He points to the PICC line in his chest, his flesh folded and knotted around the catheter. "It wreaks havoc on the body. You don't really get it unless you've been through it, you know? I don't feel up to it."

Hugo appears ready to argue further, and Martin is almost curious to hear what he will say next. But he stops himself. He stares at Martin's PICC line, his bed, the newly cleaned bedpan the nurse left beside the bed right before he entered. He seems to have just realized where he is—not in the heat of a negotiation, but in the oncology ward of a hospital.

"I understand," he says finally.

"Let's just enjoy this, hein? Tell me more about the blue wood."

Hugo nods, and they go on speaking for a while. Eventually, he checks his watch and excuses himself to try to beat some of the traffic. Martin's final chemo session is scheduled for tomorrow.

*

The next morning at half past six, a nurse checks his vitals and administers a few premedications, anti-nausea drugs, steroids, and the like. There is a light breakfast of tartines and fruit that he forces himself to eat. By eight, he's in the chemotherapy infusion unit, a large open room with many oversized reclining chairs in a wide ring against two-toned walls that give off the same mood as an airplane gate with a delayed flight. Despite the near-constant nausea, for which the meds they administer have no noticeable effect, and the unpleasant neuropathy he began experiencing on the second day—hot, tingling, and sometimes shooting pain in his hands and feet—and all the other nasty side effects, the routine is something he can depend on, grip with both hands, for the duration of his time in the hospital.

He has spent every session seated with Jean-Luc, the only friend he has made since his arrival, and today is no different. The nurses placed the two of them next to each other for Martin's first session, and Jean-Luc had greeted him with a curt nod. Then he leaned over, almost conspiratorially, and said, "They have warm blankets around the corner. All you have to do is ask," while he patted the blanket across his lap.

The blankets are, in fact, warmed, and the company, congenial. A retired detective, Jean-Luc is matter-of-fact and direct in all responses with just a hint of bravado, the latter of which comes into sharper relief whenever he has the opportunity to flirt with a nurse.

"How are you feeling today?" a nurse asks Jean-Luc as they transfer Martin to his chair.

"Much, much better, actually. Almost like new. But I can't tell if it's the drugs or your smile," he says.

This is how they pass the time: flirt with the nurses and poke fun at the other patients. There is nothing else to do. Some patients have small televisions set up, while others scroll endlessly on their phones. Almost everyone reclines the chairs as far back as they can go until they're basically beds. It's not uncommon to see patients out cold, surgical masks hiding their mouths, the same oversized gray hospital knit caps covering their eyes.

They're all slightly withered versions of their former selves. No one comes into chemo treatment on a winning streak.

The nurse flushes Martin's PICC line with saline and then hooks him up to the infusion pump. Jean-Luc greets him the same way he has every morning: "Ferrand, my friend, *we* are the luckiest men alive."

She keys in the dosages and presses the start button. There it is. The dirty, gritty, metallic taste, like he's licking every handrail on the metro at once. Then comes the aftertaste, overwhelmingly chemical. The summer he worked at the lake, one of his jobs had been to maintain the chlorine levels in a small swimming pool near the lodge. His friends used to dare each other to hold a chlorine tablet, a little brick about the size of a bar of soap, in their mouths for as long as possible. None of them ever did it. But now he imagines the sensation is somewhat similar. Aside from the taste of the chemo agents, a distinct impression arises that his actual sense of taste is retreating, like flower petals wilting under a blue flame.

Food turns to ash in his mouth now, everything smells off. The medications don't just infiltrate the body, they alter something deeper about you. It all makes sense when considered this way. Every awful symptom and unpleasant side effect. The neuropathy is unlike any pain he has ever experienced. Not so much that it is the worst pain, but rather just unlike any other pain. He's been burned, stabbed; he's broken bones, jammed fingers, taken punches, and all other manner of injuries. But nothing feels quite like the fire that lights up the nerves during chemo. The intensity alone makes it hard to think. It starts with a quiet numbness on the periphery—his fingers and toes, then hands and feet—and grows to a sustained burning so acute that every cell, every nerve, fluoresces into his perception. He feels that if he tried, he could almost count them. This awareness is the gift death gives.

"*We* are the luckiest men alive."

"The luckiest," Martin responds.

The clock on the wall above, an old two-hand model housed in a protective cage that protrudes like a great eyeball, may be broken. At a quarter to nine, Martin thinks about his old crew. They are already several hours into their day. The trucks have been checked off. The itinerary for the day, reviewed. In fact, not a day has gone by that he doesn't wonder what they are up to. The whole team—his team—is still out there peeling back the land and yanking another iron crop from the soil. There are things to do. Yes, there are always things to do. The inventory needs updating. Several pallets need to be packed and secured for disposal at the end of the week. There are always a few reports that need finishing. There are most certainly things to do. They are rolling from location to location. Responding to calls or cataloging the day's finds.

Meanwhile, he is here. Stuck in a chair pumping poison into his body. Although what they are doing is work, it seems more like freedom in this specific moment while he stands trapped behind the hospital window. How many times had they moaned and groaned about how they couldn't wait until this holiday or that holiday, the beloved three-day weekend. Too many to count. He would trade anything in this now for another day out there where things make a little more sense.

The room gets surprisingly good light, but it is always too cold no matter what the nurses do with the thermostat. The cart man arrives to deliver snacks and brings with him a noticeable shift in the mood of the room, smiles and laughter. Hardly anyone takes chips or candy from his cart, but he is someone to talk to and it is a way to mark time.

Halfway through his cycle, Jean-Luc tells him about a special club he has joined.

"Today is a special day. Do you know why?" asks Jean-Luc. "Today, I finish my final cycle of doxorubicin. The red devil, as they call it. One of the worst chemo drugs out there. It is so toxic, they try not to even give it as regularly anymore, my doctor told me. And if they do give it to you, you can only receive it so many times before it becomes too dangerous to keep using. Bad for the heart. I had it about fifteen years ago the *first* time I had leukemia. Ironically, they think I relapsed because of one of the other drugs they gave me that go-around. So, I'm on a tighter leash with the doxorubicin this go-around. After today, even if I don't get better, they have to come up with a different plan."

"Sounds like a special club," Martin says. "How many others can say they've accomplished such a feat?"

"The doxorubicin graduates. One-percenters, as we're known."

"Not just anyone can join. Look at you," says Martin.

"*The* luckiest man alive."

Martin watches the glimmering lights of Paris, the way they pulse through the windowpane.

"What will you do when you get out? Have a drink?" Martin asks.

Jean-Luc shakes his head. "I don't touch the stuff. Nearly killed me. I was a terrible alcoholic. Always kept a bottle on me. My car, an altar. The glove box, a tabernacle. That's where I received the sacrament."

"Good man," says Martin. "I was a similar way. I haven't had a drink in years."

"I used to wait outside the liquor store every morning, shaking. You know you have a problem when you're greeting the liquor store owner before he's unlocked the front door of the shop. I would park my car around the block so he wouldn't see me waiting when he arrived to open the store. My hands, shaking. A slight tremor. I would chew a thumbnail to stop the shaking. Pinch it between my teeth and hold on. Sweat on my brow. The flesh on the inside of my cheek, raw. In my ears, I could feel it throbbing. The rhythm of my own heart. It continues on, endlessly. Quicker than it should be, I knew that much. When I focused on the beats, I could follow it down from my head, through the raspy wheeze of my throat, and into the cavern of my chest. Just left of center. It sounded steady. That was good. But labored. I could feel it working harder than it should have to. My own fault. Maybe partially genetics. Bad backs and worse hearts. That's my legacy. All the men in my family from my great-grandfather to my own father have it in common.

"The store always opened late. Maybe five, ten minutes at the most. But it made me hate him. He was a lazy son of a bitch. I was mad at myself too. I ran out again. How? How could I let this happen again? I knew better. At some point it just got easier to stay away from it entirely."

Jean-Luc looks at the patient beside him. She's been here longer than both of them and has been the fixation of many, both the medical staff and patients alike. A young Chinese woman of about twenty-five, incredibly frail and in a head wrap many of the women take to wearing once their hair falls out. What little information they have gleaned, all from secondhand sources, is that this woman had been traveling alone through Europe and had fallen ill after arriving in Paris. She brought herself to the ER and was admitted, and then the story becomes familiar to everyone: the symptoms, the tests, the results. As of yet, they have been unable to contact her family or anyone close to her. She doesn't speak French, and every time the nurses need to communicate with her, from checking her vitals to using the bathroom, they need to call the translation line for a Mandarin translator.

What luck.

One of the nurses has the translator on speakerphone, and they are trying to work through some administrative issue involving billing and insurance. Martin wonders why they wouldn't give her the courtesy of a private room or wait until after her infusion. The nurse appears frustrated and out of patience.

"God. What a headache. I hope they can get that translator up and running for her last words. You'd think they would have gotten a little quicker by now."

"Hey, come on now," says Martin, taken aback. "There's no need for that."

Jean-Luc waves him off. "C'mon. Don't be soft. She can't even understand me."

"Don't be cruel. What's the use of that?" asks Martin.

Jean-Luc smiles. "Hey, do they all look like that? Or is that just the chemo? I can't tell."

"You're just being a dickhead now."

Jean-Luc stares at him and then leans over in that same conspiratorial way as the day he told Martin about the warm blankets. "We're not like her. It must be nice. What is she? Thirty? Maybe? Daddy probably paying for her to travel the world over. Come for the sightseeing, stay for the chemo. Guys like you and me, we gave everything, and for what? Nobody cares. No appreciation."

"Nobody made us do it," says Martin. "And that's not a fair assumption. What do we know about her?"

Jean-Luc erupts in anger, and several other patients look their way. "That's not the point! I've been shot at. I shot people. I've had six friends killed in the line of duty. Really good, honorable men. One time, I got stabbed during a routine call. A family dispute. Pulled up, knocked on the door, he opens up, and wham! Right in the gut," he says, and lifts his sweater to illustrate the point.

A gnarled, whitened scar traces its way up Jean-Luc's abdomen, and Martin observes it with the same interest of looking down at a mountain range out the window of an airplane.

"Never had a chance to react. What was any of it for? The guy was un sans-papiers. He wasn't even supposed to be here. It was for nothing. We were used up, the best years of our lives. Time we will never get back. What do we get in return?"

Jean-Luc gets down this way sometimes. They all do. The day in, day out of chemo, the constant state of feeling like a wet, empty trash bag, it wears one down. But still. The door opens and the cart man rolls in again. A lady across from them in a purple head wrap cheers. Martin is speechless. He considers his words carefully.

"I'm sorry you went through all that. But I don't feel that way. I wanted a simple job, something outdoors. Something that helped the community. I chose it," Martin says. "It wasn't easy. I lost friends too. But I would do it all the same tomorrow if I could. I don't feel owed anything."

Jean-Luc grunts in response but says nothing else. When the cart man passes, Martin stops him and grabs a pack of Dragibus. He offers a handful to Jean-Luc, but he declines. Martin chews thoughtfully. They settle into a strange silence and watch the light change on the floor until the nurses come get them. They both know this is the last time they will see each other here and they had made plans to keep in touch. But they don't exchange any information.

Later, back in his room, Martin still feels unsettled, and it is not the chemo. There is something beneath the generalized malaise that keeps him from relaxing. He watches his television but takes in nothing. The exchange with Jean-Luc has shaken something deep inside of him. The suddenness of his outburst, the sheer acidity of his tone. But more so, he feels disappointed in himself for not saying more, for not pushing back harder. For although he did not agree with anything Jean-Luc had said, the heat of his anger felt familiar and righteous to Martin, and that scares him. He has not realized until this moment how that vileness has grown unnoticed inside him until this moment, and he feels suddenly alert and strangely panicked, as if he just awoke on a train and realized he'd missed his stop.

*

That night, Martin wakes and has no idea where he is. All he feels is pain and subsequent terror—a bald, faceless terror where the only thing he can do is stare at the shadows on the wall, unable to name any of the shapes they create, and lie in his confusion as his skin burns with chemo rash. It takes a few long minutes to get his bearings. It starts with recognizing the bed is not his own. Then the rest of the room takes form around him. And then he stands and walks into the hall, and the window is, as always, the first thing he looks to. He is taken by surprise by how much time has passed. The window is dark and black like a hole punched through a sheet of paper. It takes a few steps before he feels like himself again. Not too much different from waking up in a hotel you forgot you stayed in the night before, expecting everything to be familiar and then finding everything foreign and strange. He sleeps fitfully the rest of the night.

In the morning, he phones Hugo.

"I've thought about it a little bit more. If you can still make it happen, I'd like to join the team."

He has a final meeting with his oncologist a week later. Everything looks great, his body has responded very well. All his numbers are well within range of what they wanted to see. Promising results, it's a start. The team has reviewed his case and approved his release. There will, of course, be follow-ups and other appointments. But for now, he is free to leave. Just like that he exits through the same lobby he entered a lifetime ago. A pale spring day. Feathery trees sway, and despite the chill that remains in his body, the sun feels soft and warm. He closes his eyes and turns his face to the sky.

5

When he arrives at Château de Vincennes on his first day later that month, his car is the only one in the lot. Endless maintained lawns and green spaces take up the view, with the château a several-minute walk away. Directly ahead, ornate gateways adorn the central pavilion along with arched colonnades. Beyond, a structure of light-colored stone dominated by tall, cylindrical towers and turrets pocked with narrow windows. Hard to believe he will continue this work in an actual castle.

Martin waits in his car and dozes uneasily until the academics arrive. He has never been one for a fat morning, and so he gets up early like he always has. Hans set him up with a cousin to stay with in a small house with a guest room, which is very kind of him, but he feels less comfortable than he did in the hospital. Martin suspects they don't expect him to last very long. Hugo's offer was one to help soften the blow of everything he's about to experience: the end of a career in which he found purpose and the aftermath of a god-awful treatment. They will probably show him a few interesting things, maybe the type of things a démineur never gets to see, like what Hugo told him about his day at the mortuary. Some research they are doing, and then maybe they figure he will get bored or too weak to come in. Do the academics really expect a grouchy old démineur to want to spend hours in front of a computer going through old census reports and tax filings? That is, as it turns out, the real work of academics. Archives are their playground. The démineurs pull bombs from the earth, and the academics pull forgotten letters and government mandates and audits and so many other documents that you could not pay people to read from databases.

Dr. Margaux Garnier, the lead historian and archivist, takes him aside at one point to speak in private.

"I do appreciate your willingness to volunteer your time, especially with everything you have been through," she begins. "But I also want to set realistic expectations for this project. I realize this is very different from anything you've ever done before."

"In some ways. You might be surprised."

"Of course. What I mean is there isn't any guarantee we will find this family. There's no way to know for certain when or even if we will locate them. This is the fascinating part of history. We have all these stories, all these monumental moments and events that we know definitely happened. We know for sure that these moments happened and there were people involved who contributed—they were all a part of it in some way or another. But then you look a little closer. You start pulling up a magnifying glass and you stop for a moment to really look at these people. Who were they? Where did they all go? And then you quickly begin to find just how difficult it is to know anything about them. There are glimpses, fleeting glimpses, and that's it. That's all that is left. The rest of who they were—the real human side of it—is often gone. They've left no trace of themselves at all."

But day after day, Martin arrives and parks his silver sedan in the small lot, not even in the handicapped spot (he never really considers himself sick the entire time he works with the academics), and by the time the academics arrive, he is already inside at the desk they set up for him in one corner of the front office.

The interior of the Service Historique de la Défense exudes a certain cleanliness that takes Martin by surprise. It is the type of place that receives daily cleanings, with a large dumpster in the back that gets emptied twice a week and checkered marble floors that get waxed weekly. Air fresheners dot the rooms. Freshly cut flowers populate a few of the desks. In short, a far cry from the grimy wartime condition of the depot. He passes fireplaces big enough to fit his entire crew. Outside every window, symmetrical courtyards with cobblestone walking paths. They pass from one tower to another using suspended walkways above the courtyards.

It's nice not having to don the coveralls and boots that had been his daily uniform for many years. Now he arrives in whatever he pleases, which most days is a black Adidas jogging suit with white stripes. The epitome of comfort, as far as he's concerned. The rest of the team finds it amusing, although that never gets back to him.

Martin feels somewhat out of place, but he never remarks on anything in particular. He actually adjusts quite nicely. It would be much more difficult to go from the cleaned-three-times-a-week château to the cleaned-whenever-the-démineurs-feel-like-it (that means never) depot. The dented, rusted signs labeled *DANGER! ENGIN DU GUERRE* nailed to trees replaced with Post-it notes labeled *Mon d*éjeuner. NE PAS TOUCHER! in the break room refrigerator. The one thing Martin does remark on is the silence. It's a constant silence that holds the place. Even the voices are kept quiet. There are no slamming doors. No boisterous voices arguing over last night's match or belches or flatulence erupting from down the hall.

Martin tells the academics he had expected a dark, cavernous place with rows on rows upon rows of books and files stretching all the way to the ceiling several stories above. The kind of place that was meticulously organized with intricate labels but somehow also a bit of a mess to anyone who did not understand the organizational system.

"I imagined long days spent at the top of a ladder near the ceiling, craning my neck and reaching all the way over for a single set of papers that might hold the answers," Martin says.

Instead, what he finds is a single room with two computers and a potted bamboo plant. He shares the office with an intern named Theo who spends a lot of time sitting around, scratching his scalp. Small, intense scratches concentrated in one specific area in a roaming pattern all over his head. Theo's hair is thinning badly even though he is only twenty-three, and he believes scratching in this way encourages growth.

"Everything was digitized about ten years ago," Theo says. "We can access the whole world through those computers. We still have access to the physical archive. It's housed in the catacombs of the building across the courtyard from here. If we need to pull anything, it's right over there."

"Ah," Martin says with a deep nod, unconvinced. The whole world might be an ambitious claim, he thinks.

Martin has to ask one of the interns for help on how to log on to the computer. Of course he has his own at home, but all he ever uses it for is ordering a few things here and there and responding to emails. But he has to be told only once. The academics do everything they can on that first day to include Martin as they begin setting out their plan.

One of their PhD students has located a promising record of a family with the surname Caledec in Nantes who had several military-age children during the war. It is a great start. Martin jumps in right away.

The computer screen requires a level of focus to which he is not accustomed. The light hurts his eyes, and everything goes a little blurry after an hour or so. But it is a fairly simple and easy-to-use system, and it isn't long before he is wheeling through centuries' worth of virtual records in kaleidoscopic fashion. The square plate of glass is the eyepiece of a periscope, and when he leans in, he can look into the past. All the refractive light collects in his mind, and it has a way of easing some of his discomfort. Every computer screen in the building appears to be a type of viewing portal to another place that is otherwise completely inaccessible. These screens amplify his sight far beyond the walls of the ancient castle. Martin finds himself falling into it. When he concentrates, he can see objects moving in the far distance. What at first appears to be static characters on a flat piece of paper suddenly become an animated story leading him to a place he never honestly believed possible.

A computer's language is unique and abstract. This language, a language of keystrokes and commands, file formats and search terms, is not Martin's. He speaks with his hands and the movement of his body. He has seen the depths of the oceans and combed through the French countryside for deadly munitions. The idea of sitting still in order to move forward baffles him. That all the world can be accessed through the screen in front of him seems a fabrication. But though somewhat complicated, once he understands a few essentials, he can unlock the past in a surprisingly simple way. It is all so much simpler than the ordnance in the ground. If only a few keystrokes could pull back the soil and show them exactly where every last shell is hiding.

Most of what he finds is garbage. Tax receipts. Rosters. Useless trails of discharge paperwork with cross-outs and misspellings and tears and burnt corners and smudges and all sorts of details that validate the artifact is nothing more than a useless shred of virtually preserved paper. That's what almost all of it is: useless. Not to mention the variations in name spellings typical at the time, *Caladec* or maybe *Caldéec*? There are inconsistencies in various record systems, all sorts of gaps, and delays due to record requests they submit for files they do not have access to. They wait two weeks for a stack of military files only to discover it does not contain a single piece of useful information. Some days are spent entirely untangling a database or file to assess whether it is even useful.

"These tags weren't even standardized in the French military at the time," Theo explains one afternoon. "It varied by unit, depending on who took the initiative to make them and maintain them."

Martin finds himself making stories from random details. He connects names to faces in photos that have no connection to one another at all. He imagines lives for them after the war that always involve a quiet house in a green part of the country and a good woman. He allows them to find love and leave the war far behind. Each story ends the same way. Purpose and peace. The lives destroyed become whole again in his mind. Fathers and sons return after years away. They return whole and unscarred as if they had only been out running errands. They take up their jobs in paper bag factories and cider mills, and they make a little extra money on the weekends playing the accordion for wedding ceremonies held in the town square.

Martin's coffee cools, and the world keeps moving somewhere else without him.

But no one is keeping him here. He knows that. Returning to life on the truck is impossible. He knows that as well. At any moment, he could pack it in and go home. *Thanks for the opportunity. I appreciate the gesture. I'm going to sit the rest of this one out.* He never says it. Instead, day after day, he makes the short drive before dawn down to the Vincennes, he finishes his first cup of coffee in his car, and then he makes his way inside, where he prepares a cup of coffee and takes the long hallway to his office, turns on the computer, and opens up another collection of files, looking for a clue—to where Caledec's family might have gone off.

The research allows him a way into another world where he can leave his body for a time. Sometimes he goes so deep into the archives that he loses sense of himself, his actual physical body, and when he comes out of it, it is like he is feeling the pain again for the first time. Dull and aching. It is always in the first couple of seconds when he breaks from the glowing screen that he realizes how truly sick he is. The pain feels new again.

Some days are better than others. It is surprising how vastly different he can appear from one day to the next. He appears to gain or lose a decade of age in a manner of a day or two. It could be all the time in front of the computer, but every now and again, he experiences a few scares, moments of extreme lightheadedness or shortness of breath. Out of an abundance of caution they send him back to the hospital twice, and both times he is kept for a night that lasts a century, the same hallways that lead nowhere except to cold windows showing him the world he is missing. Each time he returns to the Service Historique de la Défense, he quietly fights the nausea, the growing headaches.

By the time each day ends, and Martin reaches his car and retrieves his keys from his pocket, he feels like himself again, and then he wants to return to the computer. But feeling like himself comes in the form of an unsteady gait and a dull ache from deep inside his chest. A quiet drive back. No radio. Windows rolled up. He follows the road to the house with the guest room, the unfamiliar sounds of Paris swirling around him.

Martin has never reckoned with the full weight of his body until now. It took illness to make him stop and recognize his complete physical form. Its limits. Its exactness. The amount of space it takes up just sitting in a chair. He is feeling things in ways he had previously felt only at the end of extremely arduous physical labor or intense workouts. Never before has he considered something as simple as a single breath and all the life it carries and all the effort it requires. Waking life is now a daily fight against exhaustion so deep that it twists his body and one shoulder dips. He develops a perpetual grimace and one eyelid droops. Martin is always looking up at the world.

*

There are several moments when he thinks he has it. One document leads to another and a timeline emerges. He starts with the military records. This database is surprisingly uniform and orderly. He doesn't know what he was expecting: if there are any institutions that would place emphasis on orderliness and uniformity, it would be the military. But something about his own time in the army suggested that bureaucracy could do nothing but harm. Each image flashes across the screen, clear and crisp. The immaculate handwriting of some sergeant long dead reflects off Martin's face in the darkened room. Skimming these records demonstrates for Martin that penmanship is a dying, if not completely dead, art.

Each file he opens is a step forward. To open the archive is to solemnly nod one's head and be forced to admit that bureaucracy has its place in the world. Bureaucracy actually might benefit certain systems. So many forms, so many signatures. It is all here. Every little piece. After several days he knows several facts that shape the rest of his search. He writes them in a notebook and takes pains to steady his trembling hand and focus on his print:

1. Private Augustin Caledec was recorded as killed in action on October 11, 1916.

2. His family was notified on November 1, 1916.

3. His family filed for bereavement pay on January 8, 1917.

Martin cannot locate their letter requesting the payment or the form they filed if there was one. He can only locate the army's side of the correspondence. But armed with these crucial bits of information, Martin is able to push back from the computer and return to reality with the knowledge that the next day he will begin again, one step closer to locating this family and eventually its descendants. It feels real. It feels possible.

Then it comes. The good find.

A locksmith.

A good find.

It is Martin who puts it together.

A single muster roster from the 306th Infantry Regiment that not only lists the names of the soldiers but their hometowns and prewar occupations. Great initiative. Great research. It rarely ever has anything to do with discovering secrets or long-lost documents. Rather, having the patience and discipline to sift through what no one else wants to and slowly building a pile of evidence. That file was in their own database and had been set apart the day before Martin even arrived. It was at the virtual top of the pile, so to speak. But it is Martin who takes the time to read the lines.

He cross-references it with the original family he found in the census, which also lists an Augustin Caledec, age twenty-four, occupation: locksmith, and he has his man. Or he has a man. Martin just needs to find a way to connect his findings to the body.

But then comes another good find.

A day laborer. Also named Augustin Caledec.

He lived several hundred miles away in a tiny city called Ripont that no longer even exists.

What are the chances?

"We must follow up on this one," Theo tells Martin with both documents in each hand.

"I'd rather not," Martin replies.

Every cell in his body knows it is the locksmith. But this is not how research works. Begrudgingly, he digs deeper and, sure enough, corroborates the name with an individual listed on a roster for the 246th Infantry Regiment, which was also present at Verdun and, unlike the 306th Infantry Regiment, was recorded as having been in the vicinity of Fleury for several weeks, only much later in the battle, suggesting it unlikely that anyone could have died and been left after the worst of the fighting had died down.

It didn't matter anyway. Several days after, they have quite another *good* find. It comes in the manic late hour of a night they stayed past when the rest of the building's lights have been shut off. Just a single desk with a single computer, and in the feverish glow, Martin rubs his eyes, certain he must be misreading the scanned document on the screen before him.

A railroad engineer. Augustin Caledec. And this one was a German. Magdeburgisches Infanterie-Regiment Nr. 66.

What are the *chances*?

All at once, they have gone from a blank-page void with a single clue to three compelling possibilities identical in name. The lines blur together. The words collide. He is deep in the woods and turned around now, no way of knowing from where he came. The only thing to do? Dig deeper. Start again fresh the next day. Never underestimate the power of a good night's rest.

But he arrives the next day later than usual to find the room empty, the computers off. Martin looks around and hears conversation coming from the break room down the hall. He enters to find the team seated around the table, leaning against the fridge, propped on the counter with the type of deflation that comes at the end of a long day, even though it is only a quarter to nine in the morning.

"You're here. Great. Have a seat," says Dr. Garnier. "Now we can begin."

She thanks them all for their hard work, their dedication, their willingness to stay late just to audit another ream of tax records. But their funding has run out. There had, yes, been a last-minute appeal, but unfortunately, it had been rejected. This will be the last day. After today, the bones and all their findings will be turned back over to the prosecutor, who would, in turn, pass it over to the military, which would handle the interment in the ossuary.

So that's it.

"There's nothing we can do?" Martin asks.

"Unfortunately, no. This case has potential. But it also has serious interest from powers much greater than anyone here. As you know, this Armistice Day will commemorate one hundred years since the battle in 1916. They want these remains interred at the Douaumont Ossuary. His identity is irrelevant to them."

The thing that had been floating above this whole operation had been hope. The possibility of a firm conclusion. Concrete resolve. A final answer resolute as gravity. Something they could point to with a single extended finger and say, *There! There it is!* They wouldn't get that now. Neither would those bones. After three months, despite the miles of ground he covered, despite all he managed to reveal, so much of which was due to his inexhaustible energy, the investigation is closed and the burial date is set.

"If it makes you feel any better, I'm incredibly impressed with this entire team. We made real progress, and if we had more time, I honestly believe we would have solved this man's identity. It's amazing what they can do now. With another reference point and some mitochondrial DNA, you can find basically anybody. They did it a few years ago when they discovered King Richard III under a parking lot in England.

A team of amateur historians. They tracked his lineage through sixteen generations on his mother's side, and they actually found a match to prove it was him."

"That's what you get when you're a king," says Theo.

He knows he will never return. What for? This is his last time in this building. The realization brings the type of hyperawareness where every sense is heightened and absorbing all the things he's never noticed. The faucet in the break room drips. The streaks on the marble floor from so many shoes crossing over the surface. Crumbs from an unknown source in the crevices of the table. The persistent high-pitched whine of some appliance on the counter. The imperfections in the painted walls, the streaks of the brushstrokes, the petrified bubbles. The subtle aroma of printer ink and warm desktop computers. These are all the details suddenly available to him now that he knows this will be the last time he will ever sit in this room with these people in this building ever again. He exits through the same door he came in the first day and takes the cobblestone paths through the neat courtyards one more time. An unseasonably cool late summer morning greets him, and the artificial scents of office life are instantly replaced with something much heavier and familiar. Dead leaves. Soil. The outside world.

6

The Verdun City Pacers meet every Saturday morning at the landing of the Monument à la Victoire, the heart of the city. Lots of steps. Great view from the top. There's a crypt up there always surrounded by fresh flowers. It houses the Golden Book of the Soldiers of Verdun, which lists all the names of the French and Allied soldiers who received the Médaille de Verdun, and once a year, the flame for the Unknown Soldier is brought from Paris as a symbolic gesture of remembrance. Around 7:45, the group gathers from every direction and angle, from one side of the street or the other, exiting parked vehicles jingling coins for the meters and traipsing down the steps of Monument à la Victoire itself, which is something of a shortcut from deeper in the city, if you can tolerate the seventy-four broad steps to the landing. They come mostly in pairs and groups of three. They are of all ages and body types. This is not an exclusionary group. Here, running is for everyone.

By 8:00 there are just shy of thirty individuals in running attire, all sinewy muscle and smiles, bare legs protruding from shorts and vibrantly colored sneakers. Romain Blanchard, nearly sixty but there every weekend, bounces while alternating his feet in a kicking motion. He's built like a beanstalk, but there's a youthful springiness in his tendons. Amélie Roussel keeps both her hands on her hips and lunges around him in tight circles, with each step causing her to almost touch her opposite knee to the pavement. She's half Romain's age with a rosy complexion. They carry on a conversation about Amélie's recent vacation to the Riviera, restaurants, and the best place for coffee. Tristan Dumas, a local university student, blends yoga moves and calisthenics with the grace of a farmhand, all muscle and force. Painful just to watch. Everyone seems to know one another or almost everyone in the group, which gives them a congregational look, like a tour group waiting for their guide to show up. He always shows up last.

Hugo tries to arrive right before they are set to step off so that everyone will have to look around and locate him and therefore focus on him, their leader—they won't forget that way—and so he can grab their attention for a few valuable seconds. This is when he makes a little speech: he'll announce any upcoming races or changes to races people might have signed up for; he will congratulate anyone who has recently competed in a race and have everyone give a quick cheer. He usually gives updates on members' life events: marriages, births of children and grandchildren, if anyone has returned from a long vacation, that sort of thing. This builds the camaraderie and intimacy people are looking for when they come to a running group in the first place. This tactic gives him ample opportunity to sneak in his own personal updates, such as last month, when he announced the successful sale of a large portion of blue wood to a local developer. Light applause followed with smiles all around. Public image is everything. Rome wasn't built in a day, but neither was Verdun. People need to know what he is up to. Many of them know of him only as the mayor of Fleury. Today, he will announce the big news about Armistice Day: for the first time in well over a decade, a French soldier who was discovered in his village will be laid to rest in the ossuary.

But when he arrives, he finds his pacers already gathered around someone else on the street. As he gets closer, he sees Gabriel Moreau,

Camille's husband, at the center of the group. He's standing beside a shiny baby-blue Citroën DS, grinning from ear to ear. When Gabriel first joined the Verdun City Pacers, not long after Camille and Hugo began their tryst, Hugo was certain he was being stalked. He almost quit altogether, as much as it would have pained him. He had grown it from just four people to its current number of thirtyish all on his own. But he stuck it out, watching Gabriel's every move, searching every off-hand comment for double meaning, hidden messages, anything to let him know that he was here to expose him as an adulterer. The moment never came. Hugo came to realize after a month or so that Gabriel had absolutely no idea. He's as clueless as they come. A handsome guy, there's no denying. Even bundled up in joggers and a hoodie, he draws the attention of nearly every lady in the group. He has the type of smooth bronze skin made for beaches in the summertime. Hugo could easily see him trotting shirtless on some shoreline with the surf coming in around his ankles, a volleyball under one arm.

But Hugo has to smile. Camille has a bad habit of going on at length about every aspect of their sex life she detests, many of them details he has absolutely no interest in. The shape and size of his penis (weird and, surprisingly, too large), his strange habits (he always rubs his genitals and then smells his fingers after they finish), and the very specific way he jerks his dick (a birdlike flapping she theorizes he learned by watching too much pornography). The great thing about being forced into close proximity with your lover's husband while every woman fawns over him is knowing so much of what they desperately want and will most likely never get.

Gabriel spots him and waves him over. The crowd opens, and the vehicle comes into full view. It is a thing of beauty, a true work of art. A streamlined body with a sloping rear roofline and protruding headlights—designed by a forward-thinking artist who thought the whole future world would look this way one day, all curves and elegance.

"Hey, Hugo! She's a beaut, isn't she? I've been searching for this car for *years*. I almost had one a few years back, price was just too high," Gabriel tells him.

"You don't typically see this shade of blue on a car like this, but it doesn't look half bad," Hugo says.

"Here, get in! See how she feels."

Hugo slides into the driver's seat, grips the wheel. A single-spoke steering wheel, minimalist dashboard. Everything about it feels intentional and ergonomic.

"She feels nice, eh?"

Hugo smiles. "Oh yes, she feels lovely. I wouldn't mind taking her for a few rides sometime."

"Absolutely! You let me know," Gabriel says, and claps Hugo on the back as he gets out. "Any time you want, just say the word."

Hugo calls everyone together to open today's session. He goes over the route and a few minor updates.

"Last thing before we get started," he says. "As you all know, Armistice Day is next week, and this is a big year. A century. One hundred years since the Battle of Verdun. Not only will we be paying our respects to all those who fought here, we will be laying to rest a French soldier who was recently discovered in my village, in Fleury. Yes, that's right. Despite some incredible efforts on the parts of many, they were not able to identify him. On November eleventh, we will be laying him to rest in the ossuary. President Hollande will be there as well. I can't stress the significance of this moment enough. They have not opened the ossuary for interment in nearly a century. For decades, any remains discovered have been buried in the necropolis out front. This is a truly unique and special moment for our city.

"I want you to do something for me when you go home. I want you to think about the most important person in your life. Could be your mother or father, or maybe your child. I want you to imagine what it would be like to have them go to the other side of the world and never come back. Imagine that. Then think about the tens of thousands of young men who had that exact thing happen to them here. All their families. All that pain.

"Moments such as these give us the opportunity, the rare chance, to rectify those tragedies. I hope you can join us."

He's right at the end of this speech when she arrives. Elisa. A few minutes late and the last one. Maybe that's why she approaches with an uncharacteristic timidness, and everything about her—Hoka sneakers (a top brand), fitted leggings, a GPS watch, an Amphipod Hydraform ergonomic water bottle—says shopping spree for expensive gear she probably doesn't need.

"Welcome, welcome, Elisa! Just in time. Glad you made it!" Hugo exclaims, and gives her a hug. "Please, introduce yourself."

She half waves and addresses him at first before turning to the rest of the group. "Hi, everyone, my name is Elisa. Sorry I'm late. I work for the forest service. Thanks for including me."

"I think you'll find you made the right choice! We're all accepting here. Except for Gabriel. Stay away from him."

Gabriel gives him a knowing smile, and a few in the group chuckle.

"Are we all ready then? Quick one today. Three miles. Do we have any questions? We will do lunch at Le Bar after. All right then? Let's go!"

There are no clouds, and the sky is a piercing, depthless blue. Soft legs and light hearts. The group bunches, runs cheek by jowl at first, until they get a little ways down the road and begin to spread out. The stones under their feet feel springy. It's a good day for running. They make their way down Rue Mazel, every person finding their own rhythm, some pulling a little ahead, others falling a little behind. This is Hugo's favorite part. The group homogenizes into a blob awash in a sea of glossy neon, stretching limbs, and bounding bodies. To be one of the pack gives him a level of comfort he finds in few other places. Many in the group are training for the annual marathon in the spring. Others are not. The route sometimes winds through various parts of the battlefield, passing the old trenches with their buckled retaining walls and uneven support rods, the wood crumbling to felt, as well as the surrounding farmland, and ends on the main drag through town.

Running groups often split into smaller, compact groups based on speed called "pods." After this point, members tend to stick within their pods, and some unfortunate individuals end up entirely on their own if there is no one else who runs near their pace. It is rarely a competitive environment save for a few of the more experienced runners at the very front of the pack who might have a friendly rival they try to beat to the finish. But more often than not, this is an event focused on individual effort, not a race.

Hugo loves it because it gives him an opportunity to not only display his physical stamina (he was a gold medal runner in high school three years in a row) but also showcase the many projects he has going on around the city. Every route is designed by his hand, and every route passes at least three or four storefronts under construction. On this route, there's the crepe place that just opened seven months ago, as well as the new commercial space that he recently renovated and is currently seeking an occupant. Every route they run means free advertising to his curated group runners. It is no coincidence that of the thirty or forty regulars to the group, eighteen hold some type of government office related to zoning and construction. Romain has been the historic preservation officer for almost twenty-five years; Amélie is the environmental compliance officer. It pays to have friends in the right places.

Elisa slips beside Hugo in the lead and then glides a few steps ahead. Perfect timing. He picks up his own cadence and is quickly within step of her. The others in the lead pod maintain their speed and begin to fall away. Spry and graceful, she clearly is more experienced than she let on. Hugo takes note of her form in quick side glances. This is the first time he is seeing her in anything aside from her uniform or the sweatshirts she favors. Thin without looking malnourished. She's put her hair in twin braids that bounce with her stride, strands slipping out around her temples and nape. What else has she been hiding? Probably does yoga too. His wife, Léa, looked like that maybe five years ago.

Léa didn't mess around. She took everything from her studies to her daily routine (the gym, grocery shopping, paying bills) seriously. That was what attracted him to her in the first place. For as long as he knew her, Léa had the type of no-nonsense attitude toward life that created something close to stability. There had been other women—*many* other women he would tell his friends all about after the third or fourth drink—before Léa and even one or two after, but she possessed a certain gravity that kept him close. They weren't the sort of couple that dreamed. After university, Léa took the first nursing job she could find, and Hugo became an auto dealer for a time. These were opportunities within reach.

Over time her face took on a sort of pinched look, maybe from a few too many overnight shifts. Then came one night several months after Emmanuel was born when Hugo looked down at Léa while she slept and realized he didn't find her very attractive in her sleeping state. For some reason, in this position, he could see how she would age, where the skin would eventually become loose and flabby, and a sudden flash of ice ran through his chest.

Is this it? Is this what life becomes?

The next morning she came to the table while he fed Éloïse, and to his relief he found that whatever creeping sense of age and sag he had seen last night had miraculously vanished. Some time spent in front of the mirror with the clear morning light and a good powder brush had played a not unvital role in the transformation.

His first affair was a minor thing, but it nearly killed him in the immediate aftermath. It was an indiscretion so insignificant that some might not even consider it a *real* affair. He kissed one of the front desk girls—a quiet, mousy little girl named Anaïs who had awful breath—at the Christmas party. He knew it was wrong. He knew he should not do it. He did it anyway. No one forced him, he was not coerced. Hugo saw an opportunity, and in the boozy haze of a late hour, he took it. Even before their mouths separated, he recognized in a very distant and logical way that he would feel very, very bad about this. *Before you finish crossing the street when you leave this party,* he thought. He was painfully correct. Each step closer to home brought him deeper into a swamp of his own soul. Within a mile of his house he almost threw himself into the river just to avoid having to go inside and face Léa. But he didn't. Instead, he cried like a child and exhaled great, vaporous clouds into the frigid night air until he could hardly feel his fingers. Then, with his tears frozen to his face in spiderweb-like rivulets, he quietly entered the house, closed the door, and found Léa fast asleep. Hugo almost slept on the couch, a self-inflicted punishment, but realizing that might be more suspicious, and also, he was *so damn* tired, he timidly crawled into bed, careful not to wake her, and slept a deep black dreamless sleep.

He woke less hungover than he expected. A strange shift had occurred. Once the guilt and shame had evaporated along with his hangover, the sun was still shining, Earth still spun on its axis. All was well. He felt that fidelity was much more complex than the priests and nuns of his school years had given credit to the concept.

An abrupt shift, no doubt. When had it happened? Hard to say. There was a time when he and Léa shared everything with each other. Their trust was formed around the philosophy that nothing was off-limits. They could ask each other anything, they could share anything with each other.

"One time, I fucked three guys in the same night," she told him.

"At the same time?"

"No," she said, and smiled.

"I've had two threesomes," he told her.

"Say your body count on three. One . . . two . . . three."

"Twenty-seven."

"Forty-eight."

These were the conversations he remembered. Free and irreverent, and therefore nothing could come between them. He would learn quickly the true death of the honeymoon isn't marked by arguments over who was supposed to load the dishwasher or any of the other mundanities of daily life. It's the realization that although you've grown closer through the most important moments two people can experience, like having a child, in many ways, you've grown further apart. Both parties have settled into roles both unfamiliar and comfortable. Certain things were just no longer his business to know. He wouldn't dream of asking about any of her past sexual experiences now. It was out of the question. The proximity shifted without either of them realizing. He had his first sexual affair a few months after Éloïse was born. The orgasm he experienced that night punctured the shell trapping him and released him into the world again. There was no going back.

The group comes to a corner and waits for a break in the traffic before cutting across the street and onto the bridge on Rue Beaurepaire over La Meuse and then down several wide, shallow steps onto the banks. A nice, even gravel path rises to meet them as they run along the river.

It was Hugo's personal view that until relatively recently, males had sought to and, what's more, been encouraged to have sex with as many partners as possible—he'd heard this on a podcast—for the betterment of the species. It was only natural for these desires to pop up fairly often. In fact, monogamy and chaste fidelity to a single woman was a novel phenomenon and more or less unnatural in the biological sense of things. He, for one, believed it was possible and easy to be a good husband and a good father, an all-around family man and provider, while still giving in to his more base and natural desires every now and again.

"You have great form!" he says to Elisa.

She snaps her head in his direction and has an expression of mild surprise. He shoots a look over his shoulder and realizes they are quite a bit farther ahead than the lead pod now. They have already passed the new restaurant he had meant to point out to several key members and he did not even notice. There's also another thing. He feels the strain of their speed in his lungs and deeper in his chest. He can feel his pulse pounding in his throat. The coppery taste of blood at the back of his mouth.

"Typically . . . they say you should try to keep . . . a conversational . . . pace. Typically! . . . It's the best . . . way to keep your heart rate . . . low . . . so you don't . . . overexert . . . yourself."

She does not respond to or acknowledge any of his advice. This shy girl has undergone a transformation at some point in the last half mile. Her brow now relaxed, the utter picture of focus, eyes placid and containing a glimmer of some type of truth Hugo does not possess and desperately desires to know.

"This is . . . definitely . . . higher than a . . . conversational pace . . . For me . . . at least."

It is happening in degrees. She's actually picking up her pace. Elisa pulls ahead of Hugo without so much as breaking a sweat. Heat rises in his chest.

Hugo pumps his arms, he picks up his knees, he lengthens his stride and draws deep belly breaths—and still, Elisa gets farther ahead. A quick look down at his fitness watch reveals a heart rate of 198 beats per minute. Most certainly not a conversational pace. But he refuses to slow. His face burns, and he's become aware of a piercing pain in his left side, and still, she pulls farther ahead with the kind of grace and ease that might make someone believe in a higher power or at least the sheer beauty of the human body in action. Hugo thinks he might puke. And then the thought crosses his mind: *This bitch.* She keeps on moving, and now she is so far ahead when it comes time to turn, she keeps right on going. It is her first day and she was late. How could she know the route?

"You. Are. Going. THE WRONG WAY," Hugo bellows, but she does not hear him.

Elisa continues along the gravel path that will take her farther into the farmland and eventually back toward the city, a solid eight-mile route if she takes it all the way. Hugo doubles over at the turn and dry heaves into the grass. His entire body throbs, and his shirt and shorts are plastered to his skin with sweat. He walks in little circles while he waits for the rest of the group to catch up with his hands on his head, until he looks down to find two parallel streaks of bright red blood down the front of his shirt. Nipple chafing. *Great.* Far behind, the lead pod approaches, all smiles and buoyant joy.

He skips lunch with the group afterward and drives home. They usually all go out, but he's not feeling it for some reason. He parks outside his house but does not get out immediately. Instead he sits in silence. His heart won't stop racing. He takes out his phone and texts Elisa. He types and deletes several messages before sending one.

"WOW! You just like to run for fun, huh? Lol—" No.

"Thanks for leaving me behind, JERK! Friendship card revoked. Lol—" No.

He taps the steering wheel, then nods his head.

"Great run today! Any chance you are around tonight? I wanted to run something else by you. New opportunity."

Send.

She responds in seconds.

"Yeah :) 8?"

A smiley face? That's new. Perfect. It's only after he sits there for a moment, when he senses the guilt, the slight twinge of regret in his near future, that his heart slows down. Yes, tonight. It will happen tonight. He gets out of the car, and the air feels electric with possibility. He suddenly has a profound sense of appreciation for the things in his life. Simple things. Having enough food in the pantry. Not worrying about if he could pay a bill. The weight of a full bag of groceries and the way that weight made him feel just a little more grounded to the earth. He opens the front door, and the smell of fresh drywall and the sound of a child's cry greet him. What a life. What a beautiful life.

*

Elisa's house is, more or less, what Hugo expects. A light beige duplex in a single-street village possessed by the utter silence only found in vacant school auditoriums and abandoned parking lots. An easy twenty-minute drive outside the city. All utilitarian, no ornate aesthetics. Smooth plaster walls with a simple facade. Neutral and subdued. Everything in rectangular shapes with the same tiled roof found on every postwar house in the country. Practical and affordable.

Hugo parks his car beside an empty playground, a small jungle gym that looks recently renovated, across from a darkened church. He gets out and pulls the hood of his parka up and wraps it around his head. His heavy boots on the wet leaves is the only sound on the street. Every house, darkened and shuttered windows. He climbs the steps to her front door.

Hugo goes to ring the doorbell but pauses. It's always the moment right before you ring the doorbell when the crisis of confidence hits. He doesn't have to do it. No wrong has been committed yet. Yet. All he has to do is step off her front porch, walk back to his car, and drive home. That is it. It is still possible in this moment. No need for apologies or guilt or shame. But that's the thing—this is all part of the process. He will be sorry. But of course he will be sorry. Everyone is always sorry afterward, for a little while at least. It's part of the rush. It almost wouldn't be worth it if he weren't sorry. Almost. It's not just the act of adultery in itself. The anxious beginning, the rollicking middle, and the regretful end are essential. It actually might be easier to remain faithful if the regret went away. Like a favorite dish that had, for some reason just out of reach, lost its appeal. If he just wanted sex, he would just fuck his wife. Where's the fun in that? These weighty considerations slip from his mind the moment he presses the buzzer.

Elisa answers the door, and from the way she holds his gaze for only a moment, he knows they are both complicit in this act. Even merely meeting at this late an hour at her house is unacceptable. There is no reason for him to be here. He enters.

"Thanks for coming over," she says. "I appreciate you being flexible. I know this isn't the most convenient time."

"No problem at all! Glad I was able to finally catch up to you," he says, and smiles, holding up two mini bottles of Hennessy clutched between his fingers.

She wears fitted joggers with slippers and an oversized wool sweater. He speculates whether she might be wearing a bra and decides probably not—a titillating thrill dampened by his realization he has probably overdone it by arriving freshly showered, shaved, and cologned. He even wore a dress shirt and slacks. A little much, he recognizes now, but easy to explain, if necessary. Straight from the office, working late, you know how it goes.

Once inside, a sense of comfort and ease washes over him. She has a dog—a small, annoying thing that looks like a cartoon drawn by a child. She closes the door, and they exchange a few niceties while the dog jumps on his leg repeatedly. He can already feel the mood shift within him. They are entering the meaty middle, the fun part. This is no home; it is a stage, and he has just taken it as the lead in his own life. They make their way into the dining room, where they sit at a table littered with papers—various reports and graphs. Shuttered windows and lamplight; he notices she leaves the can lights above dark. Alcohol helps. She gets tumblers from a cupboard, and he opens the bottles. Drinks in hand, they talk about the blue wood, they talk about the bones. Elisa has already found some connections who are interested in discussing the possibility of wholesale purchase of the damaged trees. It's very promising. Hugo shares some ideas he's been toying with for publicity. He wants to shoot a documentary short using people from around town.

"I already have the tagline. *Nous sommes le bois bleu*—'We are the blue wood.' Think about it. We end the segment with a montage of everyone saying a word of it. I think it will work beautifully if we can get the right videographer."

"Absolutely," she agrees, but he can't tell if she means it.

"This is a beautiful home you have," he says.

"Ah, you think so? It's all right, I guess. This is one of the original buildings built after the war. There was a village here too. Even smaller than Fleury or Houaumont. Leveled like all the rest. The only difference is the residents didn't listen after the war. They came back. The government said, *No, it is too dangerous*, and they all said, *Where the hell else can we go?* They rebuilt this place right around the ruins. I like that. Move on. Get over it. There's none of this wallowing in the misery of the past. The only way you would know is that little sign you passed by the playground."

"I didn't even notice," Hugo says. "When I moved here, the first thing I tried doing was renovating all the facades of prewar buildings. Almost every one of them has chips and cracks from the bombs. No one would do it. They wouldn't let me. Protected historical sites, what they told me. It looks terrible."

"People want reminders of our mistakes so we don't repeat them in the future," she says.

"Well, it doesn't seem to be working very well."

She refills both of their glasses.

"Nine entire villages wiped from existence. Think about that," Hugo says. "Parks. Bars. Homes. Storefronts with hand-printed lettering and churches with bell towers that the sun shone on. Real buildings with doors and windows and histories and legacies of generations passing through their archways—all pulverized, never to recover. And to be honest, I don't think a lot of these people want to recover. There was life and then there was war and now there is nothing. But the wreckage, it's still all here. People do not want to move on. I'll never understand it."

"Really? I wouldn't say that. I think a lot of people want to move on. What about the trees? There's a tremendous amount of life out there. They designed it that way, planted them with intention," says Elisa.

"Yes, but in between the trees? Craters and rubble where the buildings used to stand. Smashed foundations."

"Do you know why they didn't try to rebuild them?" she asks.

"It wasn't safe. It still isn't," he says.

"True, that's probably the most practical reason. But Albert Lebrun gave a speech in 1932 when they dedicated the ossuary, about what they would do to reclaim the wasteland that so much of the country had become. And in that address, that was exactly what he said: these villages died for France, they can never be rebuilt, just like all the dead of the war can never come back. So they planted trees. Millions of them. Every species that would take root in the soil. They looked out over the soupy wasteland and decided it was better just to cover the whole thing up."

"You can't just start over. Have you ever seen some of the old photos of these villages from before the war? They had buildings that dated to the Roman Empire! I wonder how the light might have looked on a Saturday evening—the walls of those buildings, the sunlight against it while the sun was setting. You know the inside of one of those churches is still intact? Sort of," Hugo says, and tips his glass back.

"Yes, in Ornes?" She leans back and runs a hand through her hair, glossy and full.

Hugo imagines himself running his own fingers through that red hair like so many strands of pearls. He wants to know what it feels like to tangle his fingers in it and pull her head back while she's bent over in front of him.

"Correct," he says. "It still has a few columns among the trees. It's not hard to imagine the old church there. The hollow spaces where decorous stained-glass windows once sat and the incense hanging heavy in the air. How many weddings, how many funerals, passed through that narthex? I swear sometimes I can hear them. The whispered prayers."

She stares at him. "The past is the past. There are more pressing things to be concerned about. This bug is going to destroy every last tree in this country eventually. Everything that is left is what matters. It's happening now. All around us. There will be real, dire consequences unless something is done."

Elisa takes her glass to the sink.

"What keeps you going then? It seems futile, the way you describe it," he says.

"You just have to love the process of this work to really stick with it. Does that make sense? Seems a little strange. Maybe masochistic? I don't know. Originally, I went to school to be a nurse, but that didn't last. Being a ranger is just not the type of job where you can look forward to a conclusive end. We are stewards and protectors. The work just keeps going. It's difficult to understand."

"But I do," Hugo says. "I think I know exactly what you mean."

She looks exhausted. Obviously, it is the end of the day, and who doesn't look a little out of it at this time of night? But it's the same weary determinedness she had during the presentation she gave about the blue wood. This seems to be her natural state: a little exasperated, always tired around the eyes.

"It's a bizarre little mission, but you might be surprised by the little moments of joy it gives you," she says.

A draft rattles the windowpane above the sink. They hold eye contact.

"Come upstairs," she says. "I want to show you something."

She takes one of the mini bottles off the counter and carries it. He follows her through the kitchen to the stairs. Off the landing, they make a right to a closed door. He places a hand on her lower back for just a moment in the narrow hallway as she opens the door. He's about to tell her to leave the lights off when she flips the switch.

Backlights illuminate a row of shelves on the far wall in front of them. He sees immediately they are not in the bedroom. A variety of containers of all kinds line the shelves in no discernible order. Fish bowls, glass orbs, demijohn bottles, spirits bottles, rectangular aquariums, and more, sealed with cork plugs. Vibrant green plants pack the inside of every container, some almost bursting from the sealed tops. Each glows with the soft white LED light from the striplights above. Tools and various jars of soil and plant matter crowd a table against the wall to their right.

"What is this?" Hugo asks, momentarily distracted.

"Terrariums," she says. "I've been making them for years."

Closer examination reveals a world of life underneath the glass. Movement. Twisting and churning and energy vibrating in the pitch-dark soil.

"Most of these will outlive us. Once they're shut, I never reopen them. Sealed for eternity. Every one of them is a self-contained world, perfectly balanced in those glass walls."

"There are bugs in there?" he asks.

"Yes, springtails, wood lice. They are great custodians of the soil."

"They look like fleas."

"They're actually not even considered insects anymore. They've been reclassified as arthropods. Specifically, they're crustaceans. They've got more in common with lobsters and crabs than any insect."

"How does one get into assembling terrariums?" he asks.

"Everyone needs a hobby, right?"

Hugo reaches out and lightly taps the glass. The world beyond his fingertip pays no mind. "But what keeps it filtered? These are going to end up developing mold at some point."

"They won't, actually," she says, and frowns. "That's partly what the springtails are for. It's a bioactive environment. The water is deionized, and it's enough that it will continue to recirculate over and over again. Endlessly. It doesn't need us in order to function. It can carry on just fine. I think that's part of the appeal for me. I spend so much time watching our world burn, it's nice to just set one of these up and watch it thrive."

His stomach turns. All he can think of is the hot summer several years before, when the waste collectors went on strike, and after nearly three weeks of piling bag after bag into his trash can, he lifted the lid to find the heaps literally crawling with maggots. He'd vomited on the spot.

"Must be relatively simple to make. What do you do? Go out back and shovel some dirt into one, toss some grass in?" he asks.

"Not at all, actually. I've tried to use materials around here with poor results. Everything is so toxic that nothing lasts. I have to special order mostly everything. Pea gravel, moler clay, akadama. I won't bore you. Do you know there are still spots of land around here where nothing grows at all? Permanently altered war soil. They've even found perchlorate ions in the water tables in the last few years. A by-product of explosives."

His thoughts immediately turn to remediation. There must be a way to treat the water, some type of filtration system that might separate one from the other. If only he had endless capital, the kind of fuck-you money where you could follow whims and fancies for fun. He'd invest in some way to repurpose the perchlorate ions, an incredibly valuable material. They are found in everything from fertilizer to rocket fuel. If only, if only.

She picks at the corner of the label on the Hennessey bottle. It comes off easily with minor residue.

"Can you hand me those tweezers?" she asks, and points.

He passes her a pair of long tweezers. "I don't know. More than all the iron bits and the chemicals, it's the bodies that bother me. I can't believe they are just gone. How is that possible? How do so many just disappear?" he asks.

"Well, they are still out there. Some of them, at least. We just can't see them. But they are there," she says.

"I'm surprised it doesn't help with the plant life. You know, like fertilizer."

She gives him a quizzical look and mixes together several soils from different bags on a piece of wax paper. They blend together easily when she picks up the corners and rhythmically rocks the paper side to side.

Then she puts one edge to the open mouth of the bottle and coaxes the new substrate down the bottle's neck.

"Back when I thought I wanted to be a nurse, before I dropped out halfway through my final year—my parents were so angry. I couldn't do it, though. It was not for me. Better to realize it while still in school. I needed to be around nature. But I remember the first time I ever saw a body taken away for procurement. Organ donation. I was behind on my hours, so I picked up a last-minute shift. The ER was a mess that night. I didn't stop moving from the moment I walked on the floor. Every time I turned around, another room needed to be cleaned, another patient arrived. This physician needs these labs, take this patient there, someone bring me this Foley unit. Chaos."

She picks up a pitcher of water and pours in a few drops, holds up the bottle to gauge the amount, turning it in the light, then adds another drop.

"The medics brought her in just before midnight. Twenty-three. Car accident. I was twenty-three. Same age. We all knew the moment we saw her on the gurney that she wasn't going to make it. Car accidents are weird. People flip and wrap their cars around trees and are walking around by the time the cops get there like nothing happened. And then other times the body just comes apart on impact. We're mostly made of water, you know.

"They were breathing for her all the way to the hospital, and she still had a faint pulse. We got her in and transferred her to the table, but she only lasted a few more minutes. We couldn't stabilize her to move her to the OR. Doctor called it a few minutes later. We all stepped back. Someone placed a sheet over her. Twenty-three. I was twenty-three. She had probably been on her way to meet up with her friends to go party or check out a trendy wine bar or whatever, and now she was here. Naked. On the table.

"But the next thing that happened was a surgeon walked in the room. I had never seen him before. He was very serious and already gowned up. Moving quickly. An older, wiry kind of guy. 'Let's move, let's move,' he said. The whole room sprang into action. I wasn't even certain where we were going or what we were doing. Nursing school is like that. Always new experiences. Ventures."

She laughs.

"We wheeled her out of the trauma bay with a sheet draped over her body. Here's the really crazy part. We head into the hallway. The world is still falling apart with a million other patients and tragedies. All happening right there. But the moment they see us with the surgeon, I swear the whole world ceased moving. I had never seen anything like it. The chaos of the ER stopped in an instant. Every doctor and nurse paused, and they stood facing us as we passed, lining the halls all the way to the surgery room.

"I found out later it is a custom for those who have donated their organs. She was a donor, which was apparently becoming something of a rarity. People are opting out in higher numbers every year. That's how much respect these people had for one body—a single young woman who probably didn't even think to opt out of organ donation when she was getting her driver's license. I didn't know she was a donor until we got to the room. An entire ER stopped what they were doing to render respect for a young woman who was about to be harvested for everything she had. I'll never forget it.

"And when we got into the room, they did exactly that. It all happened so quickly. Opened up her chest and then dove right in. Incisions here and there, and then out comes the heart, out come the kidneys, all the rest. So quiet. So efficient. Speed was their friend. I just helped in any way I could; anything they told me to do, I did. Apparently, the window for the organs to remain viable is pretty small. And then it was over. Organs packed away into coolers and taken out of the room, and her body was rolled to the morgue through a separate door where it would stay until someone was able to get in contact with her next of kin.

"I've always wondered where all those organs ended up. They don't last forever, you know. They actually don't last long at all. Not that it's hard to find someone in need of a vital organ transplant. Wait-lists are years long. But not everybody is a good match. Not every surgery is a success. And even if the initial surgery is successful, things can still happen. Infection. The body can reject it weeks or months later. Sometimes people just die.

"She left that room one piece at a time. Right in front of me. All the special, important parts go in containers here and there. And she's still probably leaving the world. Slowly. One piece at a time. Maybe her heart is still out there, beating, in someone else's chest. Delivering oxygen to someone else's brain. Or maybe they all went bad before they found recipients."

"I mean, what do they do with the organs that go bad?" asks Hugo.

She picks up the cap and screws it on, taking a moment to evaluate her work. "Medical waste. They go into special red bags with scary hazard signs on the outside, and then they get taken away with the rest of the trash. Who knows where they go after that. Do they burn them? Toss them out at the city dump? I have no idea. In some ways, to be swallowed by the earth might be more fitting. In that way, at least. Natural."

Elisa hands him the mini terrarium.

"For you," she says.

He leans in to kiss her. She recoils and puts a hand on his chest.

"What are you doing?" she asks, her words like bollards.

The shock of rejection paralyzes him for a moment. The outcome is so foreign to Hugo that he has not even considered what to do next should he be rebuffed. They stare at each other for a painfully long time, both of their hands still holding the mini terrarium. And then, inexplicably, without any thought or reason other than that, on some level, Hugo believes everything he wants already belongs to him, he tries again.

Elisa slaps him, hard and swift.

"I should go," Hugo says, his heart pounding.

But he doesn't move right away. Elisa lets go of the terrarium and squares her shoulders to him. He holds his terrarium with both hands, and it is so quiet he thinks he can hear the springtails crawling through the clay and cork bark behind the glass. Without another word, he turns and leaves, taking the stairs two at a time to the front door and then jogs to his car. Hugo doesn't pause for a moment; he starts driving and tears back to town without so much as a thought. It's not until he's minutes from his house when he realizes he's left his parka at Elisa's house, but he doesn't even care. He lays on the accelerator and takes those last few minutes at breakneck speed, his mini-Hennessey terrarium rattling in the cupholder beside him, drowning out Elisa's voice in his mind, the sting of her hand still hot on his cheek.

Dr. Margaux Garnier, Lead Historian and Archivist of Personnel Records, Service Historique de la Défense (SHD), Château de Vincennes

Augustin Caledec. Certainly of French origin. Catholic, probably. Although that doesn't narrow it down much. *Augustin.* Aristocratic. Latin. A remnant of the Roman Empire. Also very popular among Catholics of a particular persuasion. The clergy and scholars. Saint Augustine of Hippo, the pagan turned bishop. The one we can thank for the doctrine of original sin and the idea of a just war. Strong chance he's from northern France, Brittany or Normandy. Probably a farmhand or something of that variety. Though he could just as easily be from one of the major cities. Île-de-France or Saint-Denis. Urban migration and all that. The possibilities are many but not endless. The soft irony here is it is easier to find the body than the man.

We never expected Ferrand to last. We were all honestly impressed with his efforts. He adapted rather quickly. There are so many things we didn't know about him. Even after all these months holed away in the same building, much of what we know about him hasn't come until now, after he's left us. We never knew about his time as an underwater welder. Or how he quit drinking years ago. Or how his wife had left him. Those aren't the types of things one asks about even after you get to know someone a little bit, but still.

There's a person, and then there is the idea of a person. What we remember. What we think we remember. And what surprises us upon recognition of a difference from our idea. It could be the subtlest, most inconsequential detail: the shape of their head, the direction they comb their hair, the angle of the bridge of their nose. Tiny, tiny details. Once noticed, the mind conducts a minor revision. These minor revisions are happening continually. All the time. Even with people we've known for years and years.

At any moment in the day, millions of people are looking—really looking—at their closest loved ones and saying, maybe out loud, maybe just to themselves, *Wow. I've never noticed the way Loved One only really smiles with the left side of their mouth. How have I never noticed that before?* And so all these people we think we know so well—better than anyone else could possibly understand—are really just ideas that are constantly changing shape right before us. It has nothing to do with how much we care about or even love them. The affection we feel toward them is genuine. Most of the time. Many of these moments pass subliminally, without a single pause. A minor line added to the manuscript of our day.

A person wakes up one morning and suddenly everything is different. They look around and recognize nothing. When did that happen? When did everything change? Enough small details go unnoticed for too long, and suddenly they register all at once. The whole world feels foreign and unfamiliar. Life can literally pass a person by if one is not careful.

The First World War was a compressed version of this phenomenon. Overnight, the French countryside transformed into a barren hellscape. Around Verdun, these little villages, sites of former Roman villas that eventually became communes with buildings dating back 650 years, disintegrated under the relentless pummel of German artillery. People returned and could no longer recognize what the place had once been. And still today, the land is thoroughly scarred. It never fails to make me pause, when I see the lumpy pastures and meadows. I took my time putting the photos from the investigation away, pausing over the 75mm shell they initially discovered at the site.

How can you not marvel at the thing? It juts magnificently from the clay. They removed the nose cone as a precaution, but the missile's body remains firmly planted above the remains of the soldier. The natural world has a way of projecting the slightest abnormality at a higher frequency.

The outer casing was ruptured. The husk, cracked. Soil spilled from within. Little buds had taken root and—could you believe it?—grew green and wild up toward the slate-gray sky above.

This is the world we are interested in. The world of cracks and fissures where life manages to find root. Everything in between. Not necessarily the solid world itself. Who cares about that? It is so boring. Leave the world of the whole and complete for those who can't bear to stare into the void for more than a few seconds. It's in those gaps and spaces and cracks and fissures where the truth resides. We are here to draw it out in the open. We want to pull that truth out into the light and make something more of it. Is it possible to make the truth truer?

Outside of the calm green pastoral fields, with their quiet German forests that the mushroom pickers love to wander through and their poisoned soil and infinite sadness, Verdun is a place of piles. Piles of munitions. Piles of artifacts. Piles of relics. Piles of bones.

There's a man who maintains a museum in his house less than an hour's drive outside the city itself. It's just a collection of every item he has found in the last forty years while living in the area. He takes walks and he picks things up. Sometimes even the bombs, if the démineurs declare it safe. He places these objects in piles. That's the power of his museum. It's a place of abundance. Its power is not in the presence of the artifact itself but in the sheer number of the same artifact copied a million times over. The same standard-issue fork that came with a million different mess kits could be argued to be the least interesting object to come out of a world war. But when you walk into his museum and see a waist-high pile of them massed and grouped together, it has a certain effect, a curious effect, on perception. To see the objects piled in one place does not make us think of the enormity of the objects themselves. None of us thought, *Holy cow! That's a lot of forks!* Instead, we think about what is not there. We imagine their adjacent objects. The object to the object. The hands that gripped them. The mouths they fed. The food they impaled and brought to those mouths. It is in that referencing and contextualizing that the true image forms. And then that leads the mind another degree away from the artifact itself to a much wider and fuller picture. All the fingers that might have wrapped themselves around each of those triggers. All the feet that might have stepped on the rungs of the ladder. All the hoofs that were once attached to each of those horseshoes and the weight each step bore on that horseshoe. Every drop of water contained in each canteen that made its way back to the ground and then the ocean, from a hole in the canteen itself or as blood from a hole in the body.

This is the real effect of the piles: not what is there, but what is no longer. It's what is missing that adds the true enormity to the overall picture. There's more truth in the missing than any story you can tell about this battle. The stories are all myths. We need our myths. It's how we come to understand ourselves. But the myths get cooked into the history. It changes the truth. Have to be careful of that. Very, very careful. A little is okay. Too much? After a while, you can't tell the difference.

It's a level of anonymity that is becoming rarer every year. When they decided to create a tomb for an unknown soldier in Paris, they pulled several unidentified bodies from the cemeteries of major battlefields, including Verdun, all over France. A soldier was selected to lay a bouquet of flowers on one of the coffins, unaware of anything about who rested inside. Truly anonymous. Unknown. But now, the technology has advanced so far that it's almost impossible to remain in such a state. In the United States they actually disinterred their unknown soldier from the Vietnam War and were able to identify him using DNA samples. The key, of course, is the availability of DNA.

The interment goes smoothly. President Hollande arrives with his motorcade right at seven in the morning. He is here to light a flame with the German chancellor. Another anniversary, another ceremony, another opportunity to reflect on how far the country has come. A color guard from the army arrives at about nine and spends the morning rehearsing. News crews materialize out of nowhere. Quite a crowd gathers in the hours leading up to the interment. The quiet fields are alive once more, and a parking lot becomes a parade ground with flags and rifles and paper flowers pinned on every lapel. In attendance are members of the Australian parliament, British royalty, the French defense minister, the French education minister. Politicians and celebrities of some renown take up most of the photographers' interest. In fact, there are more photographers than anything. So many that it feels like the point is to capture photographs rather than the memorial itself. A local confectioner has made little chocolates molded like the ossuary that melt in the children's fingers.

An entire regiment's worth of reenactors arrive fully kitted out. Strange behavior, if you ask me, grown men playing dress-up. They approach in tidy columns with shouldered rifles. Nearly every country is represented in the many different styles of uniforms, even Zouaves. They all walk around like the ceremony is for them, pissing in the open urinals, which they used with machismo.

Everyone appears to be reverting to their child-in-church self, no one entirely sure of what to do with their hands. They stand before crosses, kneel to place a bouquet. Finally, the remains arrive and the procession begins. One woman cries in the crowd. Real tears. The display is so visceral I have to stop a moment and wonder if it is possible for her to have known this soldier or any other soldier from that time period. People want connection. Give them a ceremony, and they will show up in full force.

French soldiers line the walkway, at arms. All the mayors of the Villages That Died for France stand in their own group near the entrance to the ossuary and are the last ones the bones pass before they enter the doors under the care of several French soldiers. Once again, passing from the sun and open sky into the shadowy space of a dank crypt. Interred again. President Hollande and Chancellor Merkel walk down the long corridor bathed in copper light. Together, they extend the long ignitor over the wide basin and light the flame together.

When the ceremony ends, the crowd wavers and then breaks off in various directions. They furl the flags, place the instruments back in their cases. Car engines start; headlights cut tracks across the parking lot as people leave to go back to daily life. There is an abruptness to it all that feels simultaneously natural and bizarre.

*

A few other facts:

1. In 1986, the consumption of locally sourced drinking water was prohibited in 544 municipalities due to high levels of perchlorate, which was used to make World War I ammo. All of those municipalities are located close to former battlefield zones.

2. Experts warn that mushrooms, game meat, and even food cooked over wood collected in Zone Rouge or former affected areas might be a source of toxins.

3. Experts have established that the livers of wild boars roaming the forests around Verdun contain abnormally high levels of lead.

4. The relatively elevated levels of lead in certain French wines may result from the wood of the barrels in which they matured, from oak harvested in former red zones.

Originally, the task was to clear the affected areas of ammunition and corpses. This involved the efforts of German POWs, foreign workers from as far afield as China, and Quaker volunteers, among others. But there were so many explosives just lying about, scattered over the ground or partially buried. Too many to just sidestep or walk around. Something had to be done. And thus, the government formed the Département du Déminage.

*

Many months later, while we were rearranging the study he shared with Theo, I discovered the journal. We found it bound with twine, wedged between the wall and the lower part of the desk we had given him. Did he mean for us to find it? Did he forget it? Seems odd to have forgotten it, tucked in that tight space between the desk and the wall. All entries were written in the same handwriting, unmistakably his. Possibly even the same pen. It appears to have been a fountain pen and, furthermore, a fountain pen used by a person who was not accustomed to writing with one. The ink is smudged and runs in several places. An amateur at practice. But written carefully, each letter of each word formed with the intention of being readable.

It is a curious experience reading through the journal. Some entries are pages long; others are fairly short, a couple of lines, a paragraph. But he dated each one so we are able to read them from first to last. He begins each entry addressing a woman named Charisse. Possibly the name of a family member of Augustine's he found? Or maybe a placeholder until he found an actual relative's name? We can find no record of anyone named Charisse, but we can only assume these entries were addressed to the family and maybe he planned on giving the journal to them once we located them.

They are at times poetic and deeply introspective. He wrote many of those final entries with a level of candidness none of us saw in the time we worked with him. One line that stands out:

They leave crater-shaped holes in our lives. Sometimes, even though we didn't know the person directly, that crater is still with us because it affected someone we love.

There's enough of his soul on the page that we have the urge to look away and destroy such personal musings, and yet it feels wrong to do so.

One simply says:

It is done.

The entries become less formal over time, more familiar. He was priming himself for the real thing, in case he didn't make it before the day we found them. The final entry is almost illegible, the handwriting cramped and messy. The words are all crushed insects on the page.

We can see him waiting for the family in their living room with the news anchor. Ferrand pats his brow with a handkerchief. It's a brightly colored room with too much lace covering every surface. Not exactly the space he was imagining for the occasion. Floral-patterned wallpaper overwhelms. A loud room with loud people, but no one says a word.

Ferrand and the news anchor sit at the table and stare at each other. This guy is supposed to be a big deal in Paris, and he certainly carries himself like he's a big deal, but Ferrand has never heard of him. In the other room the family members are being prepped by the producer. They haven't been allowed to meet prior to the filming. *It's imperative we capture the raw emotions, the natural reactions, as spontaneously as possible,* the producer tells him. She's a wiry lady with thin-rimmed glasses who seems blown from person to person by an invisible wind. The way she's treating the whole production makes Ferrand feel that it is he who is the ancestor and not the bones that will arrive tomorrow. The body will be accompanied by its own personal funeral detail. The army has sent the soldiers specifically for this occasion, and he will be laid to rest in the family plot with full military honors.

A slim crew of two continuously prep the set. There's an energy about the whole house that does not match either of their moods. Ferrand opens the folder for the thousandth time that morning. All the work from the past several months boils down to three pages and the single identification tag found months ago in the dirt.

And then it's time. The cameras are rolling. The door opens and in walks . . .

All the things we keep tucked away in drawers and boxes. Our secrets and confessions. When did he write them? None of us ever saw him writing anything but notes in the little leather-bound notebook he filled with his research. Was he at his desk? Or maybe at that window that he spent so much time watching the outside world float by? Or maybe the break room? Although he rarely ever spent any time in there except to refill his coffee every few hours. Maybe he wrote them at home after a full day of research at the château. We could see him quietly walking into the kitchen, the windows darkened and cold. Everything outside the window cast in a bluish-green quality. Night has an aquatic feel to it in Paris. Of course he pauses for a moment. We doubt Ferrand ever walked past a window without pausing a moment to see what was out there. He was never one for indoors. It was out there that he belonged, walking the streets of Verdun where the walls look like the inside of a heated kiln in the moonlight, they glow and burn, and cats roam freely.

A flock of birds tears across the sky. The flapping of their wings is lost as a truck passes by, groaning its way over the narrow street. The open journal and a fountain pen lie on the table behind him. One that had belonged to his father.

Ferrand pulls out a chair, then tucks in. He lights a cigarette, picks up the pen, and stares down at the blank page. The pen feels unwieldy in his grasp. Top heavy—a weird thing to say about a pen, but true. He isn't comfortable using a fountain pen. The ink might run. He picks at a wilted leaf of salad that lies stranded on the table. With a sigh, he uncaps the pen and begins.

There is one entry at the very end of the book. We almost don't bother reading it because it is much longer than the rest, and what is the point? We know how this all ends. But in that entry, Ferrand reveals more of himself and his family than anything else we had wished to know. His wife. His daughter. Everything no one wanted to tell us. It almost seems a final act of respect to put them all in the shredder.

It always stands out to us that whenever people picture what this town used to look like, they imagine it during the battle, when it was all but destroyed, with dead horses in the streets and barbed wire barriers blocking passage, and not when it was still a village. A sleepy village, but a well-off one, where the lanterns were always lit and the shelves at the grocer always stocked. Every now and again, there might be a wedding in the town square and a local shepherd would bring his accordion. Almost everyone in the village would be there, and the festivities would continue late into the night until the first soft bands of light illuminated the sky. That's what we would prefer to use our imagination on. Not on bloated corpses in mud so deep you could drown in it.

There's an old story in my family. About the war. How, when the German troops got closer to Douaumont and everyone began to panic, many people left in the dead of night. Just up and left with what they could carry. My family stayed. My grandparents, they stayed. For a while, at least. And my grandfather, he was a very smart man. He looked around and he saw the chaos. The Germans were taking everything! He knew food would be scarce. It would be the first thing to go. So what he did—what he did was he took sacks of grain, and in the middle of the night, he and my father—just a boy at the time—they loaded a cart up with them and hauled them out to the forest, and they buried them. It took all night. Dug the hole and dumped the sacks in. Just in case they needed them later.

But they never went back for them. They ended up leaving too. Everyone did. The whole village disappeared. It was destroyed, and they never rebuilt it. My family did move back, but they moved to Reims.

I still think about those sacks of grain. All these démineurs, digging every day. I mean, I know the sacks are gone. Disintegrated into the earth. Of course. But still, I find myself wondering . . . what else might they find out there? What else is waiting to be found? What other secrets does that earth hold?

War is the only violent phenomenon I know of that attracts man over and over again. It pulls us in. Car crash. Plane crash. Factory explosion. Nobody wishes they were a part of those. Nobody says, *Gee, I wish I'd gotten a chance to be a part of that catastrophe*. But declare war? They come flooding down to the recruiting stations in droves. Men will grow old and hold a lifetime of regret that they didn't go. There are more anti-war novels, memoirs, films, paintings, and cultural artifacts of all kinds than anyone knows what to do with. Each one is almost identical and can be boiled down to a tagline of "War bad, make me sad." Yet everyone keeps going to the war whenever it comes.

There's a project they're working on at the Imperial War Museum in London. It should be ready in time for an exhibit in 2018 to commemorate the centenary anniversary of the end of the war. See, no one knows what the war sounded like. Only novel recording techniques existed at the time, none of which could be carried to the battlefield. All we have are images. The closest thing we have to audio recordings are some sound ranging film strips—a type of rudimentary seismograph—that captured the vibrations of the artillery fire through the ground.

This exhibit revolves around a short strip of old film. But there are no images on it, just six scratchy lines. Imagine a seismograph for an earthquake but older and more brittle. It's a relic of what they called "sound ranging." They buried oil drums underground and ran crude microphones that captured any disturbances in the earth caused by sound waves through which a needle scratched out waves on rolling film in the form of these lines. So you can't hear it, but you can see the sounds of war. Heavy artillery, explosions.

This particular bit of film captures the moment the armistice went into effect on November 11, 1918, at exactly 11:00 a.m. The frenzied six lines between the tracks of sprocket holes jump erratically on black-gray gradient until exactly 11:00 a.m., at which point, the lines instantly become straight and even. Silence. It's expected to attract millions of visitors. The moment the guns went quiet, or rather, the moment the war ended.

We want so badly to believe there is a narrative arc where the war just ends. Proof that you might be able to just turn war off. *War.* What a tiny word. Three letters. But war is only a beginning with no middle and no end. War silences but it also amplifies. War obliterates but it also creates. It echoes forever in the minds of those who have experienced it, settling into their cells until it is as much a part of them as any other piece. It carries through the bloodline, it carries through the generations. War is much more than what a three-letter word can contain.

PART III

TO THE MEMORY OF WATER

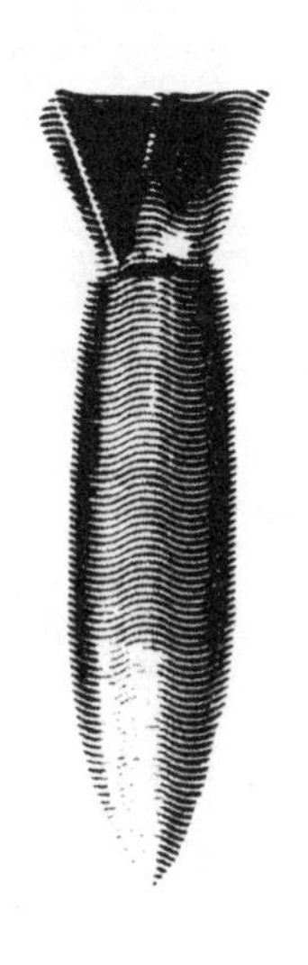

The Souls

ON DAYS he has the strength, Ferrand Martin goes for walks. Usually in the morning. Not anywhere in particular. A nice, leisurely two or three hours. Aimless walks have always seemed something widowed old men did when he was younger. But now, things are different.

These walks are always solitary, and he never has any real destination. He stops at a few different places, a café and a corner store, where he will talk with townsfolk and exchange some pleasantries. Every now and again, he will spend some time watching the trains come and go at the station. And he collects trash. He picks up piece after piece of trash with a mechanical claw trash picker he bought at a hardware store. Mostly in the parks, around the trash cans and underneath the cement Ping-Pong tables covered in graffiti both illegible and phallic, but some days on the streets too. There is so much to clean up.

Everyone wonders where the man with the claw lives. They speculate. They fantasize. They let their imaginations run wild. Maybe he squats in one of the abandoned pillboxes around Fort Souville or he camps out in the woods behind the ossuary—many claim to have seen a shadowy figure walking among the tombstones late at night. They are all wrong. We know where he lives, we know everything.

We came here one miserable year very long ago—former cobblers, ragpickers, wool merchants, laborers, metal polish factory workers, night watchmen, Limousin stonemasons—and we never left. They dropped shell after shell, which walked their way across the land like footfalls from invisible giants and snuffed us out. No longer able to distinguish friend from foe, they stacked us in spindly piles until we dwarfed the black-robed priests who stood by, solemn-eyed and quiet. They stacked us until those piles slumped and buckled and threatened to come crashing down. They constructed makeshift vaults under a clapboard building with crooked signs where the wind whistled through the thin walls. The wind swept across the open expanse, unimpeded. Where there were once great forests, there were only endless stretches of sodden clay and silent polished black cannons, all barrels pointed skyward.

Our friends returned home; we stayed. They carried us in fragments, a slouching procession of changed men bent forward under the burden of memory. Forever the same age. Forever our last conversation, our last cigarette, our last joke, our last, our last, our last. They returned to become husbands and fathers, rich and destitute, landowners and vagabonds, roaming the city, pulling the levers of vending machines for change. They grew older; we stayed the same, petrified in silver tones in a frame on the corner of a mantel and, eventually, in the trunks of forgotten corners in attics all over the country.

Memory fails us. Words fail us. Promises failed us. The church failed us. Our priests failed us. The world failed us. God failed us. Our boots failed us. Our coats failed us. Helmets failed to stop bullets. Bandages failed to stanch the bleeding. Never victims, but not heroes either.

We notice things no one else does, we who have lain in the ground a century while the world runs around in its daily shuffles from here to there. We see it all. We watch as the man picks up a piece of trash with his mechanical claw appendage and drops it into a small garbage bag he carries in his other hand. He grabs an empty soda cup, cracked and caved in along one side. And then a crumpled wax wrapper balled up against the curb. He even takes the time to pick up the cigarette butts, which require extra care because they are so small they barely fit in the pincers of his claw. He doesn't just grab a few things as he passes. He takes his time and carefully scans the spots he walks through for trash. What inspired the man with the claw to begin collecting trash? A small protest, perhaps? No one knows the answer, but it is a deliberate and time-consuming process he performs for the community at no one's request. In many ways, life for the man with the claw continues on virtually unchanged after his treatment. It is perplexing how utterly normal everyday life insists on remaining. There is the pain, of course. But there had been pain in one way or another before the illness, so that isn't much of a change. Who doesn't have some form of discomfort or irritation in their body past the age of twenty-two? Clues, differences, come in the small, almost unnoticeable details.

At the end of a long walk, back home with his claw hung by the door and his shoes kicked off and the sky darkening outside, he feels a quiet sense of accomplishment. A peculiar sensation, for sure. The garbage bins all over town are a little fuller because of him, and while he certainly doesn't expect any recognition for his actions, he can go to bed that night knowing his town, this ancient fortress city, is at least a little cleaner than it was when he stepped outside his front door that day.

What was the first piece? A Styrofoam soda cup, the worst kind of trash there is. Takes a millennium to degrade, and it is almost impossible to destroy. It only crumbles into smaller and smaller pieces that at some point just become the texture of the ground. There are very few things less natural than Styrofoam. The longer it sits, the more damage it causes. It can sit so long that it leeches into the water tables.

From above, he can see inside this discarded soda cup. Whatever it had once contained has leaked and dried, leaving behind a sticky residue that attracts a dark layer of fuzzy filth that both repulses him and drives him to action. The next natural step, of course, is removal. He bends down and picks up the cup without a second thought. There is probably a garbage bin a few feet away. The man with the claw grumbles to himself about the inconsiderateness of the average person, and how difficult is it to just walk to the garbage bins? They are literally everywhere. We imagine that immediately after, he notices, with an unpleasant realization, that his hand is now coated in that same sticky residue. Enter the claw. He can now pick up pieces of trash with ease, without having to actually touch them or even bend over. Never again will his hands feel violated and soiled by someone else's lazy decision.

The claw makes it too easy to do something about the trash, and so he collects more. In picking up various bits and pieces from the sidewalks, bushes, and gutters, the man with the claw is beginning to see Verdun in a new light. Even after all these years, he still learns new things about the city. Like, for instance, one might think that Gauloises is the most popular brand of cigarettes at the moment, given the number he finds every trip. But that probably isn't the case. Who smokes Gauloises anymore? Or maybe the lesson is that people who buy those cigarettes are the biggest litterbugs. We doubt he ever counts the pieces, nor does he keep any type of log about what types of things he is tossing, but he finds himself drawing conclusions based off what is left behind in the streets. There are, he comes to believe, ways to tell what has been dropped by accident and what was intentionally dropped by someone who couldn't care less.

*

One day, the man with the claw blew his life to bits. Long before his illness, long before the forced retirement, when he was still a young man but old enough to know better. No one saw it happen. He didn't mean to. He was out in the woods with his daughter, woven baskets dangling from their arms, picking mushrooms. Just like his father had done with him when he was a boy. She carried with her a magnifying glass, a notebook, and a pencil. Martin took peeks in it every time they returned home. The pages were covered in meticulous, misspelled notes. Their baskets were full of morels and porcini. They were going to take those home, and Charisse would sauté them in thick slabs of butter and save the rest for hearty stews all winter. Then he turned his back for a moment and ignited history.

The incident occupied everyone's mind for weeks. Seven years old at the turn of the century. She wasn't alive during the battle. The Rouge had been declared and cordoned and cleaned for generations by the time she was born.

"Papa, j'ai tellement froid! Tellement *froid*!" she told him, her shivers felt through a coat too thin for the weather.

They had been out there all day and lost track of time. It was another hour's walk back, at least. The red splotches she always got when she was truly cold were coming out on her cheeks. It had rained recently, and the ground was wet, as were the sticks and bits of bark he'd gathered, but he was a man of resource and could find a way to start a fire at the bottom of the ocean. Just a small fire. Just some warmth before they walked back. Did he forget? Did he think, *Well, just this one time . . . Can't hurt*. Did he think at all? A mistake. No one makes a campfire on the battlefield. Everyone knows that.

The Rouge claimed his daughter all the same. It was like a sponge. The soil just drew her all up and soaked her in. They found almost nothing of her, besides a foot. Blown right out of the boot. The skin was thin, almost translucent, and torn in some places. The toenails, freshly trimmed. The skin around the ankle bunched up and folded to the heel, like a sock partially removed. He was untouched save for a piece of him, a very vital piece of his soul, which had been sheared off in the blast and will forever remain wedged in this exact moment:

They tear his hands away. Floating arms slip under his right shoulder and then his left. The wind sucks his voice away and into a vortex, with every sound leaving him in silence. The blood dries in cracked flakes on his hands and face.

His waking life is a hard shoulder against the locked door of the future. In some ways, Martin will forever be stuck here, frozen at this precise moment. Past love, there is no law. Past hope, there is no God.

The démineurs went out to inspect for more munitions, to make sure the area was safe. The rain impeded their search. Officials wanted to call it off, cordon the area and wait until the rain ceased, but the démineurs were not receptive. This was one of their own. To shorten their recovery operation was to admit loss, and they weren't ready for that. Where there is one, there are usually more. They came along the ridge line slowly. A single file. Four men spaced fifteen meters apart. The ground, uneven. Steady hands. Careful steps. Not there. Or there. Or there. But *there*. In each hand, a metal detector, swinging side to side. Smooth and balanced. Four separate metronomes, each moving to its own rhythm. A thin cloud of mist shrouded the group, obscuring their legs so that, from a distance, they appear to float—lost specters wandering toward the night.

The leader of their group strode out ahead, lacking any sign of fear or concern as he examined the area. His beard hung like icicles. The ground felt alive. Electric. Every step might be his last. Of course, the odds of stepping on one are very low. And it is true that the majority of them are dead. The *vast* majority. But would that make you feel better?

This was entirely different. They'd had the odd farmer lose a hand or have his bell rung. Those were grown men. A child? One they knew? Entirely different. Unthinkable.

All they found was her foot. That's it. Coroner had already left. The gendarmerie had already left. He had to carry that foot all the way back to the station. He felt the rhythm of the foot in its bag bouncing on his thigh. It swung from the front to his side like a twisting pendulum. The sound of the bag's fabric scraping against his trouser like a fluttering of cockroach wings colliding with each other. Every few minutes he readjusted it by untwisting it so it did not become tangled. It was just high enough that it missed his knee with each step. On one attempt to readjust it, he grabbed lower than he meant and he felt the foot inside. It surprised him, even though he had been carrying it for almost an hour at that point. He fought the urge to exclaim in disgust and swallowed his surprise. He must have flinched, but if anyone noticed, they didn't say a word. He imagined it growing rigid inside the bag, hardening and bloating with each passing moment.

There are just some days that stick with you in this job. Or to you. Like tar. You can't ever rid yourself of it entirely. It leaves a residue on you for the rest of your life.

The other men follow, more out of the fear of humiliation, of looking scared and weak, than out of concern for their well-being. No one wants to be humiliated. There won't be any more today. What has happened to Martin hasn't happened in years. It is a fluke. A random chance. Bad luck.

In the city, the buildings still show the war. Chunks of walls missing where shrapnel sprayed. But in the rural areas, it is always different. The land slopes and waves, and at first glance, it just looks like rolling hills. Rolling hills unlike any you've ever seen before. Dramatic and steep with sudden drop-aways that don't feel quite natural the longer you look at them. But rolling hills nonetheless.

In fact, they are craters. Big bombs vaporized human bodies into atoms and made crying babies of grown men along with these craters. It is a sea. A vast sea calmly rising and falling to the gravitational pull of the moon. The way the landscape has adapted is serene. The deepest craters have filled with water to become ponds. Little things swim and live in there now. The dry ones are carpeted with delicate, little wildflowers. But if you look at it too long, stare too deeply, you might find your vision clouding over from the deafening silence of the place where a million souls were torn apart. Every once in a while, lightning strikes a field and causes a buried shell to detonate. The buildings in the city wear their wounds with a certain permanence. *Look at me. See where I have been. See what they have done to me. Bear witness to my pain, to my attempted destruction.* The forests quit that long ago. Instead, they say, *This is me. This is who I am. You can be like this too. We can be whole again.*

So, one day, the man with the claw blows his life to bits. It is like any other day. So plain as to be boring. No one thinks anything of the morning. There is nothing about it to suggest it would be anything other than a boring Tuesday. Just like yesterday. So boring and normal that it is possible to forget what happened out here a century prior, what we are all sitting on top of.

It is so quiet. That's what everyone will remember. How quiet of a day it is. And then the sky splits open, or it seems to split open. Quiet, and then an open gash in the clouds like a great boulder being split in two. Quiet, and then everyone remembers exactly where it is we are in this world.

All cities have their characters. The ones who are ubiquitous fixtures but remains distant mysteries. We see them but never interact. An interaction might ruin our ideas of them. Who we think they are. He looks older than he actually is and appears very frail. He tells us little bits and pieces, but we never ask him for them.

*

The forest around Verdun is envied by mushroom enthusiasts all over the county. Always full. Bursting with luxuriant variety in a part of the world where some places still lack floral growth due to the level of toxic chemicals in the soils.

These are the jobs they are called out to. Not just when the shells failed to do what they were made for and are found so many years later. But when a bomb does its job. They come out and assess the wreckage. Nothing to be done. The damage has already occurred. The death of Martin's daughter is one of those moments where the job just means standing there and absorbing all the trauma into that innermost part of your soul like a beam of radiation. No way to fix this situation. Their task is to witness the horror. Not that any of them can remember reading that in the job description. Almost like it is their fault: *You should have prevented this. Isn't this the whole point of your job? To prevent stuff like this from happening? Clean it up. This is your mess.*

7

Martin awakes in the tangled, twisted mess of his bedcovers. The ink-blue night coats his bedroom's windowpane. Disorientation grips him for a brief moment—the peculiar sensation of feeling lost in one's own bed, feeling foreign in the most familiar place. He reaches for a glass of water on the bedside table. Can't find it. Did he leave it there last night? He thinks he did. The sweat dampens the pillow under his head. He turns one way, then another. No position offers relief or comfort. He twists the sheet fabric in his hands and focuses on the tension.

Slowly, the world settles around him. And then comes the pain. Everywhere. His chest, his stomach, his legs, his head. He has never in his life known pain like this before, somehow worse than the treatment. It radiates from inside his bones. Things inside him feel swollen and bloated, and there's not enough space. He can sense it. Hiding. Growing. Everywhere, the sense of increasing pressure. He scratches his arms and then his legs. His skin burns with itching.

There are other things too.

Light feels harsher. Rooms are always a little too cold. Food has lost all appeal. He always feels just a little nauseated, like he's been reading in the back seat of a car on a long drive. And illness has a smell. Everything smells unwashed and soiled. It contaminates every fabric, every mattress and pillow. Infection. But what affects him most is the realization that he's shrinking. It started with his sleeves. One morning, Martin slipped on a shirt, a shirt he has had for years, and the sleeves felt a little longer than they did the last time he wore it. Without a thought, Martin rolled them back once and started his day. It was two or three weeks before he had to roll them back twice. Two months later, it took four rolls before the fabric was out of his way. Same shirt. Same body. Different fit.

The world around him is exactly the same in the most brutally mundane ways, and he can see that those mundane moments are absolutely beautiful now. All these boring little precious moments. But he is shrinking. His physical existence continues to diminish, and he doesn't even feel it. It's entirely separate from the pain and nausea and exhaustion, yet on some level, he knows they're all part of the same thing, but that's the logical side of things entirely separate from his physical being. It's only when he looks down on yet another normal morning and discovers—but how? again?—that he must roll his shirtsleeves one more time than the day before in order to feel comfortable that he notices any real change.

The pain follows him into the bathroom. A look over his shoulder, catching sight of his hairless back in the wall-length mirror mounted beside the doorway. The broad expanse of his back has shrunk considerably. A moonscape, gnarled and pockmarked. He has a difficult time recognizing it as his own at this point. Alien terrain. He urinates in a stinging stream that burns so bad he stops several times. Another UTI.

He returns to bed and tries to sleep, but it will not come. A shadow shifts in one corner. Martin props himself on his arms and strains his eyes in the darkness. The lamp on his bedside table feels just out of reach. A dull pounding rises behind his eyes. His heart quickens, and a fine coat of sweat dampens the sheets. The night sweats come this way, sudden and swift, almost like they're annoyed with him. He has had the audacity to live another day, and the ache will not abide such gluttonous declarations. He loses the warmth absorbed in the sheets as he sits up. The cool air brings out gooseflesh on his bare arms and chest. The room remains silent and empty.

He braces himself and slowly swings one leg over the edge followed by the other. They sink to the floor in a slow arc that sends piercing jolts of electricity through his entire body. Martin sets both feet on the floor, the surface cool enough that it distracts him from the throbbing rebounding in his body. He grips the edge of the bed and closes his eyes. The ache recedes in quiet waves, and there is nothing for him to do but let it simmer.

Life is all about pauses now. The full weight of illness rests somewhere between his head and his heart. Somehow nowhere and everywhere at once.

These are my lungs. This is my heart. They are still mine. I am the same man.

"We may try an experimental study. There's one being conducted at Institut Curie right now," Dr. Corbin had offered.

Absolutely not. He would not even consider it. The mere thought of his chemotherapy treatment makes him shudder. Everything had been fine, relatively speaking, up until they started the treatment, and then it all got worse. And for what? Irreparable damage to the only body he had.

Meat suit. That was what Jules, an engineer on the oil rig, had called bodies. Meat suits. Jules was the exact type of oddball you expected to meet working on offshore oil rigs where you spent months at a time isolated from the rest of the world. He looked taller than he actually was, and he had a tattoo of a squid wrestling with a 1950s-style UFO in vibrant colors that took up most of his right shoulder and biceps. He had to be told to shower, but, oddly, his breath always smelled clean, even pleasant, a fact no one felt comfortable admitting. It was sweet and just faintly minty, no matter the time of day. He called everyone "baby," and when he wasn't on shift he spent most of his time in his bunk, donning headphones and listening to some sinister brand of heavy metal that some of the other crew members labeled Satanic. Martin did everything to avoid interacting with him. Early one evening Martin was smoking a cigarette down on the lowest level of the rig, one of the few places they were allowed to smoke, and staring over the railing to the sea below. A straight twenty-story drop. Even after years of those jobs, the sea still had a hypnotic effect on Martin. The water shimmered with light, and the nature of the light changed as the day progressed. On certain days, it was still and clear and he could see almost all the way to the seabed. Jules appeared beside him.

"You hear Caleb is telling everyone he seen a dinosaur tooth come up once? On some other rig he worked?" he asked Martin.

"Caleb is full of shit," said Martin, unfazed.

"He said it came right up through the separator, and he gave it to his son when he got back home."

"Sounds like a story he would tell," said Martin.

"Yeah, a bullshit story. He didn't give his son no tooth. We're tapped into the reservoir *under* the rock. That's the wrong layer to be looking in."

They stood there smoking and gazing down at the water below.

"They all came out tonight, haven't they?" Jules said.

A crew of welders moved from spot to spot, completing whatever task list was lined up for the day. Above them, the sharks. They swam lazily in circles, noting the movements of the divers beneath them. Martin did not respond and instead took a drag of his cigarette.

"Ah, they're harmless. They are not stalking prey. They've never once attacked. They don't even seem that interested. Not from up above or from down below. They are just there. Must be like watching TV for them,"

"We're in their living room. They're kind hosts. If we are polite, they will stay that way," Martin said, and flicked the cigarette over the railing.

"Meat suits, baby. That's all we are. Meat suits suspended on stalks of calcium with a little bit of electricity to make it jiggle," Jules called after him as he climbed the stairs back to the control room.

All that experience had taught him was you only get one meat suit, and while it might be hard to find where the soul fit into that meat suit, he suspected it was somewhere in the avenues where the electricity flowed from cell to cell and made things jiggle. No meat suit lasts forever, but what was the sense in destroying yours just to extend it a few painful years? No, no to the bone marrow transplants, the pills in translucent orange bottles with black box warning labels, the experimental treatments, all of it. No.

The world stops spinning. It's the dead part of the night. The brief pause between everything that was and will be. Tonight, his heart is working even harder. Beating loud and clear in his ears, thrumming against the walls of his chest, pressing the limits of his ribs. He dares not look at the clock on his bedside table. What would be the use? He has been here before. He knows there is only one way out of this hellscape, and that's through sheer force of will. Grit and determination. He's been through worse. Many times, in fact. In another few hours, the visiting nurse will stop by to check in on him—monitor his vitals, administer a few meds. He releases a deep exhale like a wave recoiling from the shore.

Martin grew up on a farm outside of Nantes, and at the end of harvest, all the grain silos would be emptied, their contents carried off for sale to make room for next season's haul. Martin used to climb the ladder on the outer wall all the way to the very top and peer through the narrow hatch on the dome. The space seemed infinite. He always felt he was staring into a shaft that went to the center of the earth. Fine, almost invisible splinters of grain would float into his nose and make him sneeze. They gave the abyss a silty appearance. Light could not penetrate it. It refracted and scattered and then was swallowed whole. Such a powerful darkness, where light could not survive. It held its own gravity. And if he stayed there for too long, he began to get the sensation that he was being pulled into it. Grabbed by it—its grip tar-like and firm. He felt attracted to it while knowing this darkness meant him harm.

The same darkness holds him now. The same silky-black ether that renders him immobile. Paralyzed. Martin stands and walks to the mirror. He looks at his reflection and into his face, but he doesn't believe he is really seeing himself. This man wears a mask, and there's a part of him that wants to reach out and lift it, but the time for revelation is long past. There are only so many chances a person gets at honesty before they settle into themselves.

Where does disease begin? In the body, of course, but where? It begins with a single cell. It develops and spreads to the others. Could it really be that simple? Could an entire life come down to something as fragile as a single cell? Out of the corner of his eye, a shadow moves again. Martin looks out the window. A simple courtyard boxed in by a wooden plank fence that will need to be replaced in another year or so. Odds of him being here at that time? Not very high. Leave that job for whoever moves in after. He makes his way out of the bedroom to the back door, where he dons his coat and leaves the mechanical claw hanging from its hook.

It's a cold night, much colder than he was expecting, and he immediately shivers in the open doorway. He cuts a striking figure against the seafoam walls of the house. Barefoot and shirtless, he continues forward, slowly. He gasps involuntarily, and his breath escapes in large clouds.

He must pause for a brief moment before continuing forward, slower and more steadily. The shadows surround him, and everything is utterly silent.

"Charisse!" he calls out, desperation weighing down his voice.

"Hush!" comes an immediate response.

Martin flinches and recoils from the voice. But he sees no one in the direction it came from.

"Get down before you get yourself killed!"

Martin lowers himself to one knee and places a hand on the cool pavement to keep his balance. He cannot locate the origin of the voice. The dizziness returns. It washes over him, and he places his other hand on the ground to keep from falling over. His heartbeat crowds his mind, and he closes his eyes.

When he reopens them, the shadows return. The bayonet emerges first. And then the Lebel rifle to which it is fixed. And finally, the man. A French soldier. His capote waistcoat, stiff and caked with mud under the crisscross of his harness with his ammo pouches and canteen. His Adrian helmet, dented, the unmistakable flaming grenade infantry insignia stamped across the front. He approaches Martin slowly and views him with suspicion.

"Come," says the soldier, and waves a hand.

Martin follows him, keeping his head low, and steps carefully, almost the exact spot where the soldier steps. They come to a minor embankment. The soldier peers cautiously over the edge. A thin band of moonlight illuminates his face just below the lip of his helmet. Martin can't tell his age. He might be in his early twenties, but the longer he studies the soldier's face, the less certain he becomes. He has a thick, unruly mustache and a day's growth of stubble on his cheeks. Fierce eyes, haggard at the edges, scan whatever lies beyond the embankment. He could be thirty, maybe even older.

"Do you hear that?" the soldier asks.

"No."

"He's still out there. He's still alive. I need to get him."

Martin strains his ears. A light wind catches in the branches around them. "I hear nothing."

"He's out there."

"What is your name?"

The soldier does not reply.

"Are you Augustine? Is your name Augustine?"

"He's out there. I must get him."

"I am sorry," Martin says to the soldier, "do you hear me? Please, forgive me."

"He's still out there," says the soldier. "Cover me."

There's a wild look about him, and it's mostly in the way he moves—careful but sleek, almost insect-like. Without another word, he slinks up the embankment and crawls so quietly it is like he is part of the earth, and then he is gone.

"No!" Martin cries, and reaches for him, but a jolt of pain runs through his body, and he slides down the embankment, the dirt and grit scraping his face and hands. A moan escapes him, and he comes to rest at the lowest point.

His lungs try to keep up. Martin lies there panting. How does every little thing make him so tired now? The only thing he longs for in this moment is to be back in his bed. Martin pushes himself up, and the ridge of something hard and curved digs into his palm. He flinches, rolls onto his side. There it is. Right underneath him. Unmistakable. A shell. The cold seeps a little deeper and large clouds escape his mouth, momentarily obscuring his view of the rim. Martin claws at the clay and the bits of grass and shredded leaves around the shell, and his fingers go numb. He can feel the dirt compacting underneath his fingernails until one gives way under the pressure. It stings and throbs, but he keeps going, the pain a minor inconvenience. The sandy soil coats his wound, and whatever blood flows from the nail bed mixes with the earth, all the pebbles and crushed snail shells and fragments of shrapnel. Martin claws until his arms ache, until his breath leaves his body in exasperated gusts that wash over the now mostly exposed moineau en colère—another 75mm French one—like a blessing from a martyred saint. His frozen breaths dissipate, and he kneels there for a moment, his hands curled from the exhaustion, settled in his lap staining his pajama pants. A whole artillery shell. He must call it in.

Martin looks up and around and realizes he's wandered much farther from home than he thought. *Where am I?* All he can see are trees. He can't leave it. He will never find his way back here. No chance. He's not even sure he can stand up and look around without falling. And if he does manage to stay upright, there's no way he's kneeling back down for this tortue sinister. Martin wraps his trembling hands around the body and lifts it one attempt. For a moment he falters, his legs struggle, and he teeters back and forth, the newly freed shell cradled in his arms. There's no going back now. In the distance, off to his left, he sees light. Streetlamps? A road? It's a start. He takes one step and then another and another.

8

If a démineur is killed retrieving a shell that was fired with malicious intent a century ago, during a war he wasn't alive for, let alone a combatant, should he be included in the final casualty count for the battle? This question, a conundrum worthy of investigation, has occupied Hugo's mind for the better part of a week. An accident. No one's fault, really. These things happen. Yannick Basille, after only eleven months in service as a démineur, died when a shell spontaneously exploded in one of the vaults at the depot. The first death in over a decade, according to the département.

Live by the sword . . .

It's so very strange to him to risk life and limb without any potential for reward or recognition. Something. Anything. None of them will see this job completed in their lifetimes, not even close. They show up day after day for an entire career—a lifetime—of drudgery and backbreaking work. For what? Very, very strange.

The creases under his eyes tell Hugo that, yes, he is becoming a father again and, yes, this will change him again and, yes, it will take some things from him. Many things. The most immediate thing so far being sleep. He has not slept in over a week. Neither has Emmanuel.

Which is why he is behind the wheel of his Reneault Espace, driving around the outskirts of Verdun at eleven thirty on a Wednesday night, when he has to be up at five for a meeting in Reims at eight.

Emmanuel lets out a disgruntled cry from his car seat.

"Fais dodo, Colas mon p'tit frère," Hugo sings with his eyes on the rearview mirror.

He wants to turn around and go home. But Emmanuel is so close to sleep. So close. Tucked into his car seat, Hugo can see his half-closed eyelids in the rearview mirror. They grow heavier by the second. Soft murmurs escape him.

Hugo sings softly, just above a whisper. It isn't the words or even the melody but rather the way he sings that has the effect. His voice sounds like the last faded thought before sleep arrives.

He is becoming a father. *Becoming*. It is not an instant but a progression. The same way the changes happen so quickly in these early months. Emmanuel goes to sleep one way and wakes up another person. The photos on Hugo's phone look like there are five different babies. There had been an immediate difference in his mood at the moment Emmanuel was born, of course. Holding Emmanuel for the first time bathed in the fluorescent delivery room lights, Hugo was willing to give up anything, fight for everything, kill anyone who came between him and the delicate bundle of life in his arms without a second thought. This had happened the first time with Éloïse as well. Becoming a father. Unlocking chambers of his heart he hadn't known existed. All of that. Which was true. Undoubtedly. But it doesn't last. This is also what happened last time. Time has a way of quieting those long-enduring emotions. Once the rush wears off, once the disorienting shuffle of bringing a new child home calms down and returns to some level of normalcy, there comes the question that has haunted him for most of his life. So, what now?

The Département du Déminage must continue on as well. Although without Ferrand Martin, things appear to move at a different pace, which is to say his absence is felt within the département. In this case, instead of things slowing down, they actually speed up. "It is not a race," Ferrand would tell them daily while they went from site to site, methodically evaluating each piece of ordnance. This was one of his many sayings. "We've got all day. There's no prize for getting back first in a twelve-hour shift when you have another ten hours to go." Now they're down two démineurs. Henri has been promoted to supervisor. Hugo stopped by yesterday to see how everyone was doing.

According to Henri, they had just finished cataloging a recent deposit of mixed munitions—several 75mm, a few 105mm, HE, shrapnel shells, grenades, and the like—and Basille was in the vault alone. Henri had just walked out mere seconds before. Then, from nowhere and everywhere, a tug on a great cosmic zipper peeled away the air's atoms from each other. The explosion throttled everyone. The shrapnel was contained to the vault. But the blast wave racked every human body in the building with a pressure none of them had experienced before. It stretched their brain matter like putty for an instant, rearranging millions of neurons, before it all snapped back into place. Barbeaux, whose mouth happened to be closed at the exact moment of the explosion, stumbled around, nose bleeding profusely, struggling to breathe with a collapsed lung. Several alarms sounded, not that any of them could hear—they were all temporarily deaf. Henri ruptured an eardrum. All these moments amounted to a chaotic scene: the whole crew stumbling around in a thick cloud of dust with a faint pink hue that clogged their eyes and choked their lungs.

What survived the blast proved more surprising than what was destroyed. The door to the vault, buckled outward and knocked from its track. A single exposed light bulb swung pendulum-like from the ceiling, still operational. But Basille? He had been all but vaporized. A celestial snap of the fingers, and man and shell vanished. Abruptly ripped from existence. The only things left were several goopy chunks of a piercing yellow red that had to be scraped from the walls—the organic stuff that makes us all, yet we are unable to recognize by sight.

"We thought the whole roof was about to cave for one terrifying moment," Henri admitted, unemotional. "I swear, they really knew what they were doing when they built these places."

"But you lived," Hugo said.

"Yes," said Henri, and twisted a finger in his ear.

Vaporized—as in, literally made into vapors. Henri mentioned several times that the pink hue in the air lasted for days. The single bulb was still lit as Hugo stood there in the midst of the vault listening to Henri recount the incident. A silty haze hung in the air and he squinted into it, and it occurred to him it might, in fact, be the same flotsam from the detonation. Fine particles of dust swirled around his head. Might this be . . . Could it be . . . He realized he was trying to hold his breath. He began to take short, sharp breaths through his nose, keeping his mouth shut tight.

Feeling especially bold, he asked a question or two.

"Did it hurt?"

"It was weird. I saw it before I heard it. Flash. Crack. In that order. Felt the sound of the explosion more than I heard it, if that makes any sense. He was gone. Wild," said Henri, standing in the open doorway.

"What was the last thing you thought of? Do you remember?" he asked.

"No. Not really. I reverted back to Wolof, talking a mile a minute. I couldn't speak anything but Wolof for the following few hours after that," Henri said, shaking his head and laughing. "There wasn't much of a thought. No specific memory or person, at least. I thought in a moment like that I'd think of my kids, my wife, my mom. No, nothing like that. It was more of an intense feeling. A bold swath of neon red. Burning. There was nothing else in my mind but that vibrant color."

Hugo noticed a spot on the floor. He crouched to study it more closely. They aren't imprints so much as terminal scuff marks. The slate is irreversibly altered. That much is certain. But it is hard to say exactly how.

"What is this? Slate?" he asked.

"No, it's concrete. A special type of concrete they made back in the day. Napoleon times. Made for reinforcing military structures," Henri said.

Hugo immediately comes out of his memory as he makes the final turn onto his road, a narrow, quiet country lane, the kind of road where you hardly ever pass another person, especially at this late hour. He brings his vehicle to a slow stop. Emmanuel's soft, whistling snores can just be heard over his idling engine. The dregs of an early snowfall encrust their short driveway and the streets beyond. There, in the milky beams of his headlights, is a baby-blue Citroën DS parked right outside his driveway. The lights in his house are all dark save their bedroom light on the second floor. He checks his phone. Nothing. The Citroën remains parked, engine and lights off, the windows too dark to tell if anyone is inside.

Odd place for an ambush. He can't imagine Gabriel is trying to surprise him by parking right in front of his driveway. His headlights are on, which means Gabriel can't tell it's him at the moment and won't be able to until he's pulling into the driveway. *A strange, strange bet you've placed, my old friend,* he thinks.

Unless . . .

Unless Gabriel is already inside. Would he be that bold? No, he wouldn't. What sense would that make? Blow the whole affair up and run amok of everyone's lives? That's not how men handle things. You come to him directly, meet him out in the open on neutral ground. You don't walk up to his front door like a child seeing if his friend can come out to play.

Hugo's phone rings. He pulls it from his jacket pocket. Léa. Yes, yes, he is certainly between two fires. What to do.

He lets up on the brake and rolls forward. His phone continues to ring until it goes to voicemail, which is immediately followed by a text and then another phone call. He allows it to ring again and drives right past his house. Back on the main road, he makes a turn that will take him through a stretch of forest and put him out near the ossuary in about twenty-five minutes. Buy himself some time. He needs to think. Another text pings, and he switches his ringer to silent.

"Fais dodo, Colas mon p'tit frère. Fais dodo, t'auras du lolo," Hugo sings quietly.

The gentle hum of the truck's engine has a sedative effect on the boy unlike any other thing Hugo has found so far. It is the only thing that seems to work. Drop him into his car seat with his stuffed giraffe and head out onto the road. The car feels like an extension of Hugo's body. The seat forms perfectly to his frame. The wheel and gear shift are some vital organ system he only recently became aware of. In truth, he doesn't mind not sleeping. He has always had the ability to go for long stretches without sleep. He has a motor in his brain, just behind his eyes, that never stops humming. He gets sleep when he needs it.

Accidents are accumulations of smaller things. Many, many little careless decisions. He thinks about the marks on the concrete again. They just looked like two minor dents in the floor. The flotsam, Henri in the doorway. The empty vault had a stale odor that made him want to pull his shirt over his nose.

Hugo looked closer. A pair of boot prints. An imprint set into the concrete. Blackened around the edges.

When Hugo was a boy, the city redid the street outside his home. Men in coveralls came and ripped up the road. Trucks and shovels and jackhammers broke the hard surface to pieces like a ginger cookie and carried it all away as though it had never been there in the first place. But then they returned.

A different crew. Different coveralls. Same attitude. They laid the new road. A large pot on wheels that rumbled and turned around and around. The mixture that spilled from its mouth steamed sulfurous and toxic. Hugo watched the crew spread it and smooth it with screeds held by three men at a time. Later, after it cooled, but before it hardened, his mother took him to the edge.

"Be careful, don't step there," she said.

He kneeled down and examined its surface. Just like a fresh snowfall, soft and moldable. His mother took his hand and pressed it to the fresh asphalt, still warm. When he pulled his hand away, the print left behind was almost perfect. Maybe a little wider, a tiny bit cartoonish, but a perfect replica. A stark outline pressed into the surface of the new road.

But these imprints were somehow different. They weren't gentle the way he remembered that handprint. The curves were not smooth or natural, like they were meant to be there. The set of footprints was odd and out of place. Dark and violent. Cut into the stone. Forced into their permanence the way a wound forces itself into the body. Raw.

It was interesting, though. Those footprints and their permanence. Hugo stared at them a long time. Part of him figured they were just scuff marks on the floor. A trick of the light. But the longer he stared at the dents, the more details he began to notice. The way the edge of the dent curved perfectly in the shape of a boot heel. And how the bottom of the dent rippled in striations, not unlike the lugs of the work boots the démineurs wore. Could easily be a size 10. He stood. Placed his own booted foot in the dent. Almost a perfect match. Snug and fit.

He smiled and then laughed softly. The funniest part to him: These dents would be here longer than any of the rest of them. These dents would outlast them all. How depressing was that? Hugo knelt down and then crouched farther onto his hands. He lowered his face closer to the marks.

An infinitely held breath.

On his way out he noticed someone had taken the time to engrave a few words in the wall:

Here stood a man

For a moment

For eternity

"Hey, every man sees noon at his own doorstep. We were all having a moment. In the end, we all have to find our own way to move on," said Henri, and then he turned and left.

Hugo picks up his cell phone. Now there's a missed call from Camille. *Oh, Camille. You fool.* The glide of the steering wheel over the long stretches of farm roads, smooth and pleasing. The speed limits in their red circles, and the blinking electric-blue lights of the crosswalks. Each roundabout propels him a little farther, with each one he gains momentum. It has just enough resistance to make him feel like he is moving against a force much larger than himself but is easy enough that he feels like he is accomplishing something. It feels nice and satisfying in the same way the lace of his mother's dress had felt when he was just a boy and he would run his hand over it, at dinner, in church, on the train ride into town. Seated under the fan in the pew at the small service every Sunday, he would run his hand over the lace while the priest spoke of Saul struck blind on the road to Damascus and the scales that fell from his eyes after Ananias laid his hands upon him, until his mother reached down and grabbed his hand. She held it still against the lace, and his attention would turn elsewhere, usually to the fan above and the way the blades were a little loose, and underneath the priest's quiet and steady voice, he could hear the rattle they made as they spun around and around and around.

More text messages. He thinks about reading them, lifts the phone, then decides against it and puts it back in the cupholder.

There are moments throughout the day when he will sit and count the few hours he has slept and wonder how he is still able to function. On certain days, he wonders why he sleeps at all. When did he sleep? Twenty minutes here, a sweet half hour there. The scarcity of it becomes the mind's obsession. It is difficult to think of anything else. Exhaustion is a special kind of high. It brings a particular type of aching to the body unlike any wine or spirit he has ever had.

Hugo eases the wheel to the right, and they take a turn onto the main road into town.

All the long-term health effects that long-term sleep deprivation may have on the brain meander through his mind. But it can't be that bad. This is all very common for babies and their parents, from what he understands. If it were really that bad, he would have heard of more people dying or going blind or sinking into diaper-clad dementia. It couldn't be that bad. Just one of those things.

There is a utility box on the first block when they reach town, and spray-painted on it is a crude drawing of a penis. It has been there a year. No one has done anything to remove it. There is another attempt beside the first penis, but it is rushed and lacking the same character and precision of the first one. The artist must have hurried under duress of being discovered. The only real explanation. Hugo might have found it funny—no, he definitely would have found it funny—a few years ago. He would have laughed. What's funnier than a crudely drawn penis? It always serves as the first marker that they have moved once again back into the modern world. Hugo doesn't mind modernity so much. There is something comforting in this suburban existence: the golden sulfurous glow of the McDonald's arches on the corner, the Supeco's darkened signage and empty parking lot, the heavy canvas curtains pulled down over the front of the smaller shops, and the clanging of church bells every hour.

This world is so far away from the one he came from, and yet it feels something like home. About as much as any other place could be called home. Not the people or the town or the land itself, but what they have created here. Emmanuel. The cool calmness of the late autumn nights. Passing the empty planting fields that speed by their window in a blur. He loves the way the fields erupt on either side right after they cross the river. It is like crossing some threshold into another time, an immediate step into another era. The fields out here bear no resemblance to the petrified earth of the Rouge. They contain no trace of the ten million shells dropped or the hundreds of thousands of soldiers who killed one another for ten months because someone told them to.

He passes over the Canal de·l'Est and makes a left onto Allée des Wées. It is a nice, quiet road that keeps them out of town just a little bit longer. Hardly a car in sight. Many of the houses dark. They pass the darkened bungalows nestled in the crooks of the road, and he imagines the people deep in sleep inside. It's the same route every trip. It works. Before they are even halfway through, Emmanuel is fast asleep.

Such a strange little town. In Lyon, no one ever went to sleep. It simmered after the night came and the little outer neighborhoods went dark, the side streets erased momentarily for a few hours. But the city kept breathing every hour of the night. It is hard to imagine a town where things just stop for the night. *Where do they all go?* Hugo thinks. *Do they all really just get in bed and turn the lights out? Climb in between the sheets and shut their eyes until dawn?* Something about it seems so odd.

At another roundabout, he eases his foot off the gas and hovers above the brake. The car seems to fit into a groove that follows the bend around smoothly. The second turn takes him on the last stretch of road before he crosses once more over the Meuse and into his neighborhood. He checks the rearview mirror. Sure enough, Emmanuel is out. Eyes closed. His mouth open just slightly. Hugo immediately thinks of the baby Jesus in a manger, then laughs to himself. Doesn't every parent look at their child and think of baby Jesus?

As his turnoff approaches, he continues on. No reason. It's almost like someone else is in control for a moment. Just one of those things. Hugo takes the next turn instead, which sends him northeast, away from Verdun and even farther from his home. At the next opportunity, he bears right onto a dirt road with the vague notion that he will use it to make a U-turn, but the road is too narrow. It is an unpaved farm road, and there are now lights other than his headlights, which seem dimmer in the dark countryside.

Hugo pulls to the side and gets out. He opens the back door, and a stuffed giraffe tumbles from the car seat and lands at his feet. Emmanuel remains asleep, the deepest kind. Hugo bends down on a knee and picks the giraffe off the wet ground. He places it back on Emmanuel's lap and quietly closes the door and walks to the edge of the field. The folds of night consume everything. The air, heavy with the scent of burnt wood from cooling fireplaces all over the commune. The darkest time of night. Ink in water. Impossible to separate. It touches everything, and at this time of night the boundaries between fact and memory, history and now, all feel blurred. Hugo holds his hand out in front of him and notices all the ways his skin blends with the night and the ways it differs. Because most people fear the darkness.

In the distance, Hugo sees movement. He lowers his hand. A figure moves slowly along the road before him, hunched and staggering. Hugo turns and gets back in his car. He follows the road until he sees that it is, in fact, a man hobbling along the shoulder of the road by himself. He presses the accelerator. They approach the bend in the road, and the figure takes shape. An old man, but something so familiar about him. He clutches an object—a vase or a sculpture or . . . one of the artillery rounds?—to his chest and doesn't acknowledge them, and then they are past. He dares not shout. He cannot wake Emmanuel. There is no one else in sight. Just a lone man Hugo is almost certain he knows from somewhere, from some other time in his life, but he cannot place him. He's tempted to turn around but decides against it. There's no telling what kind of weirdo he might be, wandering around with strange objects at this hour. Someone else will notice that bizarre man and give the authorities a call.

This is the dangerous time of night. The moment he is most at risk of drifting off. Right before the dawn. When he is moving, he is fine. But if he stops too long and stays stationary, he might fall asleep. That would be incredibly bad. To run off the road and be discovered slumped over the wheel with his infant son in the back. A drunkard. A common street urchin. Out this late with his sleeping child. All-around suspicious.

The first turn puts them on the road toward the city. A left turn toward Dugny, straight through the roundabout and across the Meuse.

The snow that remains has a slushy consistency to it and lingers in crevices, the edges of the steps and the eaves of the roofs. The checkered patterns it creates add a dimension to the neighborhood not normally visible. Everything looks a little more pronounced, a little more real. A lone, stooped crane juts out over the skyline. The sun is about to reappear. Just one more lap, he decides. Whatever is happening at home can wait. The streetlamps lining the road glow with halos of grainy saffron light. They switch off one by one. There will be morning light in another few minutes. Another sun, another day. Emmanuel stirs and lets out a wail. It just never ends, does it? He rubs his eyes and suppresses a groan. Steam rises off the shadowed fields to his left, and the horizon is a seam ready to burst. Another call, this one from Camille, followed immediately by one from Léa. Hugo holds the power button on his cell until the screen goes dark and turns onto the autoroute going west with the hope, the desperate hope, that if he drives long and fast enough, he might be able to beat the sunrise for another day.

9

Martin looks down at the bank from the bridge over the railroad cut. He has carried the shell for at least an hour, if not more, and it rests on the stone railing beside him. His nose runs, and he stopped being able to feel his feet miles ago. The slippers he threw on before he followed the soldier into the night are now the color of the earth, mottled and saturated with water. None of it matters. He's back on the oil rig again, looking down into the ocean.

Oftentimes, the job would take only three weeks, but they told management it would take six. It was better to have the time than need it. Martin and whoever he was working with would drink all night and then suit up for their shift. The first half they would spend curled up on either side of the clump weight, sleeping on the seabed, a flurry of bubbles escaping their Desco helmet each time they exhaled.

Then the transmitters in their ears would erupt with life.

"Wake up, assholes."

They would stir, each one unfolding his arms and legs, adjusting his weighted belts. Time moved just a little bit slower down on the seafloor. Not unlike the phenomenon he experiences from his place on the bridge. Martin's been walking all night, or at least it feels that way. The flimsy boundary between day and night is irrelevant now. Down on the seabed, there were sunken ships. Old carcasses of freighters and commercial fishing boats slumped in the distance, just far enough to be out of reach but always there. The way the ships looked down there on the seabed, it was very similar to the way ces petite moineaux look here in Verdun. Water for dirt. That's the only real difference.

The water resisted their motions and slowed their movement as they unpacked their gear. The silt swirled in their wake, rising higher to where the open ocean yawned above them. He would then test the connection.

"Line."

"Check," came the reply from the surface.

"Hot," he said.

"Green," said Control, and the circuit was live.

Martin squeezed the trigger of his welding arc, and the stinger ignited white and then glowed a blinding phosphorescent blue. They conducted maintenance and repairs on the system of lines for the drill. Each shift spent welding individual beads onto the pipes to keep all that machinery going. The modern world depended on it the same way the old world depended on the whalers and fishermen. Joining metals in waters. They were more powerful than the kings of past empires. There were worse ways to make a living. In all his life, Martin never used the word *danger* to describe any of the jobs he had. *Danger*'s an empty word. Means nothing. There's risk, yeah, of course. But there is risk to everything in life.

Line?

Check.

Hot.

Green.

Martin leans forward and grips the stone railing. It might be the only thing keeping him standing. A section of the wide stone runoff ramp has collapsed. It has fallen in between the boulders that line the bank. It seems like things are always collapsing inward, back down inside the earth. Despite the land constantly rejecting ancient artillery shells, the man with the claw has the sense that it is quite the opposite. The world is actually collapsing into itself. He can see that between the boulders there is a darkness deeper still, and the collapsed section of ramp is heading there. Creeping downward. Everything will be swallowed. Slowly but surely. Eventually the entire city. Until it looks like the surface of the moon again, with the low, wavering wail of the wind curving in and out of the flooded craters.

His left knee buckles and slams against the overpass. A grunt escapes. Not much longer now. Martin adjusts himself and stands tall once more. He grabs the shell. It takes everything he has left to lift it. One step. And then another. And another. He can feel every fiber, every strand straining, and he looks up at the sky and sees all those stars, all those ancient stones hanging there, unfeeling, unmoved, and he thinks, *God, I can't take another step. Not another one. If I do, I'll die. Right here. Now.*

But here's the thing. He doesn't. He looks down, and he hasn't taken one step. He's taken four. And somehow, he keeps going. He keeps moving. And he still breathes. And he looks up at all those stars, and he realizes they're not stones. They're embers. That's life. That's the miracle inside all of us. It keeps us going. And going. It's in this walk that he feels most alive. When he know what it's like to live.

*

Dawn. First light finds Martin still standing, still walking, and now that he is able to recognize his surroundings, he realizes he's only a little over a mile from the depot. The sun hasn't arrived yet, but the muted illumination of the road around him is all he needs. He holds the shell close, absolutely numb, his hands curled and useless. He's crossed a threshold into some other state of being, and now he is just aware of the fact that he is freezing as opposed to feeling it in his body. His coat feels like a burden. The shell, another burden. His slippers, also a burden. If it weren't for the fact that he wouldn't be able to pick it back up, he would place the shell on the ground to remove his jacket. He would kick his slippers off and strip what little clothing he wears—pajama pants and an old T-shirt—until he was nude, and then he would find a way to strip himself yet further. There must be more to remove, to shed this weight, this all-encompassing feeling of heaviness that makes his feet stumble this last mile. No more. No more.

Yet he continues. Each unsteady step brings him closer. Won't be long now. There's hardly anyone on the road, but every now and again a lone vehicle drifts past, and if he weren't so numb he might notice that almost everyone has slowed or at least given him space by momentarily dipping into the oncoming lane so he has a wide berth on the narrow shoulder of the road. Traffic is picking up now. Morning commuters. He doesn't notice the faces in the car windows. The rubbernecking drivers with one hand on the steering wheel and a cigarette dangling from the lips. The children in the back seat on their way to school, their faces pressed to the glass so that their features become smushed and gargoyle-like. The stuff of nightmares. Martin doesn't even look. His focus is straight ahead, shell clutched in his arms and—something every driver would later comment on to a coworker or think back on during a solo lunch break, none of them could believe it—a slight smile curling his lips.

He takes the exit to the depot. The water in the well-worn tire tracks of the unpaved dirt road is partially frozen with a thin layer of ice like glass on the surface. Martin's feet have felt like stumps for miles, and he crashes through the delicate ice without so much as a grimace. The depot is only just down the road now. After the bend, he will see it. The fields behind him and to his sides are utterly motionless in the morning frost. Moments from now they will thaw and life will return in a harlequin display that will sway in the breeze. Martin leaves the main road behind and moves closer to the depot, the trees and the stillness they bring a welcome relief from the acrid exhaust of the passing vehicles.

The moment he sees the depot, its moss-covered walls and curled chain-link fence, he knows it's empty. The crew has already departed for the day. The trucks are all gone. Martin comes to a stop just outside the gate. The code was changed long ago. Standard procedure after an employee leaves. No point in trying. The shell in his hands becomes unbelievably heavy. It slips through his arms. Martin adjusts his grip, his arms cramp. He goes down on one knee and lets the shell down slowly. The rim strikes the earth first, releasing a dull ping. There's the churning of the clay underneath its body as Martin places the rest of the shell on the ground like tires twisting over gravel. He lets go.

It is lighter now. The air has a vivid quality to it that always comes right before the sun. Martin goes to stand but can't. Despite walking all night with the load he carried, he finds standing to be impossible. He stays on one knee and closes his eyes for a moment. When he opens them, he notices a line of little ants in the clay beneath him. They go about, doing their thing. But what is their thing? If he's honest, he's never thought about what little ants actually *do*. What are they here for? What is their purpose? What makes them kick their legs out of their little ant beds and say, *Carpe diem, motherfuckers!*

Martin leans closer, observing the thin line of ants weaving between his knees. What he sees is they are all carrying little grains of dirt. Each one. They follow one after the other. But he can't see where they are going. He can't find their destination. There's no hill or anything that resembles a home. From his viewpoint, he gets a vague sensation of being godlike and all-seeing. A solitary line of them, each with its own grain tucked to its chest, carrying it on and on, and for what purpose? Who knows? And all around them, an uncountable number of more grains. More than could be picked up in a little ant's lifetime.

His view widens, and all he can see is more. More land to cover. More grains to pick up. He imagines them arriving at their hill and plopping down their respective grains at the weak parts of their fortifications. Each one placed just right, so as to fortify the foundation—their home, a little better. And then some oaf comes along, some careless ogre (he imagines someone the general shape and disposition of Barbeuax), and steps right on it or kicks it without even realizing. All the grains go scattering across the plain. All those trips. All the work. Gone. Time to start over.

Martin feels the weight of exhaustion pull him to the earth. A body turned to stone. He bends down softly and rests his hands on his knees. The soil before him is clean and even. He notices his slippers. The seam of the left one is busted wide open, and the sole of the right one is completely torn back so that it sits there slack-jawed like a dead dog.

"I'll have to buy a new pair after today," he says to no one, and smiles.

His friends will tell stories after he is gone. First at his funeral and then for many years afterward. Misremember his words. Get the details wrong. But it won't matter. None of that will take anything away from the moment. If anything, it will make it better. It might bring him back to life. The only chance he stands at living past death. Because the stories will be theirs. And in that, he might live again.

Well, that's it, isn't it? There it is. There it is. The secret to life.

Maybe not the only secret. There are probably a few. But that's a good one.

Numb fingers. Blue nails. A mind unencumbered by the futility of it all. Martin unburdens himself. He allows the clean soil to slip from his palm back to the ground below. The clumps of soil hit the ground, and he can see movement. The ground vibrates. He reaches a hand down. Softness. He places both hands on the earth, and his knees sink. There is nothing frightening about it, though. The vibrations from the earth travel up his legs and arms. Martin leans into it. The last thing he sees before he disappears into the earth is a light very far ahead. Martin focuses on it. A flashlight? A headlamp? No. The sun.

The first rays slip through the trees, thaws his skin.

Warmth. At last.

The Souls

HUGO MADE IT all the way to Caen before the Police Nationale caught up with him. Léa had put out a missing person report. An impressive run, but ultimately pointless. What a mess. They called it a breakdown of some sort. All his affairs were dragged into the light, a very public spectacle. But even then, Léa didn't leave him. Nonetheless, conditions were set. A fresh start elsewhere. The house went up on the market, and they left with the idea that it was really the town that was the problem. They fled Verdun with the hope that another city would be different. There are no atheists. It doesn't matter if you say you don't believe in God. We all find something to worship. The LaFleur debacle would have been the hot gossip of the town if it weren't for Martin.

The news about his body was all everyone could talk about for weeks. So many questions. No real answers. There's no way he walked. All that way? With an old artillery shell on his back? Absolutely not. Clearly, someone dropped him off. But who? And why? They said they found him kneeling and bent over, forehead touching the ground as if in prayer.

It doesn't seem right or fair to them. Ferrand Martin, the man with the claw, spent a lifetime pruning the fields of Verdun, and for what? To die cold and alone outside the gate of his former employer in his pajamas.

Might there be more to it? A life spent doing the work makes the work worth it. Others come and go. Time rolls forward.

We are still here. We did things we never imagined we were capable of. Horrible things. Unforgivable acts. The sensation of feeling a stranger's flesh give under the weight of your blade. The eyes—more animal than man. Or the shrill scream escaping a friend as he's crushed to a vile jelly by one of our own tanks. The mud absorbed him all the same. It absorbed everything. At some point, the mud became indistinguishable from flesh, and we could no longer tell where we began.

But no one will know about those moments. They get absorbed into the abstract—the history textbooks and historical markers.

What did we do with all those spent casings? We took them and made them into something else. You can make anything out of metal. Crimp the ends. Flute the opening. Flip the base. Cut off that driving band and turn it into a bracelet. The ignitors make amazing rings. Stamp and poke and prod until you have something beautiful. It might be the only mark we leave on the world. The mud swallowed everything else.

Waiting in the rear, convalescing in the auxiliary hospitals. All around our friends were dying. We were all sick. Everything, trying to kill us. The earth threatened to consume us whole. We took the husks and etched elaborate designs along the sides to prove that something beautiful could still exist in such an ugly place. Focus. Patience. Persistence. Nothing else to do. One less thing that can be recycled into another weapon.

They look out their windows, storefronts, and second-floor apartments, over this town that suffered so much in the war in which France lost half its teachers, and it is difficult to deny a type of alignment we find challenging to describe. There must be a design.

Nearby, a lone woman leans against a wall, her cigarette glowing faintly. Voices of young boys echo off the buildings of the narrow streets that will lead them home. The whine of a buzz saw a block away in a storefront under renovation momentarily cuts through it all. A group of friends races by on mopeds; not a single one of them wears a helmet. Two men finish dinner on the deck of the boat docked at the pier and retire inside, where the portholes glow gold until they abruptly darken. All over town, other lights darken and shades draw closed. Little critters scurry and eat through the trash bags in the bins lining the sidewalks. A cyclist glides down the bank with his hands in his pockets, his handlebar guiding itself. He passes a bartender who drags a sign inside and locks the door. The trees lining the bank stand bare but will soon sprout life. The sky above unseals itself as the ceiling of clouds drifts away and reveals one hundred thousand distant stars, their fierce light glinting, ancient and bright. So much older than anything they illuminate below. The Meuse keeps moving.

These are all the moments that make a city a city. The singular present that we are forever living whether we know it or not. This is how it happens. Life. The voices float out of the bars and restaurants carried by warm light, and the music keeps flowing in the dark. It is always moving. The cyclist makes another pass down the bank, leaning back on one wheel, perfectly balanced. His tire treads grip the road and push him farther, forming to the stones the way an artillery shell fits in the grooves of a cannon barrel's rifling. The cyclist glides down the bank like a round sliding up the barrel, spiraling out of the mouth and into oblivion. He runs with the Meuse, keeping pace in an effortless way. His reflection catches in wavy impressions on the surface of the water along with the deep night sky. We wait for him to dip, to fall, to return his front wheel to the earth, but he keeps going without a thought. He is a miracle. The cyclist rounds the castle gate, and we follow him until he is out of sight, revolving the way Earth does, on an axis, screeching across the universe to a destination unwilling and unprepared to receive it.

Acknowledgments

First and foremost, thank you to Daniel O'Dowd who showed me what real courage in the face of the abyss looked like and who made me believe it was possible to be happy while struggling toward the heights. Thank you to my agent Mark Gottlieb for seeing the potential in this novel and running with it. My deepest appreciation to Brandon Taylor for your insights and keen intuition, working with you made me a stronger writer overnight. To Allison and Cassidy, and the whole Unnamed Press Team, thank you for bringing this book to life.

I have nothing but bottomless gratitude for so many people who made, not only this novel, but my writing life possible: Mac Caltrider and Marty Skovlund Jr. who gave *Zone Rouge* space in *Coffee or Die Magazine*. Keith, Tyler, Jessica and the Dead Reckoning Collective crew, thank you for the many opportunities to teach and learn. Tom Schueman for getting in the car with Mac and me at Logan International, destination unknown, and driving north. Adam Wilburn for your leadership and unparalleled dedication in building the greatest book club in the world. To all members of the Patrol Base Abbate Book Club—past, present, and future–thank you. Our conversations have changed the way I read literature. T Kira Māhealani Madden for keeping an ongoing email thread with me which I filled with every thought, fragment, and photo that crossed my mind about this fascinating city.

Hannah Beresford for the care she showed a draft of this novel I could not see the magic in anymore. Bret Lott for the many hours spent in his office telling me to just keep writing. Jonathan Bohr Heinen for opening your home to me and going over the very first draft of this novel when it was just a short story. Ocean Vuong for your generosity, kindness, and guidance. The VCCA for providing me two invaluable weeks where I was able to disappear into this world I had created. Wood Marchant and the CofC Collegiate Recovery Program for the Foxworth-Wells Scholarship.

Thank you, Connor Gilroy for always picking up the phone. Thank you to my grandmother, Meg Plunkett, who told me to just take the money and move to Charleston. Thank you Mom and Dad for the Great Illustrated Classics that kicked this whole writing thing off. Most importantly, thank you, Meagan, for showing me what home feels like again.